Lightning Song

Also by Lewis Nordan

⚡ LEWIS NORDAN ⚡

Lightning
Song

Algonquin Books of Chapel Hill • 1998

Grateful acknowledgment is made to the Virginia Center
for the Creative Arts, where this book was written.

Published by
ALGONQUIN BOOKS OF CHAPEL HILL
Post Office Box 2225
Chapel Hill, North Carolina 27515-2225

a division of
WORKMAN PUBLISHING
708 Broadway
New York, New York 10003

Printed in the United States of America.
Published simultaneously in Canada by Thomas Allen & Son Limited.
Design by Bonnie Campbell. Cover design by Steve Brower.

This is a work of fiction. While, as in all fiction, the literary perceptions and
insights are based on experience, all names, characters, places, and incidents
are either products of the author's imagination or are used fictitiously. No
reference to any real person is intended or should be inferred.

LIBRARY OF CONGRESS CATALOGING-IN-PUBLICATION-DATA
Nordan, Lewis.
    Lightning song : a novel / by Lewis Nordan.
      p. cm.
    ISBN 1-56512-084-1
    I. Title.
  PS3564.055L54   1997
  813'.54—dc21   96-54157
                               CIP

ISBN 1-56512-220-8 paper

10 9 8 7 6 5 4 3 2 1

For
Lewis, Josh, and Adam

1

One day in the summer when he turned twelve years old and when a fragrance of sweet alfalfa hay and llama musk was drifting through the windows and into the house on a breeze from the pastures and cool shade of the little barn where pigeons cooed in the rafters, Leroy Dearman realized that the day had finally come. What had been planned for so long could now be undertaken. Leroy's mama had company coming over, the Evil Queen, Leroy called her, who dressed all in black, with heavy makeup and real pale skin and long black hair and was known to be modern, with scary ways of speaking and smelly cigarettes from France. She was ugly, too—*U-G-L-Y,* you ain't got no alibi, you're ugly—the schoolyard phrase would not leave Leroy's head. The Evil Queen had a new baby, so Leroy's sisters wouldn't give Leroy any trouble, Laurie and Molly, who would want to hang around the baby. Molly was the little one, three years old, bed wetter first class, redheaded, thick as a stump. Laurie, she was eight, lithe and blonde, that girl could cuss, slap you, too. Leroy's palms were sweating, his heart seemed to flutter. "Creepy-crawly," he whispered, to give himself courage. The Evil Queen and Leroy's mama had made plans at coffee hour at the church. The Queen, in her frightening modern way, had said, "Lunch, okay, but not at my house. Nobody should be forced to eat in a house where a dentist has slept, it's cruel and unusual, it's disgusting, and not at that sandwich place either, not the Fly-speck Cafe, their pies are good, but oh my God, I cannot, will not, fight with that little bitch about salad dressing again today, I do not have the strength, the war is over and that lit-tle redneck in the Howdy Partner apron won, it's inedible, her ranch dressing, it's vile, it ought to be banned by law, get your butt in that kitchen and get me something not outlawed by the Food and Drug Administration and take off that stupid apron before I rip it off your ugly ass and shove it down your throat, do I sound psychotic, Elsie, I hope I don't sound sort of out of my mind, I mean, I *am* out of my mind, I just don't want to sound that way." Ugly. Creepy-crawly.

Leroy breathed in the familiar fragrances of the farm, and doing this made him suddenly cautious. He decided he'd bet-ter check one more time to see if the coast was clear. Leroy's Uncle Harris lived in the attic now and kept magazines up there, grown-up magazines with pictures, Leroy had seen him sneak them in the house along with his newspapers, inside a bag of groceries, beneath his shirt. Uncle Harris was away from the house today and Leroy meant to see those pictures, *Playboy* and *Penthouse*, he'd seen their bright covers on the magazine stand at the drugstore in the village, so he had an idea what was inside. He had been waiting for the perfect day and now it had come, and as long as he was up there maybe he'd check out Uncle Harris's shirt drawers, too, his pants pockets, beneath his mattress, it couldn't hurt. He caught a glimpse of the vast vistas of boundary violation, open wide.

He walked up to the front of the house where his mama and the Evil Queen were sitting on the shaded front porch in the wicker furniture and said, "I ain't snooping," just in case. His mama and the Evil Queen were having glasses of iced tea with some mint sprigs that Leroy's mama had picked out in the side yard. They acted like they thought they might be pretty hot stuff, which they weren't, in Leroy's humble opinion. How hot could you be, living on a llama farm? Sunshine filtered through a few low clouds. The temperature was mild, the air was leaf-green and fragrant with buttercups. Here and there a single tree beyond the pasture fence, a thick-trunked black walnut, or a slender willow or tulip, caught an occasional bright ray, like a spotlight. A breeze came up that smelled a little like rain. A swarm of bees circled, looking for a tree.

Leroy's mama—Elsie was her name—she had made tuna salad sandwiches and deviled eggs for lunch. She had cut the crusts off the bread and used sprigs of watercress on the sandwiches, in the place of lettuce, la-di-da. She stood in front of the refrigerator with the door open. She said, "How much do you hate Kool-Aid?" The Evil Queen laughed, that witchy sound like pigeons in the barn, ooh-ooh-ooh, what was that ugly woman's real name?

Elsie saw Leroy standing against the door frame.

She said, "Leroy, you scared me."

He said, "I ain't snooping."

She said, "You are the oddest child."

The two women ignored Leroy, they were taking a little tour of the farm. Elsie showed the Evil Queen the pantry, the shelves of Mason jars filled with bright fruit, row after row of tomatoes, jars of Blue Lake green beans, new potatoes, okra, yellow corn, speckled lima beans, bread-and-butter pickles. The Evil Queen was a city lady, village anyhow, she said she liked to look at the farm, it was the perfect life, and you're so lucky, and like that.

Elsie said, "Come on outside with us, Leroy."

He said, "Why? I ain't going to snoop in the attic. You don't trust me. You've never trusted me."

She said, "Don't say *ain't*, honey."

Outside Elsie showed the Evil Queen the shed with tools and fence wire–stretching equipment and farm implements hung up on hooks along the wall. Leroy had to tag along, his sisters, too. He should have gone on and snooped in the attic when he had the chance. They went in the little barn, filled with sweet hay. The baby llamas came up looking for gorp, the sweetened grain Elsie gave them as treats. Pigeons cooed in the rafters. Leroy thought the Evil Queen might rise up into the rafters of the barn and perch there with them, that woman was ugly. Elsie held out a zinc bucket of the sweetened grain for the Evil Queen to dip her hand into. Her nails were long, they were enameled with deep purple polish. The Evil Queen scooped up the gorp and held it in her hand and when she felt the gentle lips of the llama suck it away like a little vacuum cleaner, she made that funny little witchy sound again, ooh. She did sound like the pigeons. She said, "I thought it would bite! I thought it would be all slobbery! Ooh."

Creepy-crawly, it was the attic calling for Leroy, *Penthouse, Playboy*. Leroy turned and walked away from his mama and the Evil Queen and went inside the house, the call was too strong to resist any longer. He let the screened door slap shut behind him when he went inside. He stood beneath the trapdoor and pulled a kitchen chair into the hallway and stood on it. He grabbed the hanging rope on the trapdoor and jumped off the chair and swung down like Tarzan on a vine. The door pulled open from above and slid down the metal gliders into the hall. Leroy went up into Uncle Harris's attic room. Behind him as he went he heard the soft, frantic bleating of one of the llamas, a young female up near the second row of pens, not far out in the pasture. He knew the animal had gotten her head stuck between the squares of wire, one of the young llamas, trying to reach a clump of sweeter grass. He imagined her little anvil-shaped head hooked in the fence. He imagined one of the male llamas pacing back and forth. It spat several times. Leroy reached the top of the stairs and rose up into the attic.

Uncle Harris's made-up bed with two pillows, the bedside table, the little bookshelf with a few books, a rocking chair with a caned bottom and a ladder back, and the tasseled lamp with a fringed shade meant nothing to Leroy now. Not the tiny chest of drawers, the oval hook rug on the floor, the steep A-frame of the attic itself, its bare board floor and exposed beams, not the trousers on the chair, nothing held meaning for Leroy. He was looking for magazines. The magazines were there, Leroy had not been mistaken about that. They glowed in the dark, they were plutonium, that end of the attic room was bathed in a strange light, their colors shone like a cache of gold in a fairy tale, a sound of deep-throated electrical thrumming emanated from the stack. He had suspected they would be here. He had seen them come into the house, oh, he had known they would be here, all right. He just had not known they would be so easy to find, so immediately in full view. He had expected to have to search for them, maybe not to find them at all. He realized now that he had halfway hoped he would not find them. There they were. They were not strewn about, not hidden away. There were no drawers to search through. As if they were as innocent as any other detail of the llama farm, they sat quietly glowing and thrumming in a stack on Uncle Harris's bedside table.

Leroy noticed that he was trembling. He listened to be sure no one had entered the house. He knew that his mama must have unhooked the she-llama from the fence by now. The tour with the Evil Queen could not last much longer. His legs felt

weak. He sat on the edge of Uncle Harris's bed. The magazines were inches away. He could smell them, a manly per-
fume, like musk. They glowed with a rich yellow light. He
tried to regularize his breathing. He breathed deeply a few
times, and this caused him to feel light-headed. He picked up
one of the magazines. He held it in his lap, not even open.
Every place the magazine touched him felt like electricity. It
buzzed, it crackled at his touch. He forced his eyes down,
forced them not to close in fear, he looked at the magazine.

On the cover stood a woman wearing a western vest, she
had on very tight shorts, which seemed to have come unzipped. Leroy hated to have somebody point out when his
pants were unzipped, so he said nothing. He almost said, "Hi,"
but managed not to say this either. He held the magazine in his
lap. He looked at the cover for a long time. For a long time he
only looked at the strip of flesh from her throat to her belly
button, where the vest was parted. He hoped that by looking
hard he might cause the vest to open farther. It did not. He
looked briefly at the half unzipped shorts and averted his eyes.
He wasn't sure he was ready to work his magic there, it
seemed a little risky. He studied the woman's face. He wished
he knew her a little better, maybe he wouldn't feel quite so
awkward looking at her like this. She was smiling, he noticed,
a nice smile too, real sincere, she had excellent teeth, extra
white and not a bit bucked. He thought his own teeth were
beginning to buck out a little. He pushed at them with his
thumb, he did this whenever nobody was looking, trying to

coax them back in a little. Anyway, he was glad she was smiling, that was a relief, it pleased him to think she was happy. He wasn't sure why she was so happy, come to think of it. It didn't make much sense for her to be this happy, under the circumstances. Somebody had taken her picture before she really even finished getting dressed. It seemed like to Leroy she might be embarrassed, or even angry. He knew he would be angry, he'd die of embarrassment if somebody took his picture with his pants unzipped. He looked at the photograph more closely. Something wasn't right here. Those clothes, for example. They weren't even her clothes. Those shorts couldn't have belonged to her, they were much too little. Look at that, they wouldn't meet at the waist. No wonder she couldn't get them zipped up right. Somebody had put this lady's little sister's shorts in her dresser drawers and made her think they were her own, then when she went to put them on, took a picture of her in them. Man, that was low, that was mean. That really fried Leroy. This was one of those jokes that just wasn't funny, if you wanted Leroy's personal opinion. His penis was stiff and aching and he had to adjust it to one side of his pants, but that didn't keep him from feeling indignant about the practical joker who popped in on this perfectly nice lady and took her picture while she was getting dressed in clothes about ten sizes too small for her. How could you stand it? How could anybody ever go to school again, face your friends? It was awful. Boy, that riled Leroy, that really fried him, how could anybody trick this nice lady like that?

He kept looking at the picture. His you-know-what was seriously stiff now. He wondered if he ought not let it out for a little while, give it some air, it could smother in there, all cramped up. Something about this picture, though. Where did she think she was going in that outfit in the first place? Even if she'd had time to get finished dressing, even if she'd noticed these dinky clothes couldn't possibly belong to her, Leroy couldn't think of a single place on earth where she could have worn those shorts and a western-style vest and fit in. Nobody else would be wearing anything close to this, you could bank on it. Did she really imagine she could wear this getup and blend in with any group of normal people she'd ever heard of, even for one second? If you looked close you could see that the vest didn't have any buttons on it anyway, no buttonholes for them to go through. Well, see, right there. Where did she get that stupid vest? He hoped she had kept the receipt. She got gypped, man. She got gypped, and good. She went to Gyp City and took up residence, she ran for mayor. She'd never get a refund now, she'd already worn it. She should have tried it on at the store. He unzipped his pants to relieve a little strain on the fabric, to give one part of himself a little breathing room, even if there was no oxygen getting to his brain. He turned the page.

He turned many pages. Writing writing writing writing writing, some shoe advertisements. He turned the page again. Well, what do you know, he couldn't believe his eyes, here was somebody he recognized. It was another picture of the same woman he had seen on the front cover, that poor girl. What had she done with her vest? She'd lost her vest! And where were her pants, for God's sake? What on earth had she done with her pants? Not only that. She had breasts. Nipples on the ends, one each, two total, count them for yourself. She had hair between her legs, like a triangle, right on her you-know-what place. Do you really need to hear any more?

That was not all, though. She was wearing a big white cowboy hat and a gun belt. She was pointing two silvery six-shooters out into the room she was standing in. At least she might be able to make a citizen's arrest of the person with the camera. She was wearing cowboy boots with yellow sunbursts at the ankles. She was still smiling, big smile, full set of white teeth, you could count them.

Leroy kept looking at the magazine. One part of him seemed to see the six-shooters pointing at it and that part was reaching for the rafters. He patted it to calm it down. Leroy understood now, he understood something about the woman in the picture, and it was not good, not a bit, it was bad, in fact, plenty bad. The lady in the picture suffered from mental illness, was retarded possibly, deranged, completely out of touch with reality. She needed help. She would never get her pants on now, even if she could find a pair that fit her. She would have to start all over, dressing herself, and Leroy had no confidence that she could do it. He hoped she wouldn't try to pull on her pants over those damn boots. They'd never make it. Leroy had tried that stunt on school mornings, half asleep, and it doesn't work, just normal shoes, not even boots. Put the camera down, asshole. Find this lady's clothes. Where were her friends, her parents, her minister? The world seemed to be caving in around Leroy.

Just then the porch door downstairs opened and closed. Leroy heard the sound and sat still, with the magazine open in his lap. He looked at his penis and suspected it would never go back to normal. He stuffed it back inside his pants and zipped up and listened. He expected to hear voices but he did not, only footsteps. Only one set of footsteps. He closed the magazine and placed it on the bedside table. He stood and walked close to the trapdoor, the better to hear whoever was downstairs. He placed each foot on the floor carefully to prevent the boards from squeaking. He stood very still, just beside the hole in the floor. He heard the Evil Queen's baby crying a little. He heard the Evil Queen's voice. He understood now that the Evil Queen was going to kill the baby. He went to the attic window and looked out, the side of the house toward the llama lot. He saw his mother and sisters there, among the llamas. He watched a young doe go bounding away from Elsie like a spring-toy. The little tail was standing straight up, waving like a flag. Leroy walked down the attic steps without trying to hide. He didn't bother to put the trapdoor back up. He was probably too late to save the baby. He felt like he was smothering. Smothering in pain, he guessed he would have said, if he'd thought to say anything at all. He surprised the Evil Queen, whose back was to him, bent over the child, at the bed. He said, "Don't." She looked up. She was hideous, pale as a witch. He started to say, "Don't kill the baby," but then decided not to. The Evil Queen finished changing the wet diaper, it took only a few seconds, and when she finished she lifted the infant, who had stopped crying now. She balanced it on her hip. Leroy realized with a shock that the Evil Queen was not ugly after all, she was beautiful. He couldn't believe it, but she was. In the strangest way she reminded him of the woman in the magazine, though they looked nothing alike. Suddenly he knew why people fell in love and wanted to marry, he understood why they wanted to have children, to live together for a lifetime. He couldn't believe he had ever thought she could harm her baby. She was so beautiful the sight of her made him ache, her washboardlike bony chest, the downy hair on her arms. He heard his heart begin to speak in his own silent voice, it cried out to her, words vague and surprising and indistinct, I want you, I need you, I love you, he understood Elvis Presley at last. The Evil Queen smiled a warm smile. She turned around. She said, "Why, Leroy, hello. I thought I heard somebody. Did you sneak up on me?"

That evening, when the sun went down, a big yellow ball beyond the red clay hills in the hazy west, the llamas, who were many colors of brown and rust and pure white and pure black and mottled, turned to face the sun, as they did each evening, and again when it rose in the morning, and they flicked their big corn-shuck ears, they shrugged the coarse fur of their broad backs, they stretched their giraffelike necks, and they began to groan, low, low, and then louder, to sing their strange llama-song, first one llama, and then another, and another, until all the llamas were singing in their rich individual voices, blended in a strange chorus. They sang each day to the rising and the setting sun. Leroy's daddy, a one-armed man, came in on the tractor from the fields, Uncle Harris, wearing one of his Hawaiian-print shirts, looked up from his newspaper, Leroy's mama dried her hands and walked out on the porch, Laurie, Molly, Leroy, too, all of them stood at the end of the day and listened in the last sunshine to the song of the llamas.

Later when Leroy was lying in his bed, wearing only his crinkly pajama bottoms on this warm night, he looked out his window where there was moonlight, yellow as gold in the tree limbs, and thought of the naked woman in the pictures in Uncle Harris's magazine. He wondered if he could be in love with her—he thought he was in love with her—because when he thought of her face, the nakedness of her flesh, the innocence of her smile, he wanted nothing more than to stay near her forever, to save her each day from some new danger, fire, wild beasts, evil men. He wondered how he could kiss her, as she was so much taller than himself, then realized he didn't know how to kiss, not the kind of kiss a boy would need to know about if he were in love with this woman. His head spun, the retarded magazine lady and the Evil Queen had become confused in his mind, they seemed now to be the same person. He imagined kissing his mother's friend. All his dreams were heartbreaking, and all were vague in details. He found that he did not want to touch himself in the way he had in the attic, and then as he was realizing this he found that he was touching himself and thinking of her, this composite person, dark and fair, and he lay and touched and breathed hard and then did not need to do this anymore for a while.

His mama came in later, to say good night, as she always did, making her rounds of the children. She sat on the edge of his small bed.

She said, "Are you all right, honey?"

He said, "I guess so."

She said, "I worry about you sometimes."

He lay in the moonlight and could not think what to say. He could feel the warmth of her rear end against his leg. An electrical spark seemed to flash between their two bodies. He didn't want his mama's face getting mixed up with the faces of the magazine lady and the Evil Queen. He wondered if she knew he had been in the attic. He wondered if she knew about the magazines. He wondered whether she had come in before he finished with his touching and breathing and had seen him; it was possible, he had become too involved in his daydreams to pay close attention to whoever might have passed by his bedroom door.

He said, "I think something is wrong with me."

His mama said, "What is it, Leroy?"

"I don't know."

She patted his leg. She said, "Well, you're growing up. That's one thing, I suppose."

He said, "Tell me the story."

She said, "Oh, honey, no, not that old story. Not again."

He said, "Tell it, Mama."

She said, "Oh, well, all right, let's see." She told the familiar tale, the one the children always wanted to hear. She told about the day she fell in love with their daddy. "We were young," she said. "We hadn't known each other very long. Your daddy had an old car. He took me far out in the country on a long drive. He stopped beside a big field and parked the car. I thought he was going to kiss me. It was getting close to dark. Instead he said, 'Listen.' I listened and heard them running, thirty of them, or more. I thought they were horses when I saw them. Their hooves were flying. They sounded like thunder in the hills. They came closer. I saw the slender bodies, the long necks, legs so thin you wondered how they held them up. I saw their faces, the pointed snouts and big ears and bulging eyes. They were all colors. Llamas. I had never seen a llama. They were running for the fun of it. That's when I fell in love." She stopped. Leroy lay for a while in the moonlight with his mama beside him.

He said, "Is that the end?"

She kissed him on the forehead. "I guess so," she smiled.

He said, "*Did* he kiss you?"

She said, "Leroy!"

He said, "Did he?"

She said, "Oh, well, sure he did, honey." She blushed in a way that Leroy loved to see.

She said, "You *are* growing up, aren't you! Is my young man growing up? First thing I know, you'll be heading for trouble."

2

Right after Leroy's Old Pappy went into his coma, Leroy rode with his daddy from the red clay hills down to the Gulf Coast where Old Pappy had drunk the poison, and his daddy asked a few questions, did a little detective work, making sure there was no foul play involved, was the way Leroy's daddy put it to Leroy. Leroy liked the coast pretty well, palm trees, pelicans, white sand beaches. They didn't find out anything, though. Most of the men they talked to were old bozos who stayed in the halfway house where Old Pappy had been living. They were pretty unreliable. One man wore long lilac-colored scarves tied around each ankle and kept tripping over them. He claimed to have given Allen Ginsberg a blow job in the early sixties. Leroy's daddy said, "I just can't believe Old Pappy would have tried to kill himself." The man said, "I can't believe I gave Allen Ginsberg a blow job neither, but I did, gimme a dollar, son, gimme two dollars, I got to catch a bus."

Old Pappy weighed no more than eighty-five or ninety pounds in his coma, white as chicken dooky. After he drank the poison, Elsie took care of him in the attic for over a year. Each day, three or four times a day, Leroy's mama heaved down the trapdoor and went up and turned the old man in his bed. This prevented bedsores, she told Leroy. She kept the implanted catheter irrigated and the jug emptied out. She bathed the old man each day, top to bottom, with a washcloth and a pan of warm water with mild soapsuds. Once each week she washed his thin hair with Prell and shaved his tiny face. She took care of his bowel movements. She rubbed his poor, blue feet with talcum powder. He generally smelled pretty good, Leroy would give him that much.

One particular afternoon an electrical storm moved across the county. It wasn't especially late but the sky started getting dark. There was a faint yellow tinge to the air outside, it seemed like to Leroy. The rain started up. It was coming down pretty good. In the attic you could hear it on the roof like a drum. Leroy's daddy was still in the field, on the tractor, already making his way back home, so he was getting wet. Rain was sheeting off the roof. Leroy happened to be in the attic creepy-crawling. This was a game he played, snooping around. Just then Old Pappy died, Leroy noticed. He stopped breathing. Leroy noticed this as he was rifling through some stuff in an old trunk. There had been a rattling, and then it stopped. Leroy went over and sat on the side of Old Pappy's bed. He looked at him. He'd quit breathing, all right. Leroy didn't know what to do. He just sat there for a while. He could have called his mama, she would have come up and done some kind thing, would have spoken the right words. He wasn't sure why he didn't call her. He felt responsible, that was it. He felt like he might have caused this to happen. He put his hand on the old man's forehead as if he were feeling to see whether he had a fever. Old Pappy's forehead was cool, but not like death, he just felt like a regular person lying in a well-ventilated room. A little rain was blowing through the open windows at either end of the attic, but not much. Leroy suddenly felt very tired. He thought he might cry, or he might just lie down in the bed with the old man for a minute, pull up the covers and stay there. He did lie down. He stretched out. He turned on his side then and cuddled up to the old man, as he had cuddled up to his parents in their bed when he was a little boy. He was going on twelve now. He held on to his Old Pappy. He wanted his Old Pappy back, even in a coma. He stayed like this for a while, not long. He sat up then. He knew what he had to do. He heaved himself around and straddled the old man in the bed. He pinched the tiny little nose together with his two fingers. He'd seen this on TV. They'd had a demonstration at school. He manipulated Old Pappy's jaw until he had his mouth open a little. Before he put his own lips to Old Pappy's, he noticed the thin lines, like razor cuts, in the old man's lips. He needed some ChapStick, it looked like to Leroy. He was afraid the old man was going to have bad breath, so he held his own breath for a few seconds. He put his lips on the old man's mouth and breathed into his lungs. He did this many times. The tiny chest rose and fell. Rain kept falling, falling. Lightning hit the lightning rod once and a few shaggy balls of fire bounced through the room and then dissipated. Leroy's daddy was already coming inside. Leroy had heard the tractor pull into the shed and now could hear his daddy stomping his wet boots on the steps. Leroy kept on with the resuscitation. After a while he stopped. He sat back and looked at Old Pappy. Well, what do you know? he thought. Old Pappy was breathing again. That was really something. Leroy had brought him back to life. He watched him breathe for a while and then he got up and went back downstairs, where everybody was shutting windows and running about the house, making a big fuss about the rain.

"You're soaked!" Leroy's mama was saying to Swami Don as he came into the house. Swami Don was an odd name, nobody seemed to remember why he was called that. He took off his John Deere cap and shook the rain off onto the porch floor. Swami Don was a big man, with just one good arm. The other one was just a withered limp little wet rag of an arm. Old Pappy had shot him when he was a child. It was an accident. Swami Don didn't hold any grudges, he had said this plenty of times, Leroy had heard him. Leroy didn't mention that Old Pappy had died and come back to life. Swami Don shook himself in a funny way, like he was a dog, and this made everybody laugh. He said, "A towel, somebody!" and Laurie came a-running.

Later on they ate dinner together, all of them. They sat around the little kitchen table covered with checkered oil-cloth. There were big white bowls of steaming food, a wooden salad bowl with lettuce out of the garden and red chunks of ripe tomato. Leroy thought about Old Pappy up in the attic, breathing, but he didn't say anything. Elsie had made a big chicken stew, with carrots, green peas, and potatoes and onions, and served it in a big crockery bowl in the middle of the kitchen table. There were other dishes, too. She had also made biscuits, which were golden and fragrant, and placed them in a wicker basket with a blue towel over them to keep them warm. A little plate with butter sat with a butter knife perched on the side. Little Molly made a fuss and wouldn't sit in the high chair, but that was all right. Laurie got a big pillow and put it on a regular chair for her to sit on. Swami Don said, "She's growing up, that's all, first thing I know, she'll be married, they'll all be married, and I'll be a granddaddy." He smiled and winked when he said this. Elsie said, "Oh, please!" and this made everyone laugh. Leroy tried to laugh with them, but he couldn't do it. He was wondering if Old Pappy had died again yet. He grinned, that was the best he could do. He felt Old Pappy's cracked lips again upon his own.

Chicken stew and biscuits was Leroy's favorite supper. He

looked at the steaming bowl, the wicker basket of bread, the butter dish, and thought he could never eat enough chicken stew. He was as hungry as a wild dog for chicken stew and biscuits. He would never get enough, he just knew he wouldn't. He was suddenly so hungry he was ready to fight for chicken stew. He grabbed the bowl even before his daddy could get any. He dug into it with the big serving spoon and shoveled it onto his plate. He piled up his plate, he spooned it on, dollop after dollop. He grabbed up his fork and ate so fast his teeth were clashing against the metal loud enough to hear in the next room. His mama finally said, "Whoa, honey, slow down." He felt wild, he wasn't sure he could slow down. He forced himself to eat more slowly. He ate and ate. When he was finished with the stew, he buttered a biscuit, then another, and put both on his plate and poured syrup over them. His daddy said, "Guess who's hungry tonight?" He smiled at Leroy. "Is that some good eating?" Leroy ate as much as he could. He was so full he was about to bust, but he couldn't quit eating. He drank two glasses of milk. The storm was blowing, the lightning was cracking, fireballs danced through the house. He said, "Is anybody going to check on Old Pappy?" Elsie said, "I was up there earlier today." He sat at his plate, sodden with food. He didn't know what to say. When he went to bed his stomach felt like he had swallowed a basketball. Old Pappy wasn't dead when he left him, that's all Leroy cared about. If he was dead now, it wasn't Leroy's fault. Later on Leroy's mama came into his room and sat on the edge of his bed. The rain was falling and falling and making big puddles in the yard. The lightning had moved on through. A light from the llama shed, which burned all night, shined a dim glow in the rainy darkness that he could see from the bed. He could see the outline of his mama's form beside him. He could feel her weight on the side of the bed. She said, "Are you okay, sweetie? You ate so much, I was afraid you were going to make yourself sick." He said, "I didn't kill Old Pappy." She put her hand upon his face, as he had put his own hand on Old Pappy's face. She said, "Well, of course you didn't, darling. Of course not." Leroy said, "He ain't dead." "I know, punkin," Elsie said. "He's in a coma, we've talked about this, he's just sleeping right now, you remember. You didn't do anything." "Are you going to check on him?" "Well, sure. I always check one last time before I go to bed. Don't you worry about a thing." When she leaned down and kissed Leroy on the forehead, her lips felt cool on his skin. She told him the bedtime story she always told when any of the children were sick or scared, the drive into the country, the wide field at sunset, the musical sad voices coming from far off in the distance. It was llamas, singing to the setting sun. They sang and sang, this strange song. "Those innocent faces," she said.

When she was gone, Leroy lay in the bed looking out his window and listening to the falling rain. It was hard to do, but he stayed awake until he heard his mama go up the stairs through the trapdoor and find Old Pappy dead. He heard her whisper this to Swami Don. He heard his daddy crying and knew that she was holding his daddy's head in her lap and touching his hair. He heard the ambulance come and heard the men come in and take Old Pappy down the stairs and out the door. He heard the ambulance drive away in the rain.

3

It was one of those blue-sky summer Sunday afternoons in the red clay hills of Mississippi. Sometimes Elsie told Leroy to walk down to the end of the lane and down the blacktop and over to Mr. Sweet's store for her, she might need some bread or something. It was kind of far, and the macadams did have traffic sometimes, but if you were careful it was pretty safe. She said, "Ask Mr. Sweet does he need me to bring him his supper tonight. He's been poorly." Leroy looked across the llama pasture, in the direction of Mr. Sweet's store. He saw the white cottage there, surrounded by big pecan trees, a few old cars in the yard. Some new people had moved into the cottage not long ago, before that the house had sat empty for a long time. Everybody called them the New People. Nobody knew them, they kept to themselves. If they had another name, Leroy didn't know about it.

He looked over at the New People's cottage. Nobody had met them yet. Leroy was starting to have him an idea.

He said, "Can Laurie and Molly go with me?"

Elsie said, "You might have to carry Molly partway back."

He said, "Okay."

She said, "Well, y'all walk in the ditch, I don't want you close to that road. Molly, you hold hands, you hear."

Everybody talked about the New People. Nobody knew much. They seemed different from everybody else. They didn't dress like farm people, maybe they spoke with a foreign accent, nobody was sure which country. The postmistress, a woman named Lolly Pinkerton who raised and sold cockroaches to fishermen, said she heard they came from Venezuela, maybe Trinidad, though if you talked to her long enough you could tell she had no idea that these were foreign countries. She seemed to think her boy, who was grown now and lived in Arkansas, had once played football against those teams, sometime after integration, down in the Delta maybe. How did she get that government job? Mr. Sweet, the old man who ran the store and gas station out on the highway, had them mixed up with a late uncle of his who had fought in the Mexican War, which made no sense at all. Mr. Sweet was failing. Poorly didn't hardly cover how Mr. Sweet was doing. It was hard to get good information about the New People. Leroy felt the calling. Leroy was planning another creepy-crawly. This one was too big to do alone.

It took a good long time to walk all the way to the store. It was hot, too. You could work up a sweat. Leroy started wondering if he'd made a mistake dragging his sisters along with him. Laurie wore a pair of new yellow boots, even though she didn't need them, the weather was dry, and got a blister on one heel, first thing. She said, "Shit." Molly said she had to go tee-tee, and Leroy said, "Don't go in your pants," but she did anyway. It ran all down her leg. Man, that was pretty bad. Leroy cleaned her up as well as he could. When did this start up, this pants-wetting? She'd been pretty well trained. Leroy told Laurie she could go barefoot and he'd carry her boots for her. She said, "If I step on a nail, I'm going to slap the shit out of you." He made Molly take off her underpants and he wadded them up and stuck them down in Laurie's boot while she wasn't looking. They walked past the New People's cottage on the way to the store.

Leroy said, "Want to go for a visit?"

Laurie gave him one of her slap-your-stupid-face looks.

He said, "Sort of explore?"

They walked on past the house and then along the blacktop. If a car came along they all three jumped in the ditch. Leroy finally pulled open the screened door of Mr. Sweet's little store and the three of them went inside. Sometimes Mr. Sweet gave them each a cold drink, Leroy liked Nu Grape or Yoo-Hoo, but he'd take anything. The handle on the store's door was a faded tin contraption in the shape of some kind of cola drink that Leroy had never heard of anyplace else. The one gas pump out front was a brand of gasoline nobody else ever heard of, with a dinosaur drawn on the globe. A man named Hot McGee was in the store trying to buy a jar of pickled pig's feet. Mr. Sweet said he couldn't remember what they were. "Describe pickled pig's feet," Mr. Sweet was saying to Mr. McGee. "Give me enough clues and I might be able to come up with it." Hot McGee had a son Leroy's age named Screamer McGee who could lick his own penis, double-jointed, he was well known in the county. Leroy had tried that trick and got nowhere close, it was a gift. Hot was a man with strange red arms, with forearms bigger than his biceps, a funny-looking guy if you wanted Leroy's opinion. He carried a chair and a bullwhip with him wherever he went, like an animal trainer, though he wasn't one. "Pickled pig's feet, Mr. Sweet, you remember, come in a jar, real tasty, special good with beer, maybe some crackers, come on now, you can do it. Kind of pink? Got a knuckle and a toenail sometimes?" "It's about to come back to me, I think I'm about to remember," Mr. Sweet said from behind the little empty meat case. The meat case had one package of wieners and a shriveled-up fryer chicken in it. There were a couple of flies crawling around on the inside of the glass, so it probably wasn't too cool in there either. "There you go," Hot McGee was saying. "Now you're talking. You can do it." Mr. Sweet was a toothless little man with one leg shorter than the other. He walked on a built-up shoe. He rubbed his chin thoughtfully with his hand. Leroy didn't know what a pickled pig's foot was either, and proud of it.

Finally Mr. Sweet said, "Now what was it you were asking me? Seem like you were about to ask me something."

Hot McGee let out a long sigh. He uncoiled his bullwhip and Leroy worried for about a second that he was going lash the living shit out of Mr. Sweet with it, but he didn't.

He coiled it back up again and picked his straight-chair up and turned to the door. He said, "I'll come back later, when you're feeling better. Miz McGee, she'll be calling later on to check on you. I think you've got them pig's feet, if you'd just put your mind to it."

Leroy had actually seen the New People once before. Talking about Mr. Sweet's store was what made him think of them in the first place. This was where he saw them that time, right here in the store. Leroy had walked down to Mr. Sweet's by himself for some little something, milk maybe, or a dozen eggs, and there they were, standing there picking up a few groceries, just like regular people. The New Guy was what you might call skinny, although Leroy's mama saw him one time and said he was slender. His face was on the leathery side, with creases in his skin. Leroy's mama said his face had character. His hair was a silvery shade of gray and he had a short-cropped beard, stiff as a brush. Well, that part looked pretty good, even Leroy had to admit that much. He was wearing a tweed jacket and silk tie. The New Guy's wife seemed like she might be a lot younger than her husband. She had olive-colored skin and high cheekbones and black, black eyes. Her long hair was wild and wiry and black. It stood out from her head like a bush. You could have said she was skinny, you could have probably even said she was slender, it wouldn't be going too far to say she was beautiful, but Leroy's mama said she looked like a bag of bones, she didn't know what an attractive man saw in a bony old hag like that, it just made her mad to see an attractive older man just throwing his life away on a young little money-grubber, boy oh boy, did it ever make her mad. Leroy remembered hearing Mr. Sweet ring up the amount for their bag of groceries. Mr. Sweet had the New Guy mixed up with some family member who had fought in the Mexican War, a brother maybe, an uncle.

Mr. Sweet said to the New Guy, "I still got them uniforms out in the garage if you ever need them."

The New Guy took his change and gave Mr. Sweet a kindly look. He said, "No, no thank you." Mr. Sweet looked disappointed. He said, "Bayonets?"

That was an earlier day, today the children were the only customers in the store. Leroy said, "Hey, Mr. Sweet."

Mr. Sweet rocked along on his one built-up shoe behind the counter.

He said, "Well, Leroy, how are you? To what do I owe this pleasure?" He saw the girls and swept the paper butcher's cap from his head and bowed a deep, comical bow. "Miss Laurie, Miss Molly, at your service." Some days were better than others, Leroy guessed.

He said, "What can I do you for?"

Leroy said, "Mama said would you like some supper. She'll bring it to you."

"Why, my boy," he said, sincerely, "how could I resist Miss Elsie Dearman's exquisite suppers? I'd be honored, son, honored. I dine promptly at eight, your mother will remember, and I am watching my saturated fats."

"Okay."

The children turned to leave the store.

"Ah!" Mr. Sweet said, and the three of them stopped. "Sweets for the sweet, as the queen said of Ophelia."

He rocked his way along the counter to a great block table on which rested a huge slab of chocolate fudge with a gray dusting of sugar over it. He took a candy knife and slowly, meticulously sawed off three equal-sized pieces. He put each piece into a thin wrapper of waxed paper and rocked back along the counter to where the children stood. He handed each a little package of candy.

"One more thing," he said, holding up his finger and rocking over to the drink box. He pulled out three cans of root beer and handed them across the counter to the children. "Little something to wash it down," he said.

Leroy said, "Okay. Bye."

Mr. Sweet said, "Of course the queen was talking about flowers, not candy, but the sentiment remains."

Leroy said okay again.

He and the girls stood in the store with their candy and root beer.

Finally Leroy remembered and said, "Thank you."

Laurie and Molly said thank you, too.

Mr. Sweet spoke confidentially to all of them. He said, "Now if anybody asks, you tell them Mr. Sweet thought he was selling you some pickled pig's feet. Okay? Can you remember that? That'll be our joke. Tell your mama I sold y'all some pickled pig's feet. All right then, eight o'clock, on the dot, I'll be looking for that supper."

The cottage had been neglected pretty bad, that was the first thing Leroy and his sisters noticed when they got back to the New People's house. They were finished with their candy. They drank their root beers and threw their cans in the ditch. It could use a new roof, the cottage could, even Leroy could see that. The chimney was crumbling, a few bricks lay on the roof. He noticed a busted-out window screen. No flowers had been planted, no dog ran out barking, no chickens or ducks scattered in their path, no yellow cat stood ready to wind around their legs, no new paint freshened the porch, the yard was unmowed. A few junker cars sat in the yard on flat tires, Johnson grass was growing up through the engines. What kind of folks were these? The children were standing just outside the gate. Leroy was a little scared all of a sudden. He wasn't so sure he wanted to go through with this after all. He was glad he had his sisters with him, even if they were pains in the butt. Laurie's boot was beginning to smell a little like pee. Molly bounced up and down on her toes. Leroy had to hold her hand to keep her from running ahead. She said, "Go." Leroy looked at Laurie. He said, "Want to?" Laurie looked thoroughly disgusted with Leroy. She said, "Gimme my boots, shitheel." Leroy took this to mean yes. She looked inside the one boot and jerked Molly's underpants out and slung them in the ditch, along with the root beer cans. Leroy took a step back in case she was in a slapping mood. She put the boots back on her feet and gave him one of those you'll-pay-for-this looks. Molly said, "Go, go!"

They walked through the front gate and kept on walking, all the way around to the back of the house. An old garage, rank with mildew and rot, seemed ready to collapse there. It looked like it had just started to squat down to take a dump. Bamboo fishing poles could be seen racked in the rafters, decayed and ancient. No telling who they once belonged to. They walked along together in a clump, suddenly shy, even Molly. They came to the back porch, which was not screened in but open. The water well for the cottage stood near the porch beneath a little tin-roofed shed. They could hear the pump motor running under there, like a deep-throated sewing machine. Leroy imagined the cool water being sucked up from beneath the earth and sent gushing through pipes into the New People's house. They walked up the steps and stood there at the rear of the cottage. They kept standing there. No one moved to knock. No one turned to leave. They fidgeted. They looked at the door. They scuffed their shoes on the porch floor. Laurie said, "Do it." Leroy breathed one deep breath and rapped lightly on the doorjamb. He might have answered her back if he hadn't smelled up her boot with those underpants. He stepped back from the door and waited, they all did. They stood like ducklings behind a hen. No one answered, no one came to the door. Leroy said, "Nobody home." Laurie said, "Again." Leroy kept standing there for a while. All right, he'd knock again. Rap rap rap, he knocked, good and loud, he let that door have it. Molly became restless. She wriggled and squirmed and would not be held by the hand. She pulled away from Leroy and sat on the old porch floor. Leroy said, "Be good." Molly said, "Okay." After a minute or two she scooted on her butt across the porch and sat at the bottom of the steps, in the dirt, playing with whatever fell near to her hands. Leroy kept his eyes on her. She was always into something.

He heard Laurie say, "Look." He turned and saw that she was pointing at the kitchen window. Leroy looked through it. Though the cottage was small, the kitchen seemed to be its largest room. Looking at it from outside, through the window, the kitchen floor seemed endless, with a wide expanse of yellow linoleum. A heavy porcelain sink stood on one side of the room, with big old-fashioned iron faucets, and near it a cheap, grease-covered stove, so unlike the brilliant Chambers oven in his mother's kitchen. Against another wall stood a round-shouldered old refrigerator. The cabinets were cheap, too, falling off the walls practically, a hinge broken, a door sagging, white-painted metal. A kitchen table covered with oilcloth stood just inside the window. Something seemed to have congealed on it. A man was sitting at the kitchen table. Leroy's insides jumped a little when he saw him. It was the New Guy. One of the New People. He seemed unaware of their presence and not to have heard their knocking, though the table where he sat was very close to the door. He was elegant, it was the only word for it. Leroy wasn't sure he had ever heard the word *elegant,* and yet it was the first word that came to his mind. Maybe his mama had said the New Guy was elegant, he must have gotten it from somewhere. Nothing about the shabby kitchen seemed in keeping with its inhabitant. Leroy couldn't get over it. It was like finding a king in a pauper's cottage, what the hell was a pauper's cottage, every fairy tale Leroy had ever heard was required just to give words to what he was looking at. The jacket that the New Guy wore seemed made of silk, though Leroy had no idea how he knew this.

He said, "What's that, that thing he's wearing?"

Laurie said, "Ascot."

"Ascot," Leroy repeated, as if the word were part of an incantation. A red ascot. He looked at his eight-year-old sister. How did she know these things?

He looked back in the window. He and Laurie might as well have been watching television on a large screen with the sound turned off, as if in a department store window, a little family of urchins who had never seen such a thing.

The New Guy was crying. Weeping would be a better word.

Leroy was having to search through his whole vocabulary all of a sudden. Wailing, that was another word for what was going on in there. He was crying like nobody's business, like Leroy had never imagined anyone on earth ever crying, no sniffles at first, no tuning up to it, just all-out wah-wah-wah, straight out of the gate. He cried and cried and cried. He was a snotty mess he cried so hard. There ought to be a law against crying this hard, forget about it. You couldn't hear him, no sound could escape through the closed window or door, but he was truly going at it. He was howling like a dog. You could see it, head thrown back, really like a dog in the moonlight, sure enough, dog at the railroad tracks, hear that whistle blowing, coming 'round the bend. Laurie said, "Now that son of a bitch can flat cry." The New Guy fell out of his chair. Even Laurie was taken aback by this. You couldn't give this guy enough credit for what he knew about crying. He was the world's best, held the record, champeen, forget about outcrying this one. He rolled around on the kitchen floor, crying good-godamighty. Leroy and Laurie stood on tiptoes to see him down there. They pressed their faces to the window. They shaded their eyes against the glare. The New Guy thrashed about, he rolled under the table and back out again, he kicked his feet, he went on howling in silence, he banged his head on the floor. He rolled up under the windowsill, mostly out of sight now.

Laurie said, "Shit, I can't see."

Leroy said, "Okay, okay."

He put his arms around her waist from behind and picked her up and held her so that she could better see the action down low.

She said, "Better, much better."

Leroy said, "What's he doing now?"

"He just spit up a little."

After a while the howling man rolled back out into the middle of the floor and was easier to see. He got to his feet again. Leroy said, "Oh, good." He could let Laurie stand alone again. Again they both pressed their faces to the window. The New Guy staggered around his kitchen for a while. Leroy and Laurie kept on watching, their eyes shaded against the window glare. The New Guy held his heart with both hands. He tore his hair. He hit himself in the face with his fists.

Leroy said, "I don't think this would be as good without the, uh—"

Laurie said, "The ascot."

Leroy looked at Laurie, then back into the window. Every day his sister grew stranger.

He said, "Right."

The New Guy's ascot was coming undone. He staggered around for a while longer, aimless. The red tie flopped this way and that. Laurie said, "I wish he'd just take the damn thing off." He bounced slowly off the refrigerator, off a wall, the stove, like a pinball in a dream. He stopped and leaned heavily on both hands against the sink. His head was down, his back to the window. His chest was heaving. He stood there for a while, until his breathing grew more regular. He seemed to collect himself.

Leroy said, "What's he doing?"

Laurie said, "He's collecting his thoughts. He's thinking of the bleak future, he's wondering if life's worth living, whether its dim hopes aren't really self-deluding dreams and not worth all the pain of going on, he's coming to the bitter realization that we're all alone in the world."

Leroy just shook his head, he let it drop. What was the point? She was a space alien.

Slowly the New Guy opened a drawer beneath the sink and reached inside. The children peered through the window in interest. He withdrew a sharp knife with a long blade, ten inches at least. This part was bound to happen, Leroy thought. You couldn't do creepy-crawly without somebody dying or ruining their whole life, oh well. The New Guy held the knife in a stabbing position above his head and began his terrible silent wailing again. Crying with knives, Leroy noted. Definitely worth remembering. The New Guy placed the knife to his throat, the sharp point of it pressing a deep indentation into his neck. A trickle of blood appeared. No one moved. Two doors led out of the kitchen and into the rest of the house. Through the door at stage left a woman entered from the bedroom. Leroy and Laurie nodded, yes, all right, a new character. The New Lady, in fact. This beautiful dark woman was wearing only a bra and panties, her hair was wild. She too was carrying a large knife of some kind, a hunting blade, huge, gleaming steel with a big bone handle. Leroy could see a dark shadow at the crotch of the woman's underpants. Well, at least they fit, at least nobody was sneaking around trying to take her picture. And although she could have stood to dress up a little, what she was wearing made some sense. Anybody might walk around in their drawers, Leroy supposed. Now this woman was wailing also, as anguished as her husband, she was going at it, they were the perfect couple. Still, the children couldn't hear much.

Leroy said, "Can we turn up the sound?"

Laurie said, "It doesn't work."

This new character, the New Lady, or maybe even the Wild Woman, seemed to be threatening something, it was hard to tell what. Man, not hearing anything was turning into a major inconvenience, no two ways about it. Who do you call to get this sort of thing fixed? Leroy wondered. The Wild Woman was speaking to the Weeping Man and holding her knife out in his direction. She was acting like she might stab him. She might as well go on and do it, Leroy thought, get it over with, okay, stab him, go ahead. The two New People seemed to face off, to scream at one another for a while. At last the New Guy took the knife from his throat. He didn't want to quit stabbing himself, you could tell, just when he'd started to do some damage. He quit, though, he was a good sport about it. He looked like, Oh well, shit, all right, if it means that much to you. He looked depressed and defeated. He would not kill himself today, his new posture seemed to say. Okay, he quit, jeez. The Wild Woman, she lowered her knife. She looked like she guessed she wouldn't kill anybody either. No point in killing him if he wasn't going to kill himself. It could have made more sense, frankly. Leroy's head was spinning. It was never quite clear what she had planned to do with the hunting knife in the first place. A better sound system would have made all the difference in this particular case.

The man laid his knife on the sink. He was tired, you could easily see, all that bawling's got to be hard on an older guy, so yeah, he was pooped but not bad, he seemed like he was in pretty good shape, he could cry a little more if he had to, he had probably trained for this sort of thing, sort of a professional, our viewers are advised not to try this stunt in their own home. The New People stood around in the kitchen and talked for a while, smiled a little. They liked one another, you could tell that. Before long they were just chatting, kind of regular. She checked his throat where he had pricked himself with the knife. She licked her thumb and wiped a little dried blood away. He was okay, they seemed to agree, sure he'd be fine. He patted her on the butt. Though they seemed sad, they were all right. They walked together out of the room. She was still carrying her bone-handled knife.

Leroy and Laurie looked at one another. What was that all about? What could you say? Leroy looked around. He said, "Where's Molly?" Laurie looked, too. Molly was not on the porch, they couldn't see her in the yard, or in the near pastures. She had slipped away. Where had she run off to? Where had that child gone? They got down off the porch and out into the backyard looking. They started really looking for Molly. "Molly," Leroy called, not very loud, since they were trespassing. Getting caught at creepy-crawly was not one of Leroy's favorite things. "Where are you, Molly?" After a while they found her, she was okay. Molly poked her head out of the old garage. She smiled in an odd way. Her cheeks were full and plump. Fishhooks were sticking out of Molly's mouth in all directions. Leroy walked over to her. He said, "Don't swallow. Okay, Molls, that's good. Just don't swallow." He got them all out. He slung them off his fingers like snot.

4

To Leroy the way he felt was not just because he was growing up, like his mama said. To Leroy everything had seemed to change one fine summer day when his Uncle Harris Dearman had shown up on the llama farm, completely unexpected, wearing a great big smile on his face and plenty of styling mousse in his hair. This was right after Old Pappy died the second time. "There's gonna be some changes around here," Uncle Harris seemed like he was saying to whoever might want to listen to him. Leroy had just turned twelve years old that summer as he watched his amazing and sun-tanned Uncle Harris come driving up the lane, all the way from the Gulf Coast, in that fancy convertible car. He didn't recognize his Uncle Harris at first, he'd only laid eyes on him once before, but he knew something special was about to happen, he knew from the ringing-bells feeling in his stomach, and even in his face, that things might never be the same again now that Uncle Harris was here. He might get to ride in that fine little car, for one thing. That alone would surely mean he would never be the same again. Uncle Harris's little white sportster came flying down the lane trailing a dust cloud like a comet's tail, oh man, it was blaring, too, it was making music on the summer air, an ah-ooga horn and dual exhaust pipes, oh boy. Romance has entered the building, it sounded like somebody was saying. That's what Elsie Dearman would claim later on, though Leroy wouldn't have picked just that word exactly. Everything was about to change for the better, though, that was for sure, things were picking up around the llama farm, it seemed like to Leroy, anybody would have told you so.

When the sports car turned off the blacktop, Leroy was sitting in the sandbox packing sand around his bare feet to make a frog house. When he looked up and saw the car turn off the paved road and make its way down the lane, he pulled his feet out of the frog house and let the sand collapse around them. Who cared about a frog house? His two little sisters dropped their rag dolls on the porch swing and ran out the door and looked up the drive. The times they were a-changing, that was the song being played on Uncle Harris's ah-ooga horn, it might as well have been, to Leroy's ears.

Behind the wooden steering wheel of the little open-topped car Leroy finally recognized his glittering Uncle Harris, tanned face, brilliant hair, flowered shirt, luxurious upon white cordovan leather seats, his white teeth gleaming, the heel of his hand pressing the button of a horn that made some extravagant sound of hilarity, maybe it played a few notes of "Dixie." Uncle Harris had come to the farm, hot damn. For one amazing moment the notes of the horn's blast seemed actually to be imprinted on the summer air above the car's hood, with cartoon drawings of sharps and flats alongside them. The music of the car's horn filled the farm-world with alien, comic hilarity whose sound glowed as bright as a many-faceted gemstone and made tawdry everything it touched, the llama farm, the house and outbuildings, the truck crops in the field, the farm equipment, the great black walnut tree and lightning rod.

Maybe as Leroy remembered this moment years later its details were exaggerated. Much of the memory was contradictory. It was dreamlike. Even Harris himself seemed scarcely real in the memory. Everything had an antique look, and the people, especially Harris, seemed dressed in costumes, as if for an old-timey movie. Leroy's mama looked Amish almost in her simplicity and dowdiness. His daddy, who was clean shaven, might as well have worn a Mennonite's beard, his John Deere cap might have been a black hat with a severe brim. His sisters might have been selling quilts and goat cheese at a roadside stand. He himself—well, Leroy disappeared, for the moment anyway. For this exciting moment it was he himself who sat behind the wooden steering wheel of the amazing little car, Leroy not Harris, in glory, oh yes, oh yes.

He looked hard at his Uncle Harris, who seemed to have changed again. Now he wore a wide-lapeled canvas driving coat, and on his head a jaunty cap with aviator goggles, and gloves for his hands, and a white silk scarf, which flowed behind him in the breeze. An orchestra played loud hopeful music all around. Dancers with long legs, dancers with top hats and canes, announced Uncle Harris's entrance onto the scene. Here he is! He has arrived! The llamas in the pasture stood up on their hind legs and pranced. The tractor in the field went "Toot toot!" like a comical train. Funny smoke rings blew out its tall exhaust. Fish rose up out of the farm pond and sang along. Ducks flew over in a chevron and they joined in the song. Jiminy Cricket was there. Uncle Harris had come to rescue them from their dull lives on the llama farm.

None of this was so, of course, how could it have been, the world did not become a cartoon, but so it seemed to Leroy, so it surely seemed for this moment, and seemed so perhaps to Elsie as well, Leroy's mother, perhaps to Elsie more than to anyone.

At least one thing was true. It was Harris, in that car, Leroy's daddy's extraordinary brother, and his appearance on the farm was as unexpected as a visitor from another planet. Leroy blinked away the extravagance of his imagination and looked upon the extravagance of Harris's reality. He was wearing sporty sunglasses, so dark you could not see his eyes. The black pools of his shaded eyes spoke of mystery. His hair was straight and cropped short in the modern way, his face was golden brown. Leroy's own sun-blond hair and freckles seemed a loathsome thing. Harris was waving his arm and blasting away on the sassy horn. He brought his car to a crunching halt in the driveway and set the emergency brake. The car rocked forward and then back again it stopped so quickly. Even the crunch of gravel seemed filled with newness and miraculous distances. Harris's smile was white-toothed as a shark's. Leroy had never seen such a smile. His own teeth felt too big for his mouth. They felt gray by comparison. There had never been so wonderful a vision as his Uncle Harris, who sat before him like a king.

Harris did not open his door and step out in the normal way. No one would have expected this banality of him, in any case. Somehow—later it seemed impossible that this should have happened and yet surely it did—Harris vaulted, effortless, from his seat. He left the car as if by extra-human propulsion. He rose from his seat, it seemed to Leroy. He might as well have been ejected from it, with such ease he seemed to become airborne. He launched himself, Leroy might have said—over the doors of his car and through the air. He was not out of control of this leap, he was flying, he was Superman. Solidly he landed with both feet on the ground. He held his arms halfway out, palms up, and said, "Whoa, Mama!" His smile, honestly, was like sunlight.

Just then Elsie came out the back door to see what all the commotion was about. She had not yet been transformed by her brother-in-law's presence. She was drying her hands on her apron. She wore no makeup, in her fresh-faced, farmwife way. She blew a strand or two of hair out of her eyes and scratched the tip of her nose with the dry back of her hand. Leroy watched her. He watched the neat little farm, the funny ducks on the pond, the baby llamas in the lot, he imagined the yellow pound cake on the table behind his mother, fresh from its pan, all the details of his life and contentment. Everything suddenly lost meaning and strength before his very eyes. What had been expected and usual and even invisible suddenly became tawdry and stupid, a judgment upon them all.

Leroy's mama had noticed none of this, yet. She saw only Harris.

She said, "Well, would you look!"

Her face showed such joy that Leroy wanted to shout to her, "Watch out!" He had no idea what he would have meant by this.

Elsie stopped at the bottom of the porch steps and stood looking at her glittering brother-in-law like a shy girl. Her farmgirl complexion was underlaid with a blush that even Leroy had to admit was beautiful. It was a thing he had not noticed in his mother before.

Harris hauled out his carpetbag from behind his seat and stretched himself good and looked exactly like a man making ready to settle in for a while.

Leroy was transfixed. He saw Harris and his mama see one another. He saw Harris hold his arms out wide. Harris cocked his head, rakish and teasing, to the side.

Elsie twisted her apron in her hands.

Leroy ran for cover. He hid behind a crepe myrtle bush and watched. He eased out again.

Harris said, "Hey, good-lookin', whatcha got cookin'!"

This caused Leroy's mama to blush even more and to become even more beautiful.

Leroy watched, incredulous.

Suddenly Harris rushed to Elsie as if he had returned from the wars, he did this in a single sudden sweep of his whole self across the property. In a split second he was upon her. He grabbed her around the waist like a movie star, as if Elsie weighed nothing at all. He flung her into the air. Elsie said, "Eek!" She actually said that word. *Eek*. Leroy had never heard that word spoken. He had seen it in "Nancy and Sluggo" comics, when Aunt Fritzi stood on a chair with a cute mouse on the floor. What was happening to their lives? Maybe, later on, when Leroy executed his creepy-crawly, it was an answer to this question—as much as the dirty pictures—that he had hoped to find. Harris swung Elsie up into the air, up and up, her feet off the ground, and then around and around in a circle, as easily as if she were a child. Her golden hair became a halo, it swung over her shoulder. She said, "Oh, oh, oh!" Her skirt flew up above her knees. Suddenly her smile was as bright as Harris's. Leroy had never seen his mother so happy. She was no longer Amish. She looked like a teenager. She looked almost modern. Leroy wanted to be modern, he wanted to be a teenager. He had seen them on television, heard of them all his life. He was twelve years old. He would die of old age before it was time for him to be a teenager. He wanted to drive a car. He wanted to have a date. He wanted to fall in love with somebody like his mother. Like his mother? What was he saying, had he lost his mind? Elsie held on to Harris's neck and allowed herself to be held by the waist. She flung her head back in laughter and joy. She said, "Oh my!" At last Harris stopped swinging her. At last he let her come back to earth. Then he hugged her, the biggest, funniest hug Leroy had ever seen, a real bear hug, all around, engulfing her. He held her straight back from him, at arms' length. He said, "Yahoo!" then hugged her again.

Leroy was spellbound. What he saw next terrified him. Harris kissed Elsie, kissed his mama. Kissed her three times, smack, once on the forehead, smack, once on the tip of her nose, and then, smack, right on the lips. When he did this, the kiss on the lips, he actually said, "Smooch!" in a loud voice. He held her at arms' length again. The two of them laughed and laughed and said happy hellos.

Elsie said, "You're crazy! What are you *doing* here!"

She said, "The children!"

"The children!" Harris said.

He crouched, he turned slowly, he crooked his fingers in the way of old-timey movie monsters.

Laurie and Molly squealed in happiness and appreciation.

They ran in circles. Molly peed in her pants. Come to think of it, this was the first time Molly started wetting her pants again, the day Uncle Harris arrived.

Harris picked up each of the children, the two girls anyway, and swung them around and kissed them with noisy kisses in the same way as he had done with Elsie. He didn't care about wet pants.

Leroy took off running. He was out of here. He didn't know why. He rounded the corner of the house. He tore out around the side of the house and hid in a lean-to shed he had made with some spare boards against a corner of the pasture fence. He was breathing hard. He wanted to be swung around. He even wanted to be kissed. He just couldn't take the pressure. He barely escaped. There was a stitch in his side. He stayed there in his lean-to for a while, wondering. The others went inside the house with Uncle Harris. He could hear them in there. He listened to their voices, their laughter. He burned with envy and relief. The thin scraps of boards above him were safety for now. Even the house he lived in seemed suddenly unsafe. The house where Leroy lived with his parents might as well have been the water a fish lived in, so familiar had it always seemed to Leroy, a frame structure built in the red clay hills. Its underside was one of Leroy's secret places, its attic another. His grandfather had died in the attic, and so its mysteries were rich. Leroy's bedroom was tiny, with a narrow steel cot where he slept. His sisters shared a larger room. The kitchen with its enormous old Chambers stove, his parents' room, the living room with its stone fireplace from which wisps of smoke crept on fragrant winter days, the screened porch and its casual furniture of wicker painted white. Truck crops grew in the fields, tomatoes, corn, melons, squash, beans, carrots, turnips, alfalfa for the herd. Llamas stood behind rail fences. This was the world that began to fade from view when Uncle Harris arrived in it.

In another hour Swami Don came putt-putting out of the field on the tractor, Leroy's daddy, with only the one good arm. Leroy watched him from the lean-to. He was wearing Big Smith overalls and had a sweat-stained red bandana tied around his neck and the John Deere cap on his head. Swami Don didn't talk about his strange nickname. About all he ever said was he was named for a man down in the Delta who ran a salvage business. It made no sense.

The llamas fanned out, away from Swami Don, running along with such strange ease that they reminded Leroy of giraffes, necks swaying like slender trees in the wind. He watched his daddy. He regretted the limitations he saw in him. He was embarrassed that he was a farmer, that he had only one arm, that he did not glitter like Uncle Harris did.

Swami Don drove the tractor into the shed and switched off the engine. Leroy eased out of his lean-to. He watched as Swami Don got down off the tractor and squinted his eyes in the sun, looking. He was looking at the sporty little car. Leroy couldn't tell whether he recognized it. Leroy moved on around to the back of the house. He had wanted to go inside with the others but couldn't go alone. He would walk in with his daddy, he supposed. He couldn't hide forever. He wished now he'd taken his turn at swinging in Uncle Harris's arms, taken his three kisses.

Swami Don hauled his withered arm around and let it drop by his side. Leroy watched every move, felt critical and even angry. Swami Don untied the bandana with his good hand and used it to mop sweat out of his eyes. He walked up to the car and looked inside at the dusty leather seat covers. He stepped back. He walked around it. He kicked a tire. He wiped his neck with the bandana and then he wiped a streak of dust off one of the fenders and stuck the bandana in his back pocket, where it hung halfway out. What in the world? his expression seemed to say.

Leroy walked out to the drive. He walked up behind his daddy.

He said, "It's Uncle Harris's car."

Swami Don turned around. This was the first time Harris had ever visited the farm.

Swami Don said, "Oh, hey, Leroy. I figured as much."

Leroy said, "He's great."

Swami Don looked at Leroy.

He said, "I know."

Swami Don ambled on up to the porch. Leroy followed him. Uncle Harris hadn't wasted any time. There was almost a party going on up there. Elsie and Harris were sitting in the wicker furniture and talking. The girls were sitting nearby, trying to behave so they could stay forever. Everybody was having something cool to drink, lemonade, maybe, two tall glasses filled with ice, and a sweating pitcher between them on a low wicker table.

Leroy's mama's face was still flushed with joy. It was impossible to say why this frightened Leroy.

She said, "Donald, look who's here!"

Elsie had taken the wicker rocker and seemed perched there, birdlike, while Harris was lounging like a benevolent king on the chaise, hands clasped confidently behind his head. Laurie and Molly were underfoot, in love with their Uncle Harris. Leroy was no less in love with Uncle Harris than his two sisters were. He stood half hidden behind his daddy. He pushed at a little pile of dead flies on the porch floor with his toe. Before he had gone out to play in the sand pile he'd been out here killing flies. Flies came in during rains, and Swami Don had told Leroy he'd give him a penny for every ten flies he killed. Leroy was trying to figure out how many flies it would take for him to get a motorcycle. Maybe now he would go for a sports car instead.

While Swami Don had still been outside kicking the tires of the sports car, Leroy had looked up onto the porch and had seen something he knew Swami Don was not meant to see. When his mama poured the lemonade, Harris had taken a small silvery flask from his pocket and unscrewed the cap. He held it as if to offer it to Elsie. Then he smiled at her blushing and tipped the little bottle to the side of his lemonade. Leroy saw his mother mouth the words "You're bad."

Swami Don said, "Has something happened to Hannah?"

Hannah was Harris's wife. Swami Don had once dated Hannah in high school and Harris took her away from him. Everybody knew this. Leroy had forgotten, but now he remembered.

Elsie said, "Well, for heaven's sake, Donald, can't you at least say hello to your brother before you give him the third degree?"

Swami Don said, "Oh. Well— Sure. Hi, Harris."

He pulled the red bandana out of his pocket and mopped his neck again.

Elsie smiled her brightest smile.

She said, "Okay, then! That's better, you two!"

This next part probably wasn't true, but later on it was the way Leroy remembered it: in the memory, Uncle Harris now seemed to be wearing a wide-brimmed white straw hat and a white Panama suit with an open-collared shirt and a long red kerchief dangling from the suit's jacket pocket. Leroy remembered that his Uncle Harris dipped a bright red cherry out of his lemonade, gave Elsie a big wink and a white smile, and popped that cherry into his wide-open mouth, yum yum yum.

5

Later on, after the sun went down, the fire-flies appeared in the yard in numbers. The heatless light of their golden tails looked like peepholes in the darkness into a bright strange world. A sweet fragrance of insecticide wafted from the orchard, through the screens, to their nostrils. The hours passed. Leroy caught these glimpses of his old familiar world.

Conversation settled down some as evening dropped over them. The hilarity subsided. The children were allowed to hang around longer than usual to visit with their uncle. The subject of Hannah came up again. Hannah was fine, just fine, Harris assured them, don't you worry yourself about Hannah, he said. He apologized for his sudden appearance, right out of the blue, with no warning. "Sorry for dropping in like this, I should have called first, it was rude, I realize, I just thought, what the heck, it's my brother for Pete's sake, if you can't drop in on your own brother, well, anyway, I hope it's all right, hope I'm not intruding, I wouldn't want to be a bother."

This was the quiet way they had begun to talk. Leroy liked this as much as the mad entrance. It seemed in some ways equally foreign to his customary evenings on this porch.

Finally Harris got around to telling Swami Don and Elsie what he was really doing here, what had happened. He told them Hannah wanted a divorce.

For a moment no one spoke. Leroy held his breath.

Swami Don said, "A divorce?"

No one had ever spoken of a divorce on this porch before. It was an odd thing to be thinking, but it was what came to Leroy's mind. It thrilled him, in a way. The world had changed. He had been right.

Elsie said, "Oh, you poor thing."

Leroy didn't know whose face to watch.

Harris had on his serious look now.

"She kicked me out," he said.

His wife had kicked him out? It was like television. Leroy watched his mother nod seriously as if this were the kind of conversation she had every day. Later on Leroy would learn that what she was doing was "being supportive." Right now Leroy knew she was as astounded as he was.

Harris put his tanned face into his hands. He sobbed a little.

"I wanted to be near family," he said when he looked up. "For a night or two, at least."

"Of course," Elsie said quickly.

"You can understand that, can't you, I hope you can, but hey, look, if I'm in the way, if this is any bother whatsoever, well—"

Elsie said, "Oh Harris, of course—of course we understand. And no, of course not, no bother at all, don't be silly, we wouldn't have it any other way. We're here. We're family. Absolutely."

Swami Don bounced his withered hand in his good hand. A few seconds were allowed to pass. It was clear Elsie wanted him to chime in with some kind of agreement.

In fact, she said, a little fiercely, "Chime right in, Donald, anytime you have something to offer."

Leroy might as well have been watching a tennis match, back and forth, he was dizzy as a witch.

Swami Don said, "This is the first time you've ever come to see us."

Elsie gave him a look. Leroy almost said something but managed to stay quiet.

Harris nodded. He said, "I've been remiss."

Elsie let out an exasperated sigh in order to change the subject. She got up out of her chair and sat back down again. She rocked as fiercely as she spoke.

She said, "What is *wrong* with that woman?"

Meaning Hannah, of course, Leroy realized.

There was a long silence. Leroy paid careful attention.

Swami Don said, "There's nothing wrong with Hannah."

Elsie looked at her husband as if he were a stranger who had just walked up on the porch.

Swami Don did not shrink from her black gaze, as normally he might have done.

Harris seemed to know better than to let the remark about Hannah stay in the air long. He said, "Oh, absolutely, you're absolutely right. Hannah is not at fault here, please don't get me wrong, no sir, no siree, no way José, I'm not blaming Hannah, not anybody really, certainly not Hannah, blameless as the day is long, perfectly innocent, didn't mean to imply otherwise, you know that, don't you, you know I didn't mean to say anything against Hannah, sweet as she is pretty, and smart, too, of course, she's not seeing things too clearly right now, taking bad advice from well-intended friends maybe, but blame? Hannah? Me? Not a chance, not a snowball's chance in aitch ee double-el, pardon my parly voo, no ma'am, uh-uh, let me set the record straight, it's not anybody's fault, not that good woman's fault that she unfairly, unexpectedly, cruelly, and with no provocation whatsoever, save only vicious and unsubstantiated rumors and lies, kicked me out of my own house and gave my clothes to the Salvation Army and changed all the locks on the doors, no way. I'm not saying anything is anybody's fault. Not at all. Not entirely. There are things I could have done differently, too, probably, I'm sure there were. There probably were things I could have, you know— Darn straight. I'm not blaming Hannah."

Elsie put her hand on Harris's hand.

She said, "And don't blame yourself either, Harris. You're too good a person for that. I hope you will believe that."

Leroy said, "Will you teach me to yodel?"

He couldn't think of anything else to say. He might as well say this. Nobody paid any attention to him anyway.

Elsie withdrew her hand and sat back in her chair.

Swami Don said, "But *is* Hannah all right? Does she know where you are? I mean, should you at least call and let her know where you are?"

Leroy said, "You don't hear a lot of yodelers. I was thinking I might take it up."

Everyone looked at him as if he had just walked in from another planet.

Harris smiled. He said, "As a hobby?"

Leroy said, "Right. You know."

"One of Captain Woody's puppets can yodel," Harris said. "I may have it out in the car."

"A yodeling puppet?"

"Right."

"Wow."

Elsie said, "Let's don't rush him, Donald. Let's just let Harris make all his own decisions, in his own time. Okay? Is that okay with you, Harris? Let's let him teach Leroy to yodel first, okay? Is that a Swiss puppet, Harris? There used to be a yodeler on the "Grand Ole Opry" show, didn't there? Well, I don't guess he was Swiss, though. So, anyway, Harris doesn't need anybody rushing him right now, do you. Okay, Donald? Isn't that okay, not to rush him? Rushing is the last thing your sweet brother needs right now, what with yodeling lessons and all. Just tell me if I'm wrong. If I'm wrong, I'll be the first to admit it."

Harris shrugged helplessly.

He said, "She changed all the locks. On the *doors*."

Swami Don said, "You don't need a door key to dial a telephone."

Elsie gave him a poisonous look.

Leroy made a gargling noise in his throat. It was the closest he could come to a yodel.

Harris wagged his head slowly, side to side.

"I just don't know," he said. "I only wish I knew."

They sat for a long time in the silence of the deepening evening. A cool breeze blew through the screens. Heat lightning showed silent yellow reflections on faraway clouds. Leroy had started thinking about what to do if he got sent to bed.

Harris made a puppet out of Molly's rag doll. He gave Leroy that bright smile. He made the puppet talk in a comical voice. The puppet yodeled, "Hold the old man while I kiss the old-lady-oh!"

6

By the next morning Harris had moved into the attic and transformed the whole house, filled it with high spirits, flags, banners, might as well have been flying, circus horns, jugglers, and magicians. The days passed and were filled with laughter. Leroy had never laughed so much. His cheeks ached from laughing. Laughter was Uncle Harris's constant companion. He had a wonderful laugh, too, Leroy realized, loud and sturdy but also childlike, high-pitched at times, almost a squeal. A strange musical instrument with bells and banjos seemed to be playing when Uncle Harris laughed, that was how rich Leroy found those refrains to be. No matter how corny the joke, how tall the tale, you couldn't keep from laughing with Harris when he laughed that laugh of his. It was contagious, oh what a laugh it was. Leroy watched his daddy who almost never laughed. Sometimes he only stood with wide-open eyes, a scared little smile, but other times even

Swami Don could not contain himself. Uncle Harris told a tale about a blue runner snake that chased a man down and hid in his asshole. Leroy's eyes widened. "It's in a blue runner's nature," Harris said, "to hide in a man's asshole, ask anybody, look it up, it's a fact, it's science, Leroy, the asshole aspect of the Mississippi blue runner." Leroy thought he might actually faint. "Slithered right up in his asshole and nested down," Uncle Harris said, and laughed that fine big rich laugh of his, and then everybody else laughed too, even Swami Don. Leroy knew this was a joke, but he believed it anyway. He whispered, "Yikes." What health seemed to follow Harris wherever he went! Even the sad marital split that had sent Harris here became a part of the joking, the clothes in the street, new locks on the doors, the Salvation Army on the march, it was hilarious, all of it, how could anybody be so funny? Sadness scurried before Uncle Harris like geese before a child's cane. Then Hannah disappeared from conversation, from memory, almost. Harris's grief seemed to fade in the glittering presence of that laugh. People begged him to repeat their favorite stories, even little Molly.

"Tell the blue snake in your asshole," she pleaded.

Elsie said, "Molly!"

Harris said, "Not *my* asshole!"

"Yes!" Molly shouted in joy.

Harris told some stories that were supposed to be true. He claimed to have met John Dillinger, the famous outlaw. "I was just a baby," he said. "So I don't remember it well, but it's the truth, the God's truth, I've got a photograph around here somewhere to prove it if you don't believe me, swear to God, cross my heart and hope to spit. John Dillinger, listen here, the famous outlaw held me in his arms, sure did. He had on a hat, I do remember that much."

Laurie said, "Did the blue runner catch John Dillinger?"

"Nobody could catch John Dillinger," Harris said seriously. "John Dillinger was uncatchable. You might as well forget about catching John Dillinger. Even the blue runners gave up on ever catching John Dillinger. Here's a fact few people know about, historical fact, I'm glad to share it with you. John Dillinger had the only snake-free asshole in Mississippi for many years."

Elsie said, "Harris!"

His laughter was like banjo music.

"Oh, *you!*"

Every day was a party. You couldn't keep from enjoying yourself. Evenings Harris held "grog rations." This was what he called cocktail hour. It was a nautical term he had picked up from his foster daddy, Captain Woody, he told Leroy. The fact that there was alcohol in any form in Leroy's daddy's house made Leroy's head spin. Literally he felt quite dizzy the first few times he realized grog rations was becoming a regular element of the daily party, and the true amazement was that nobody really objected. Was this really his own house? Had he been transported somehow, taken to another world?

Each day Uncle Harris brought forth some new alcoholic

concoction. Each day the new drink was introduced dramati-
cally. Sometimes he covered the drink tray with a clean white
cloth that he whipped away at the last moment, as if he were
a magician revealing a hidden rabbit or flight of doves. Always
there was laughter. Frosted glasses sparkled, ice cubes clinked.
Even Swami Don looked forward to what the day's alcoholic
confection might be, so much color it brought through their
doors, so much romance, Elsie would have insisted. Of course
no one but Harris ever tasted the alcohol, no one else in the
house drank, and he made no demands. No one was expected
to drink if they didn't want to, only to enjoy the party. Leroy
was fascinated, but for this bit of permanence he felt grateful.
The fact that nobody in the Dearman household drank alcohol
was one thing he felt he could hold on to. In this way the
world still turned on its axis, the sun still rose in the east, set
in the west.

Still, the party never seemed to end. Harris produced
cocktail shakers and little paper umbrellas, cherries, sprigs of
mint, even a hollowed-out pineapple, whatever was necessary. He bought a blender. He crushed ice to a fare-thee-well.
Brandy alexanders, stingers, rusty nails, piña coladas, banana
daiquiries—these were the new words Leroy and the girls
added to their vocabulary, along with Elsie and Swami Don.
Harris was no boozer, he was not a hard drinker. Life was a
party, that was all, a big fat wonderful party with Harris on
board, man you couldn't beat it, life was good, you better believe it was. Nutmeg and citrus rinds and a fragrance of co-

conut and tropical fruits. Grog rations was as good as love, some days it seemed that way to Leroy, to Elsie, too, maybe to Elsie more than to anyone.

"Grog rations!" Harris would sing out at the same hour each evening.

Always he spoke in a funny voice that was supposed to sound like Popeye the Sailor Man. He would squint one eye hard and wrinkle his face in a Popeye sort of way. He had a stubby corncob pipe and a billed cap that made everybody laugh.

Leroy's mama would literally squeal with delight.

Harris would whistle a tune, which might sound a little like a bos'n's pipe, or sometimes he would sing a bit of a song that he called a sea chantey. Elsie and the children learned some of the words and sang along with him.

"I yam that I yam!" he would mug, and everyone would laugh again.

Elsie didn't drink the alcohol, but she was always a part of Harris's party. She piped nautical tunes right along with him. She was always as gay as he was. He never made a drink for himself that he did not make a nonalcoholic version for her. She sipped through straws, she allowed whipped cream to stay on her lip as a moustache until Harris wiped it away with a comical sweep of a napkin. Leroy kept an eye on all this. She said, "Eek!" when bubbles went up her nose. *Eek* became her favorite word. Leroy wished she would stop saying eek so much. She acted tipsy, just for fun. She put a paper umbrella behind her ear, or two cherries in her eyes, or pretended orange slices were earrings, and giggled at the smallest joke. She was positively girlish in Harris's presence, or anyway at grog time. Harris said, "Party girl!" No words could have delighted Elsie Dearman more, Leroy could read this in her face.

Swami Don joined in, in his way. He was more reserved than Elsie—always he was—and yet he was not left out. He loved Elsie's laughter. Leroy watched his daddy watch his mama and thought this must be the meaning of love. That was the main thing for Swami Don, Leroy could tell, he loved to see Elsie happy. He drank a Coke sometimes, just to join in; he raised his glass for Harris's silly toasts. He didn't drink the nonalcoholic version of his brother's drinks, though. He only said, "Aw, no, no thanks, I don't think so." He didn't say why. Maybe he didn't know. Once Laurie picked up one of Elsie's drinks and was ready to take a sip and he took it firmly from her and set it down. No one mentioned it, not even Laurie. What Swami Don really seemed to like, though, even more than grog rations, was the time he now spent each day with his younger brother, with Leroy's Uncle Harris. Leroy watched his daddy, saw him in a new way. He wondered what it was like to have a brother. He wished he had a brother. What was he saying? He didn't want a damn brother. Often Swami Don and Harris spoke quietly at night, out on the porch. They recalled living together in the hills, before the family broke up. They remembered an owl they saw once, in the moonlight. They recalled a Pentecostal minister who wore an Indian warbonnet. They talked about their Old Mammy's death, the gunshot that crippled Swami Don.

Leroy lay beneath a soft quilt on the porch glider in the cool of the evening and listened to their quiet talk.

Swami Don said, "You sure had a way with the girls."

Harris said, "I felt guilty for having two good arms."

He said, "You could have used four!"

Leroy could hear the laughter.

Later, when his mama came in to say good night, Leroy said, "Tell me the story," and Elsie said, "Oh, honey, no, not tonight, not that old story."

7

Leroy's Uncle Harris was a wonder to behold, Leroy couldn't take his eyes off him. One morning he was dressed in a brightly flowered Hawaiian shirt and white duck pants and deck shoes, and the next morning in khaki safari shorts and belted bush jacket and pith helmet. Another day he wore tennis whites; another the white Panama suit and straw hat; another a Nehru jacket and beret and double-knit bell-bottoms. Each day was a fashion statement of some demented sort. Where did all these clothes come from? How had he smuggled them into the house? Had he somehow fitted them all into his carpetbag? It was not possible. He was like Ginger and Mrs. Howell on the "Gilligan's Island" reruns. Was this the way all divorced men dressed? This seemed impossible as well. Leroy remembered that Hannah had thrown away all of Uncle Harris's clothes, given them to the poor. He had been cast out, naked and homeless, he had been desperate.

Was this the wardrobe a man with no clothes comes up with on short notice? Did he shop each day when he went out on his rounds away from the farm, at junk stores, used-clothing places, such as Leroy had noticed, places with names like Second Hand Rose and Twice Told Tales?

Each day Harris slept late and Leroy found himself waiting expectantly for his uncle's appearance. Each day when Harris finally emerged from the attic he was always wearing a long silk robe with a sash. He spent long hours in the bathroom. He used lotions and colognes. Each day he came out dressed in some new outrage of fashion. No one asked him about his clothing, there were other aspects of Uncle Harris's personality that drew similar attention. His toilette was one. His indolence was another. He did nothing, absolutely nothing. He sat, he ate heartily, he made suggestions on improving the service, he asked people to bring him things, to adjust the fan so that it blew on him without ruffling his newspaper, he made himself comfortable, no one on earth had ever been so comfortable as Uncle Harris. Uncle Harris was the laziest man alive. Anyone would have agreed. Nobody held this against him, but no one could have failed to notice. He was not depressed, he did not sleep all day, he simply relaxed, his mood stayed high, his spirits were excellent. The work on the farm went on, and he did none of it. Leroy's mama and daddy each had part-time jobs they sometimes worked at to help make ends meet. None of this bothered Uncle Harris in the least. If his brother and sister-in-law wanted to work, well, sure, work was an honorable thing, he fully approved, no need to be embarrassed, you go right on ahead, don't let me stop you. In the meantime, he better check the sports page, that midseason pitching was beginning to heat up in Fenway, it looked like to Harris, real horse race shaping up in the American League, yessiree, go right on with your business, you ain't disturbing me a bit, I mean it.

Newspapers were Harris's true love. He snuck in a dirty magazine, okay, that was true, hidden in a folded paper now and then, he had diversified interests, sure, but it was the newspaper that really captured his heart, he read as many of them as he could get his hands on, newspapers from all over the country. Uncle Harris was quick to make friends in the village, he found a newspaper supplier right away. There were so many of them, too, these newspapers. At the end of a day his hands would be black with newsprint. Why, he might have to bathe all over again. Who would have ever guessed there were so many different newspapers in the world, Leroy thought, they cost a fortune, must have, there were so many. When Harris finished reading one, he threw it on the floor. That's all for that newspaper, let's see now, where was the *Post-Dispatch*, I thought it was right here under the *Commercial Appeal*. Leroy's mama was always having to pick up after Harris. He kept the newspapers stacked beside his chair and read one after another. By the time he was finished with them they were all over the house. It looked like a blizzard.

Elsie said, "Maybe we should think about recycling."

Harris said, "I just read an excellent article about recycling scams, where was that piece, the *Times* I think, let's see, I've got it right here somewhere." Eventually he found the article proving the folly of recycling and the subject was dropped.

Newspapers seemed a constant source of adventure. He loved to read aloud. He had a beautiful reading voice, it didn't matter what he was reading. He could make serious things sound funny or even funny things sound serious. Leroy would have gladly done nothing during the day but sit in his uncle's presence, in his lap if he would let him, but of course his mama wouldn't hear of that. Indolence in others was not allowed. Harris was the only person on the property who was permitted to be a total bum. This seemed to Leroy simply to be the way of the world. Harris loved to read and he shared everything he read. He read to whoever happened to be in the room from whatever paper he happened to be making his way through. Ann Landers and the horoscope, of course, headlines, cartoons, Miss Manners, Heloise, the lives of others, in many forms, long articles on astronomy or anthropology, political pieces, op-ed pieces, book reviews, church bazaars, executions, plane crashes, disco artists, whatever caught his interest.

"I'd love to go on a dig," he'd say. "One of these days I'm going on a dig."

Leroy imagined going on a dig with him, or a safari, or deep-sea diving, or to the moon, whatever had caught Uncle

Harris's attention that day. Leroy noticed a look on his mama's face one day that told him she might like to run away with Harris, too, she might enjoy a dig on foreign soil.

Harris read the obituaries, at length. Watch out if you were in the room when Harris reached the obituaries. You were going to hear about some dead people if you were nearby, mark it down. The grown-ups knew to clear out. They had learned their lesson. The children usually got stuck with the tales of the dead. It didn't matter to Leroy, he loved every word. Even little Molly was not immune to the obituaries.

"Listen to this, Molls," Uncle Harris might say. "This guy died and he was just, well let's see, it says here he was thirty-four years old. Can you believe that? Thirty-four. Jeez. Same age as me. Whew. Makes you think, doesn't it? Let's see, it says here, oh listen to this, Molls, it says here he was survived by his mother—well, let's see, hm, his daddy must be dead, he's not mentioned, heart attack probably, men don't live as long as women, it's a scientific fact, you take any scientist off the street and he'll back me up on this—survived by his mother, well at least she's in good health, I'm glad to hear she's doing okay, that's good, and oh listen to this, seven brothers. Seven brothers! Wow! Jeez Louise! That's one shitload of brothers, wouldn't you say, Molls? What do you think about that?"

Everything was an adventure. He drove into the village most every day. He had a few other regular stops, not just the newspaper guy. The newspaper guy was real old and said he taught Elvis Presley how to comb his hair. Some things you believe, some you just have to take with a grain of salt, that was Harris's way of looking at it. He found a truck stop on the edge of town where he said they served the best breakfasts in the world. He was always bragging about these breakfasts.

"You should try it yourself, Els," he said to Leroy's mama. "You should let me take you out there sometime. You know where the place is, out on Highway 61, you'd recognize it. Try the flapjacks. That would be my recommendation. Whipped butter, real maple syrup, yum yum. I was asking this old gal, waitress, you know, with a scar on her face, marital difficulties, sad story, asking her about that maple syrup, where it came from, Vermont, you're probably thinking, that's where you automatically think it came from, I don't blame you, I fell into the same trap, I guessed Vermont myself, I won't lie to you, but nope, that's not it, not Vermont, guess again, where do you think that maple syrup was tapped, come on, take your wildest guess."

He was enthusiastic about everything he did, everything he saw or heard. He said the short-order cook at the truck stop was a one-eyed man who could sing every song in *The Mikado* in its entirety with a cigarette hanging out of his mouth, a long ash on the end that never fell off. Harris was starting to pick up a few show tunes himself, he said, some night he might treat everybody to a song or two. He said he would take up smoking if he thought he could learn that trick with the long cigarette ash. He told about another man who had been to

Hollywood and walked through Mayberry, Gilligan's Island, Fantasy Island, Petticoat Junction, and the Love Boat. "They're not real!" Harris exclaimed at the end of his story. "They're soundstages! That's even better, isn't it, better than real!" Another time Harris got started on Gary Gilmore, the murderer out in Utah. Gary Gilmore this, Gary Gilmore that. Gary Gilmore, the Mormons. Gary Gilmore saying, "Let's do it." Gary Gilmore, shot through the heart. Could there be anybody more boring than Gary Gilmore? Leroy had heard enough about Gary Gilmore. Gary Gilmore, would you please shut up.

Every once in a while Harris stopped by an old-fashioned barbershop in the old part of town and got a shave with a straight razor and a shoeshine. "It's a luxury, I know, I know, I could do without," he said. "I'm going to think about cutting back on expenses one of these days, you just wait and see. You ought to hear that strop, though, once he gets that sucker going, man, sounds like Hambone, poppy pop, poppy pop, hambone, hambone, have you heard, yeah." He said the shoeshine boy was a Mexican gent in his sixties or seventies, he didn't know how old. "Real old Mexican, name of Hernando, funny name, ain't it, Hernando, like the hideaway, I never thought about that hideaway serving Mexican food, did you, it ain't quite as romantic if you think about it being a Mexican place, them refried beans are some nasty eating, man, whew, I hope I don't sound prejudiced against our southern neighbors because that would leave a false impression, I'm not, not in the slightest, love a Mexican, sure do, makes you kind of queasy to think about it, though, don't it, couldn't speak a word of English, poor old Hernando, locked up in a cocoon of silence, you might say, don't seem to bother him, though, Hernando don't seem to give a rat's ass. It's unusual, a Mexican gentleman in that line of work, don't you think, wouldn't you agree, shoeshine trade, *habla habla,* that's how they talk, makes you dizzy as a witch to listen to it. I myself don't speak a solitary word of Mexican, but if I did, I think I'd have to ask him about his career choice, see could I help him define his goals."

Some days Leroy's head was spinning as he listened to his Uncle Harris.

Swami Don was rarely in the house for Harris's enthusiastic newspaper reading or his spirited report on his daily excursions. Swami Don spent his days in the pastures, or on the tractor in the fields, and many nights he was gone as well, working as a part-time night watchman at a sporting goods factory in Eupora. He was always looking for ways to supplement his income. And he especially liked the military-style uniform he wore to his night watchman job. He felt almost handsome in that uniform. Elsie liked it, too. She always looked at him a little different when he dressed in his night watchman uniform. By the time he got home, usually evenings, around suppertime, Harris was already in his party mode, with grog rations and puppet shows and the rest of his foolishness. He was finished talking about the newspaper and *The Mikado* for now. The children's faces were glowing, always. Leroy knew his was without even looking in the mirror.

Swami Don saw the newspaper carnage sometimes, before Elsie managed to pick up after Harris. Leroy thought his daddy might be irritated by the mess, especially by Harris's laziness. You could build a table on that man's laziness, it was so sturdy and sound. But this turned out not to be so. Swami Don didn't seem to mind at all, any of it. He was encouraged by the clutter, not irritated. He said it seemed like a mess made of happiness and enthusiasm. He said he believed he himself could learn a few things from Harris's careless life. Anybody could. Or maybe Harris was not completely careless, he said one time. We don't know, really, he was saying. Maybe the newspapers meant Harris was looking for work, a part-time job of some kind, to help out with the expenses. He might be going through the classifieds in every major city in the country, that was certainly a possibility, Swami Don said. Well, Leroy knew this was crazy. That was one idea that made no sense at all. It didn't matter, though. That was the odd part, it didn't matter a bit what Harris was doing with those newspapers. Swami Don didn't mind that his brother lay about the house and village all day. He didn't want his money. He was just grateful to have his little brother in the house after being so far apart for so many years. Harris didn't have to do one thing more than he was already doing to make Swami Don a happy man.

One night Harris got out two hand puppets he had brought

with him from the coast. One was a sea captain puppet, with a red beard and square glasses down on its nose and a corncob pipe and a little white cap with gold braiding on the bill. The other was a flamboyant woman with a great mass of red hair and huge, brightly rouged lips and big boobs. These puppets supposedly looked exactly like Captain Woody and Belle Trudy, Harris's foster parents. Swami Don had lived with the captain and the belle for one year also, in high school. The two brothers took roles in an impromptu play. Leroy looked on in amazement as he saw his father take one of the parts. Harris was the captain and Swami Don played Belle Trudy. He was good, too. He was funny. He was hilarious, in fact. Leroy could hardly recognize him. His face seemed to change, the way he held his mouth, his whole body, when he talked through the puppet. Sometimes Leroy almost forgot he was watching a puppet show and thought Belle Trudy was really saying those funny things. She spoke in an amazing falsetto, or rather his daddy did, this masterful person in Leroy's home. Was this really Leroy's daddy? It was not possible. Had the planet really turned inside out? Harris had changed their lives. This thought could not be escaped, Leroy sure couldn't escape it anyway. When the puppet show was over, Swami Don put the doll aside. His face was bright red with surprise and good feeling.

Leroy crept about on a regular basis now. He looked in his mama's purse. He went through his daddy's pockets. He poked through drawers in his parents' room. This was before he went creepy-crawling in Harris's attic room. He didn't find

anything much, his mama and daddy didn't seem to have any
secrets, nothing real interesting, well, some rubbers, Trojans,
in the red pack, they weren't real good for blowing up because
they were treated with some kind of lubricant and tasted a little funny. He took two anyway, it couldn't hurt. He had heard
about a boy, well, he knew him actually, it was Screamer
McGee, Hot's boy, the child who could lick his own penis,
double-jointed, you know, he stretched a rubber over the bell
of a bass horn in the junior high school band room one time,
took him about three hours, latex of course, forget about
stretching one of those sheepskin doogies, but school wasn't
in session now, summer vacation, so Leroy couldn't really
think of anything good to do with the Trojans. He eventually
just threw them away. He wasn't looking for anything especially when he was creepy-crawling, he was just looking.

As far as Leroy could tell, Uncle Harris didn't have much of
a life outside the family and his goofy friends in the village and
the newspapers. If you're too lazy to turn your hand, that's
what happens, Leroy had to suppose. It didn't matter, though,
it was all right with Harris that he had no real life. It made
Leroy wonder what a man this lazy would ever have had the
get-up-and-go to do that would cause his wife to run him off.
Harris was talking about getting a telephone put in his room
in the attic. This was about as high a level of activity as Harris
ever reached, calling somebody to perform some service for
him. He might need to call somebody, he said, well sure, he
might find a need one of these days to make a phone call,

transact some business, sell some stocks, see, you never knew about that sort of thing. Somebody might want to call him, see, that was another good reason he might need a phone, though he didn't say who he was expecting a call from. There were a couple of things he needed, come to think of it, Harris said. Maybe he needed a little TV set, too, nothing fancy, it could be small, very small, don't worry about a big screen, wasn't necessary; it didn't need to be color, either, although sure, he would prefer color, a little color portable would be nice, that NBC peacock, now that was something, wasn't it, a color portable would be perfect, actually, those big tail feathers.

8

Not long after Leroy saw the lady in the western vest, he saw something else almost as amazing. Out in the pasture at twilight a bright ball of fire drifted down the sky along a curious course, down, down, slowly, slowly, toward the earth. He watched it for what seemed like a long time, far out from the house, above the deep woods. Just above the treetops the fireball seemed to explode. Fire shards drifted like an innocent rain of flames into the forest. He heard no thunder. He kept on watching. He walked into the woods, to the spot where the flames had seemed to fall. There were no traces, no scorching.

The woods were clear, the trees in full leaf. The world beneath the trees seemed dim and fuzzy at the edges. The forest floor was covered with leaves. A squirrel scared Leroy by running through the leaves and straight up a pin oak tree. Leroy stopped to check for snakes. He looked for the fireball for a long time before he noticed the sun had gone down beneath the tree line and darkness had fallen. The woods were very dark, though when he looked straight up through the trees, the sky still had some dark blue light. Large birds were circling overhead in the big wide sky before dropping down into the forest to roost. Lightning bugs had come out, and out to his left, in a clearing, he could make out snake doctors in the air above the high grass. He hoped he didn't scare up a bunch of swamp elves out of the cane. They were harmless, he knew that, but the way they sounded when they ran, well, he didn't care for it, they scared him. He looked back toward his house and could see the porch light on. He looked back into the woods. Nobody would be worried, he had often stayed out like this on a summer evening. He halfway thought he might see a spark somewhere along the ground, or in the branches of a tree, or in the fork of a dead tree trunk, some small clue to the meaning of the fireball, but there was nothing. It was gone, whatever it had been. It had seemed important, he couldn't have said just how, a sign, something another. He turned and began to walk up out of the woods and into the pasture, on his way home. The problem was, he had missed grog rations. Well, shoot. He had completely forgotten about grog rations. He was mad at himself about that. Uncle Harris was probably already up in the attic, the party was over, well, doggone it.

Leroy walked up out of the woods and through a field and into the yard. He came in the house through the back door.

The house was quiet. Maybe his daddy was working late, maybe he missed grog rations, too. No, the tractor was in the shed, the pickup was parked out back. A table lamp was on in the living room, but that was it, not much sign of life. Where was everybody? Leroy walked through the front part of the house. He didn't call out, he just looked around, listened. He could hear the water running, the sound was coming from the bathroom. That's where Swami Don was, in the shower, okay, that was a little better. Somebody was home, at least. Then he could hear quiet voices from the rear of the house, in the girls' room. His sisters were playing together in their bedroom. Okay, he was just a little tense. He was breathing a little easier, everybody was home after all. Leroy looked around for his mama and found her too, right where he might have expected, in the kitchen.

And in fact he found his Uncle Harris as well. He was not in the attic after all. Uncle Harris was in the kitchen, too. He was standing right there with Leroy's mama. Leroy's mama and Uncle Harris were kissing in the kitchen. That's what they were doing, kissing, in the kitchen, right there. They didn't see Leroy, he'd been pretty quiet, and they were pretty busy themselves, right about now. Leroy stood in the doorway and watched for a while. They kept on kissing. He said nothing. He just stood there and watched.

The kiss that he was watching was not a comical kiss. Not on the head or forehead, not with a loud smack at the end or the funny word *smooch*. This was a long, serious kiss. A secret kiss. Leroy looked at his Uncle Harris's hands as they gently passed over his mama's backside and hip and leg and maybe up to her breasts. His mama's hand was on Harris's neck, the other on his shoulder. This kiss had not been forced on her, it had not surprised her. They were kissing. That was it. Leroy didn't know what had happened to the world. A memory of his lips on Old Pappy's came back to him and he pushed it away.

The kiss ended. They didn't look around, they didn't draw their faces apart, they didn't know Leroy was standing at the door. They spoke a few quiet words, Uncle Harris, then Leroy's mama. Their lips were still close. Leroy could understand nothing they said. They kissed again, brief and tender. They spoke more soft words.

Elsie's hair had grown long this summer. It was sun-blonde, like honey, Leroy realized. Just this summer his daddy had taken him to a bee-tree and showed him honey in the comb. He had watched it pull in wide strands from the nest and into the sunlight to take color. His daddy had said, "This is the color of your mother's hair." Now he understood what he had meant, that his mother was a desirable woman. He also understood that she was now betraying his daddy. He thought of the bedtime story he had heard so many times, the llamas singing to the setting sun. He didn't know what to do about any of these things. His mama's pretty hair was all he could look at or think about.

With these thoughts in his head, he watched his mother's

hair rise from her shoulders, as if by magic. It was the oddest thing. At first he doubted his eyes, and then he knew it was true. Her hair floated behind her like Superman's cape. Blue sparks leapt from her head. The crack of thunder and the flash of light came together. Elsie and Uncle Harris jumped back from one another as if they had been caught.

Harris said, "Your hair!"

Elsie said, "Eek."

He quick-kissed her again, smack, and they laughed together.

Leroy stepped back from the kitchen door and into the living room so he would not be seen. He stood with his back to the wall, like somebody was measuring his height. He heard his daddy turn off the water in the shower and fumble around in there for a towel. He knew Swami Don was getting out of the shower so he wouldn't get struck by lightning. Leroy thought it might have been better if Swami Don had been struck.

Laurie called from her room. She said, "Mommy!"

Elsie called back, "It's okay, honey!"

Laurie said, "Molly peed in her pants!"

"I'm coming," Elsie said. "It's okay."

On the roof above and on the tin roofs of the farm sheds Leroy heard the soft incessancy of hard rain. It grew harder then and fell like hammers upon the house. This had been a summer of storms. His head suddenly ached, as if the hammers pounded directly on his skull instead of on the shingles.

In the skies outside the window he saw occasional bursts of lightning, with a low complaint of thunder far behind, like an afterthought.

Swami Don came out of the bathroom wrapped in a towel. His withered arm seemed to Leroy especially small, so pale.

He said, "Everybody okay?" He was smiling to show he was okay, it was just a storm, no big deal.

Elsie and Harris were standing far apart now, Leroy noticed. They were smiling, too, nothing going on in here. Elsie noticed Leroy as he slithered himself around the doorjamb and came into the kitchen.

Elsie said to Leroy, "Well, when did you come in? I thought I was going to have to go looking for you." She said to Swami Don, "That one got us, I think."

"Did it ever!"

Harris said, "You should have seen your wife's hair."

The two girls came out of the bedroom and into the front of the house with the others. Molly was holding her wet pants in her hand. Leroy looked and noticed that his mama's hair was floating again. Just then the house was struck a second time. A flash of fire, a sudden crash. The telephone rang one long ring. The lights went out. Then the strangest thing of all. As if it were an afterthought of the huge surge of electricity, a large friendly-looking ball of fire plopped down out of the chimney, onto the hearth. It lay there, yellow and red but in texture looking like a large globule of water. It wallowed upon the floor, so it seemed to Leroy.

Harris said, "Would you look at that!"

Elsie said, "Why, I never."

Leroy thought he recognized it, it was the fireball he had seen drift down into the woods, the one he had been looking for. He looked at Laurie. He said, "The mother ship." Nobody paid him any attention. He couldn't help but look for some sign of recognition in her eyes, some explanation for everything. The fireball was about the size of a basketball, shaggy with flames. It kept rolling about. It didn't dissipate quickly. Leroy went into the living room and sat on the rug and leaned against an old leather ottoman. Molly was completely naked by this time. She had decided to take off all her clothes once she got her underpants off. Everyone watched the fireball bounce in a slow, leisurely way, benign as a sleepy otter, across the floor. It bounced right across Leroy's legs. He didn't feel a thing. It left a little yellow stain on his pants leg that faded away after about a second or two. No one moved. Before it had traveled far, the fireball broke up into a hundred smaller pieces of fire, the size of marbles. These pieces floated about the room for ten seconds or more. They rolled around on the floor and knocked into one another. Then they were gone.

Leroy looked at the frank and open expression upon his mother's face. In this moment everything made sense. The explanation he had been looking for came to him at last. He had expected to look at her and to see in her vulnerable, beautiful eyes something of her feeling for Uncle Harris, complex and impossible for a child to interpret. Or he had expected to see the field of llamas running with swaying and innocent necks. He had been very wrong about this. When he looked he saw none of this at all. His mama's expression had nothing to do with Harris. It had nothing to do with the origins of love. And it was not complex or hard to interpret. A child could read it and know its meaning, what the lightning had revealed. His mama did not love his daddy. That was it. Simple as that, a thing he had not known before. Love had not lasted. This was the message in the high voltage.

He said, "Mama—"

She turned and looked at him. Their gazes met and held. Maybe what Leroy read there now was acknowledgment, maybe what her eyes said was "Yes, it's true." Maybe yes, maybe no. There was really nothing for either of them to say.

9

One night out on the screened porch when
the evening was filled with the small songs of crickets and tree
frogs and Leroy was stretched out on the glider, with one foot
on the floor, slowly swinging, he heard his daddy telling Uncle
Harris about an earlier night, way back when they were boys,
down on the Gulf Coast, when Swami Don had woken up,
overcome with needs he did not understand. He said he had
lain in his bed, in the home of their foster parents, the captain
and the belle, and blinked his eyes in the bright moonlight. He
saw the straight-backed chair where he had flung his shirt, the
lamp shade with pictures of a tall ship in full sail, his dresser
with car keys and change spread across the top, his white sport
coat crumpled on the floor. He said he remembered that the
Gulf breeze had blown in through his open window, fragrant
as always, and so he got up out of bed and stood at the window, looking out. "The moon on the waves made you think

you could almost walk to South America," he said. "Brazil and Argentina lay right out there, just beyond the horizon, I was thinking. The darkness felt like it was sucking at the windows, like the vacuum hollowed out by seawater underneath a lee wall. It seemed it was going to pull me out." He said, "I'd had a date with Hannah. You remember. This was the night you stole her from me. Her hair, back then, was long and blonde and sun-bleached. I know it's darker now. She wore a white dress that showed her bare tanned shoulders. Her skirt stood way out from the crinoline petticoats beneath it. The whole thing threatened to fly up in her face when she sat down. She kept her hands clasped in her lap so she wouldn't be embarrassed. That's the Hannah I remember. It's no wonder both of us were in love with her. I don't blame you for stealing her. And no wonder she chose you. You were so cool. I mean it. Pegged pants, long DA, open shirt. You were the coolest guy in school. Anyway, there I was, wide awake in the middle of the night, scared out of my mind at nothing at all. There was a flat section of roof just outside my window, you remember, so I stepped out into the Gulf breeze. I had to make sure I kept my balance—with this bad arm, well, you know. I stood there, looking south. I breathed in, real deep. I could smell magnolias and honeysuckle and wild orange, and something sweet coming in on the breeze from the islands. You know what I thought about? I thought of Brazil, of the equator and the tropic of Capricorn, the great Brazilian plateau, the escarpments that end in the sea. I always was a fool for an atlas. I thought of gold mines and diamond fields and plantations of coffee and wild rubber. I thought of carnauba and barbassu palms and dark servants and stalks of bananas and icy waterfalls and ranches with a million head of cattle. I can't believe I'm telling you this. I imagined bright music and hot-blooded dancers in costumes. I thought of the Delta—not the one down around Belzoni and Itta Bena, I was thinking of the Nile, the wide muddy mouth of the Amazon. Something crashed and scrambled in the top of one of the palmettos that grew alongside the house, right near where I was standing on the roof. It was a big tree, the upper leaves stood close to my face. It scared me, this noise, brought me back to reality, you might say. I looked over at the broad palm leaves. Probably I'd heard a big rat—you remember those palmetto rats, with bead-hard eyes and tails like ropes? One of those old gentlemen had probably been lying in the palm leaves looking at me. I turned around and got control of my bad arm and ducked my head and stepped back through the window into my room. I felt like a fool, naturally. I was feeling pretty foolish already, of course. You and Hannah— At the dance, while I was inside, y'all were out in the car drinking whiskey and Dr. Pepper and making out. I was standing in front of the Red Top bandstand, bouncing this gimpy arm along with the beat of the music and singing at the top of my voice, 'I'm a lover not a fighter, they call me Johnny Valentine.' I was a proper fool, all right. What I really started out to tell you, though, was that I got this idea, there in my room that night. I got the bright idea that I needed to tell somebody my troubles. I was wide awake, remember, middle of the night, scared half to death, a rat plunging around outside my window, I had all these romantic notions about South America and love, so I rummaged around through my dirty-clothes basket and found a pair of jeans and pulled them on over my pajama bottoms. I slipped my bare feet into some deck shoes, shoes I didn't have to tie, struggled with a tee shirt until I got it over my head. I crept down the stairs like a thief in the night. I took off in Captain Woody's car, full speed ahead, down the beach road to Old Pappy's place, that halfway house for indigent men where he lived, you remember, clean beds, showers, a TV room, two meals a day, cards, dominoes, a few worthless books— I pulled off the beach road onto that dirt lane, hard-packed sand really, that we called Purgatory Lane, and crept down it for a ways, it was so narrow, with nothing but beach sand for shoulders, you could get stuck. The moon was bright, I remember that, the sand was white, the water sparkled. I hated to ring the bell and wake everybody up, all those poor old men, so I went up and tried the door and found it was open. I crept through cubicles —total darkness, almost, moonlight, that was it. I finally found him, came to Old Pappy's little living space. I pulled the chair up next to his bed, sat down next to him, touched his skinny old arm. He screamed, 'His name was Newgene Slick!' That's what he said, just coming awake. He sat up in the bed. His eyes were big as fish eyes. He looked this way and that. He finally saw me. He said, 'Hot damn, Gimp! You scared the pea-turkey out of me.' He rubbed his face in his hands. I wanted to tell him to stop calling me Gimp, but instead I said, 'Who is Newgene Slick?' Old Pappy groped around on a little table for his spectacles and finally found them and put them on his nose, hooked them over his ears. He said, 'You come out here in the middle of the night to ask me who Newgene Slick is? How would I know who Newgene Slick is? I never met the gentleman. Never heard of him. Newgene Slick, good Lord.' So I sat down on the edge of his bunk and told him the story of what had happened at the Red Top dance, you and Hannah, you know, all the details. I even told him about the rat in the palmetto, and South America and the escarpments to the sea. I confessed all my heart's romantic dreams. I told him I had thought Hannah would be the girl I would share them with. I told him that some day I hoped I would find the right girl, one who would know how to share those dreams. I went so far as to say I wished he never had shot me, that he'd been more careful with my life, even if it was just an accident. I told him I wished he hadn't given me this lifelong burden to bear. I said all that, can you believe it? When I finished we just sat there. You could hear old men snoring all down the hall. Somebody had a bad cough. Do you know what Old Pappy said? He said, 'Johnny Valentine?' I said, 'That was one of the songs, yessir.' He shook his head. He said, 'What are they going to think of next?' I said, 'I'm trying to tell you how much I need you right now.' He swung his feet over the side of the bed and dug at his crotch. He said, 'I don't know about this place.' He meant the halfway house. He was implying it had bugs. He was saying the captain and the belle should have found him something nicer. We sat for a while, neither of us saying anything. Then he said, 'Remember that man named Rafe, with the great big hairy dog?' I said, 'No, I don't think I do.' He said, 'He shaved that dog except for his neck, made him look like a lion, real hairy dog, used to live on an ostrich farm, them's some mean motherfuckers, an ostrich, kick, you better believe they will, kick your fucking teeth out, looked just like a lion, that dog, couldn't tell them apart. You can make a good living farming ostriches. You ought to buy yourself an ostrich or two when you can afford it, give you something to fall back on.' Light was coming into the sky, already morning. After a while Old Pappy got up and walked down to the toilet and peed and came on back into the cubicle and got in bed again, up under the sheet. He said he had to get his beauty rest. He said, 'Good night, Irene, I'll see you in my dreams.'"

10

One day Leroy was walking down the lane, coming back home from Mr. Sweet's store with a little bag of groceries for his mama, when he looked over at the junker cars parked in the muddy yard alongside the New People's cottage and saw the New People themselves, both of them, standing out there in the yard together. He wondered what they were doing outdoors, the weather had been so bad. Rain had fallen hard for the last few days, this was the first day it had let up at all, so everything was a mess. A bunch of trash that had been thrown up under the cottage, out of sight, had all been washed out, old newspapers, some two-liter plastic Coke bottles, a bleach bottle or two, a bedsprings, some pasteboard boxes that had collapsed in soggy heaps. A few rays of sun were poking through the clouds, but the skies were still low and it looked like it could start up raining again any time. Leroy's house had been struck by lightning three days in a row, that's how bad the weather had been. The ditches were filled with water, all down the lane and out by the macadams. Frogs were flopping all over the roadway. Snakes were looking for branches and high ground. Mr. Sweet's roof had leaked and he'd had to move his meat cooler over in a corner and sweep the water out the front door with a straw broom and then mop up the whole store. A culvert was gushing. Leroy found a baby swamp elf that had drowned in a ditch. Its scaly little three-toed feet were sticking straight up. He didn't stop to look, just kept on walking. He wondered if the swamp elf's mama was looking for him. Grass wouldn't grow around the New People, it looked like, and so there they were, standing ankle deep in red clay mud.

Leroy was still out in the lane, a good distance from where the New People stood, but he could see that they seemed to be dressed in odd outfits. Just then he noticed another man, someone he'd never seen before, a bald-headed, red-faced man mopping sweat off his face with a white handkerchief. He was walking to his big shiny new car parked along the roadside. He came up to Leroy. He said, "Is it humid, son, or is it just me?" Sweat was pouring down his neck. Leroy couldn't think of anything to say. He pulled up his shirt and started to rout out his belly button with his index finger. The man was carrying a little metal strongbox and a leather pouch with a drawstring and looking back over his shoulder at the New People like he was about halfway mad at them, put out anyway. He had several pens clipped to a plastic pocket protector in his shirt pocket. His shirtfront was wringing wet with sweat. He gave Leroy a good hard looking-over. He didn't seem to like what he saw. He said, "Y'all hillbillies ain't got no pride, is you?" Leroy didn't know what to say again, so he just stood there with his bag of groceries digging at his navel. Some of what he found there he put in his mouth. The man had on a shiny blue sport coat with dandruff on the lapels and big sweat stains underneath the arms. You could say he stunk. This was an insurance collector from Memphis, it turned out. He said, "They never told me nobody was going to die. You trust somebody, swear to God, and this is what happens, happens every time, you can't trust nobody, that's my newly revised opinion of the world, the human race of it, anyway, they's still a few pretty good redbones, I guess." Leroy cut his eyes out across the yard at where the New People were standing among the old cars. The New Guy was wearing a long warbonnet made of dyed chicken feathers, all colors, and the New Lady was wearing a large pair of angel wings, also made of feathers and chicken wire. They both were wearing boots of a kind that Leroy later learned to call Wellingtons. They were just standing among the junkers in the mud. At least they didn't have knives. The insurance guy said, "Oh, they talk fancy, sure enough"—he indicated the New People with an angry jerk of his head in their direction—"but they're hillbillies, too, you mock it down, son, down at the bone them two's just like your ownself, some ig-runt, unrefined, hillbilly motherfuckers, if I ever seen a pair."

Leroy said, "Somebody died?"

The insurance man said, "Jess look at them two out there. Ain't they disgusting?" Leroy looked. The warbonnet was so long it almost touched the ground. The angel wings were just as long. The insurance man said, "I seen it all now. Junkers and bleach bottles and chain-saw art and jug bands and a sculpture of Our Lord and Savior Jesus Christ on the Cross made out of beer cans, every goddamn redneck thing a hillbilly can think up, but I never seen no Indian and an angel, them's a new one on me, takes the cake, don't it, sons-a-bitches, anyway. You know what I heard? I heard this is the way hillbillies tell one another they in love, you know. Well, that is a joke, a big old funny joke. You mock it down, boy, a hillbilly knows not one goddamn thing about love, not one, it chaps my whole sweaty ass to hear they think they do. Makes my butt work button-holes, sho does. Half the people in the Delta don't even know about love, let alone a hillbilly. They's some people in Memphis don't know all they is to know about love. Love's an illusive motherfucker, Junior, do you hear me, do you hear a word I'm saying, what the fuck do you think you know about love? Nothing, that's what. So just shut up."

Leroy said, "Who died?"

The man looked back over his shoulder. He said, "They's both ugly, too, they think they pretty but they not, they ugly, look at them, look out there, ugly as hammered shit, both of them, I don't care what you say, not to mention dishonest, the boy dying like that, without no warning whatsoever, never been sick a day in his life till the murder, and I'm supposed to pretend like it don't matter to me? Life expectancy, seventy-six years, well forget that now, life expectancy don't mean shit to a hillbilly, it don't mean diddly-squat to a schoolboy gets hisself murdered, I don't care what kind of la-di-da airs they put on, life expectancy is straight out the window, now ain't it, just about fifty years too early. Do they care? Not a lick, never give one thought to me, my livelihood. Shit far and save matches, like my daddy used to say. You think it don't matter to me that a child gets murdered? Well, let me tell you, it does. It means plenty. It means whether I get a new car next year, it means food and drink for me and my wife. It's my livelihood we're talking about here, son. It means I'm the one's got to shell out the dough-ray-me, my company does, it might as well be me. It's the integrity of my actuarial tables that's at stake, too, they's a lot more to it than you ig-runt hill-billies ever think about. That man standing out there in the headdress, look at him, he's too old for that woman, I don't care how ugly she is. I heard people say he robbed the cradle, well, I got another idea on that subject, look like to me he robbed a grave, anybody that ugly's got to been dead awhile, wouldn't you agree with me, son, where'd she get that hair, and now trying to rob me, not trying, doing it, did it, I got to pay up, not a thing I can do about it either, the way the law's written, honest to God in holy heaven, son, what's a working man supposed to do if he can't expect children to stay alive? Look like a child would stay alive, don't it? You ain't planning

to die, is you, you ain't going around all-time getting murdered, is you, well, naw, naw, you wouldn't do that to me, I
know you wouldn't, you're a good boy, fine child for who you
are, little hillbilly shitheel without a hope in the world, and no
romantical illusions about the future, sure, but an honest boy
it looks like to me, that'd be my guess, and I'm known to be
an excellent judge of character, mock it down. Take your finger out of your navel, son, it gives me the heebie-jeebies. Like
I said, he's too old for that woman."

When the insurance man was gone, Leroy looked through
the gate and across the mud to where the New People were
standing. The old cars, the under-house trash in the yard, the
red mud, the headdress, the angel's wings, they made no
sense. When had this started, this failure to make sense of a
single thing? He tried to remember his life before Uncle Harris came—watermelons beneath the big tree in the yard,
lightning bugs at night, honey trees, the gentle llamas, no
thoughts of secret kisses. He remembered his daddy's story
about trying to tell Old Pappy his heart's pain and wondered
whether he should try the same, find someone to tell. He
didn't really know what he wanted to tell. Something about
missing Old Pappy, maybe killing him? Something about his
mouth covering the old man's mouth? The chapped lips, the
pinched nostrils, the rise and fall of the frail old rib cage. Did
he want to tell about the secret kisses? Warn his daddy that
what had happened that night at the Red Top dance with Hannah, down on the coast, was happening again? He couldn't tell

his daddy about the kisses; he couldn't stand to think of them, in fact. He didn't know who to tell. He could tell Mr. Sweet, he might catch him on a good day. He could tell Screamer McGee, or his daddy, Hot. He wished he could lick his own penis like Screamer, that was one thing he was never going to tell anybody.

He didn't exactly decide to visit the New People, he just found himself walking through the gate and out across the mud in their direction. His shoes were getting covered with the wet red clay. The New People seemed in no way surprised to see him.

The New Guy said, "Oh very well, very well, you may go along then, if that's the way it's going to be, come on then, hop in, can't hang about all day, you see, am I right, eh, what, hm, pop right in, shall I drive, dear, what do you say, would you rather do the honors, eh, speak up, what say now, my angel?" He shook his head and the feathers of his bonnet sounded like a million beads clicking together.

The angel, the New Lady, said, "You be the chauffeur, I'll be the lady."

"Oh quite right, very good, excellent suggestion, the Lady and the Chauffeur, should we go back for the other costumes, oh well, no, I think not, these are fine, just fine, we'll make do, all right then, that's that, it's all settled, let's see, let's just see now—" He was looking at one of the enormous old cars in the mud. "Let's see whether we can get this old cruiser cranking, as they say in the American South. You'll have to sit

up front with me, I'm afraid, young man, all right, no complaining, front seat it is, hop around to the other side, that
door's heavy, be careful, here we go, grief therapy, all aboard,
chop-chop, beggars can't be choosers, all that, hop in, no
more delays, agreed, all agreed on that count, excellent then,
first rate, ready now?"

Leroy walked around and climbed into the front seat of the
car and pulled shut its heavy door like closing a bank vault.
The interior was huge and his legs were so short they seemed
to stick almost straight out when he sat all the way back on the
seat. He looked at the vast expanse of dashboard, many dials
and clocks and instruments. He put his bag of groceries on the
seat next to him. The New Lady opened the back door and
arranged her wings so she wouldn't sit on them and got in. She
made herself comfortable, folded her hands in her lap. The
New Guy was last to step inside. He stood back and looked at
the car admiringly. He pulled a handkerchief out of his pocket
and made a motion as if to polish off a speck of dust from the
hood, though the car was rusted through in several places and
stained and caked with red clay that had splashed up all over it
during the heavy rains. He put the handkerchief back in his
pocket. He walked along his side of the car. He kicked a tire,
like he was buying or selling. At last he said, approvingly, "The
chap I got this beauty from is still singing the blues. Oh, I
admire this Southern vernacular of yours! Never mind what I
paid, you wouldn't believe the bargain, in any case. Oh, it's
still crying time for that unlucky gentleman, I can assure you."

The car was a Ford, and it was massive. Leroy learned that it was called a Crown Victoria. It seemed as big as the *Queen Mary*. It was the most amazing thing Leroy had ever seen. Nothing about it seemed quite real. It was a color of green that was impossible to believe anyone had paid real money for when it was new. There was no describing the color, pea green, maybe, with wild metallic undertones. The tires were slick, the rust along the underside of the car was growing like a fungus, there were rust patches on the hood and top and trunk as well. Both sides of the windshield were busted into opaque spiderwebs in the shape of the heads that had tried to go through it. The trunk lid wouldn't shut.

The New Guy said, "It doesn't need a key."

The steering column was cracked, Leroy noticed, as if the car had been stolen rather than purchased, so you could start it with a screwdriver.

Leroy sat in his seat and looked. He had never been inside such a car. He loved this car. Just sitting inside it, behind the busted windshield, beneath the tattered lining of the roof, in the stink of ancient mildew, he knew that life was good. He knew he had found a safe place, with people like himself. He had never seen a car quite so beautiful as this. What had he ever seen in Uncle Harris's little sportster? What had he been thinking when he admired Uncle Harris's puny little excuse of a car? That was no car. That was a shadow. This was a car. This was the car of Leroy's dreams. Good things could actually happen to a person who rode in this car. Dreams could come true, broken hearts could be unbroken, lost love could be reclaimed. He wished his daddy could ride in this car, his mama, too. If they could ride together in this car they would fall in love all over again. They would go away on a second honeymoon, if they ever had a first one. If they owned this car, all happiness would be theirs, enough to share even with Leroy. The person who owned this car would have a magic charm against all future harm, and grief would have no sting.

Leroy was overcome with good feeling. He said, suddenly, "I'm riding shotgun."

The New Guy had been dusting off the steering wheel with his handkerchief, finding the screwdriver beneath the seat, checking a road map for some unknown reason. His headdress kept getting in the way. Now he stopped all his busy-ness and looked at Leroy. He let out a breath, a sigh of gentle dismay. Oh callow youth, his sigh seemed to say.

He said, "Ah, well, yes, you see there, hm, all right, very well, shotgun seat, is it, hm. Perhaps we should take a step back here"—he looked at his wife in the backseat—"won't take a minute, dear, we'll be off shortly, you'll see. Ah, now, young man, it is important for you to recognize that you, in the innocence of your youth, you know not the first thing about automobile travel, am I right, you may answer truly, mustn't be ashamed, there, there now, it's all right to make a mistake, no harm done."

Leroy looked out the busted windshield. He could see the New People's cottage, with its blistered paint and torn screens and collapsed steps and a refrigerator on the porch. The cottage was in worse shape than he had fully realized. The chimney had collapsed and most of the bricks still lay on the porch roof. Through the windshield the shack looked like a badly-pieced-together jigsaw puzzle. It looked pretty much that way without the windshield. He imagined he could see his Old Pappy standing on the porch smiling at him. He thought about waving to him and then decided not to, it might scare him off.

The New Guy said, "Now are you interested in this grief therapy, young man, or not, it's your choice, make up your mind. Up to you. Don't have all day here, don't you know."

Leroy took his eyes off his Old Pappy.

He said, "Yessir."

"All right, then!" the New Guy said. "Very well indeed. First off the mark, let's get this intrusive automotive issue off the table, clear the air, don't you see, what, what? You don't say 'the shotgun seat.' That expression, my dear boy, has lost currency entirely, gone out of style, it's dated, *passay voo*, as the French are fond of saying. It's considered very old-fashioned, you see, even in the American South. You'll look, quite frankly, like a fool if you are allowed to continue saying 'shotgun seat' in this modern day and age of ours. You don't want to look like a fool, do you? I didn't think so. All right then. Straight to the point: what you say is 'the suicide seat.' Not *shotgun*, *suicide*. That's what you'd be sitting in, you see." When the New Guy said "you see" it sounded as if he were saying "you sam." "You're sitting in it right now, you sam. *Suicide* would be the proper modern phraseology for where you wish to sit, you sam. Do you understand it a little better now? I'm just trying to be of help in your time of need, you sam."

Leroy said, "Yessir."

The angel in the backseat said, "You were always wonderful with children, darling."

The New Guy said, "Everyone ready? Here we go!" He twisted the screwdriver in the ignition and pumped hard on the gas while the motor turned over.

He said, "It ain't been crunk for a while." When he said this he wrinkled up his nose and spoke in an exaggerated nasal sort of way. Then his face brightened. He said, "Oh, my, the American South! Its language! Its idiom! Its rhythms are music to my ears!"

He kept twisting on the screwdriver and pumping on the gas. The battery was low, and the engine was sluggish, the smell of gasoline filled the car. It made a sound like whuh-whuh-whuh-whuh, and for a minute Leroy thought it might not start. Then all of a sudden the enormous engine started in a rush. It sounded like a hurricane. The wilderness echoed. Oily smoke blew out the tailpipe in a huge cloud.

The New Guy hollered above the roar, "Sound like she might be 'bout ready for a tune-up. Whoo doggies!" Leroy thought the New Guy might have learned Southern speech from reruns of "The Beverly Hillbillies."

The New Guy kept pumping on the gas so it wouldn't die. It sounded like a jet plane ready to take off. The car was rocking. The trunk lid was up and bouncing. He put his foot on the brake. He slipped the transmission into reverse.

He said in a loud voice, "Are you ready, my angel?"

"Ready, dear," came the voice from the backseat.

To Leroy he said, "This always helps me in a time of grief." He floorboarded it.

The Crown Victoria was a huge car. Leroy had never realized just how big cars could be. This was surely the biggest he had ever seen up close. It was massive. It had eight cylinders and three hundred horsepower. It weighed two tons. It was sunk into a foot of wet clay mud. The wheels started spinning, mud started flying, good Lord. Leroy could hear the mud flying, slapping the underside of the car. The wheels slung mud so far up under the car it flew out the front end and straight up in the air. The sky seemed to be raining red mud. It flew all over the hood and all over the cracked windshield. The front window was completely covered with mud, it was completely opaque. It didn't matter. Leroy held on. They were in reverse. They were rocking. The tires were about to find traction beneath the mud.

Suddenly the Crown Vic seemed to take flight. It dug out backwards. They were taking off, they were airborne, almost. Smoke and steam boiled out of the hood. The trunk lid was going wild. The New Guy cut the wheel hard to the left. Leroy held on. The car went immediately into a high-speed spin. It tilted wildly, but there was no danger of turning over, the car was too heavy for that. They were roaring around in a backwards circle. Mud flew up onto the side of the house, all over the porch, the refrigerator, everywhere. The car was leaning, the tires were smoking, the noise was overwhelming. Leroy's groceries flew around the inside of the car for a while and then right out the window. They disappeared beneath the wheels and the mud.

Leroy was rattling around in the front seat of the car, which was generating all three hundred horsepower in reverse. There were no seatbelts. He fell onto the floor and climbed back onto the seat again. He looked in the backseat. The angel was pinned to the car's door. The wings were askew. He looked out his side window. Around and around the Crown Vic flew in reverse. The exterior world was a blur. The house, the well house, another car, the trees, the road, the mailbox—all the images appeared at once and blended together. The Crown Vic clipped the mailbox and sheared it off its post. Leroy looked at the New Guy.

The New Guy was just barely in control. He was hanging on for dear life, gas pedal to the floor, hands gripped on the steering wheel. He was riding it out. He was working through his grief, whatever it may have been, taking care of this boy who had stopped by, in case he had grief to work through as well. The gas pedal was on the floor. The car was roaring. The New Guy was looking not into the rearview mirror at where he was going but straight ahead, into the mud-splattered glass. He knew where he was going. He didn't have to see to get there. He was rewinding his life. He was watching his past fall

behind him, or in front of him. He was on a beeline for innocence, pre-grief. The look on his face was earnest. This was
serious work, even Leroy could see all this.

The car engine roared, the wheels spun, mud flew, and
they went backwards, backwards, in dizzying flying circles.
They drove this way for a very long time. The Crown Victoria completed many circles, a hundred at least, it seemed to
Leroy. They ran the car into one of the other junkers and sent
it spinning, they ran into the house and knocked off the porch.
You never heard such a noise. The refrigerator turned over
and fell out in the yard. The roof of the house came down on
top of the Crown Vic. A couple of chimney bricks crashed
right through the rear window and landed in the backseat.
The angel missed getting her head bashed in by about a foot.
No one seemed concerned. The car spun around one more
time and finally stopped. The radiator was billowing steam.
The temperature gauge was all the way over on H. There was
a smell of gasoline. The car could catch on fire, Leroy realized. Some mud had gotten into the car, all over the seats, all
over the headdress and wings, all over Leroy. This ride was
over. The Crown Vic was pretty much finished forever. Everyone was still alive, and there was no fire, so that was good.
Leroy sat for a while. No one spoke. The world spun more
slowly, then ceased to spin at all. It must have worked, Leroy
had to admit. Some miles must have been taken off their lives'
odometers. He looked over at the New Guy, who was sitting
behind the wheel, not fully conscious. The ride had been hard

on him, had battered him pretty badly. Leroy straightened himself up in his seat. He felt better, he sure did. The grief therapy had worked. At last the New Guy began to stir. He regained full consciousness and turned to Leroy with a smile. He said, "You won't forget what I told you about automotive terminology, will you, young man?"

11

The day the story of Aldo Moro's kidnapping in Italy broke into the news, Uncle Harris ran into the house from his car after the usual morning drive into town. He was waving newspapers and shouting. "Kidnap!" he cried. "Danger! Death threats! Romance!" To Leroy his uncle had never seemed happier. Even the kisses scarcely seemed to matter in the face of Uncle Harris's unbridled enthusiasm. How could Hannah ever have kicked out a man like Harris, with such infinite capacities for enthusiasm over death? It was too bad Uncle Harris arrived after Old Pappy had already died, Leroy thought. If he had been around for the death and resurrection and re-death, the mouth-to-mouth, the corpse spirited away in an ambulance at midnight, all the rest, well, the party would never have ended. Harris spread the papers on the table. He seemed to be offering a special gift to the family. He pointed to the headline. *Aldo Moro Kidnapped in via Fani.* He

made everyone look. He said, "Photos, page B-12. Let's see."
He turned through the pages, looking for pictures. He found
them. A file photo of Aldo Moro, in a dark suit. And then a
picture of the car, riddled with bullet holes, dead and bleeding
bodyguards lying nearby on the pavement. "Molly," he said.
"Look, honey, look, it's better than Gary Gilmore!" His face
was bright as a child's. All over he seemed to glow. There
might have been a bright light behind him.

It was impossible not to share his uncle's enthusiasm, even
if Leroy had no idea who these people were. The president of
the Christian Democratic Party of Italy? What did it mean,
even? Kidnapped? Uncle Harris read aloud from the paper.
The obituaries were old news, history, unimportant, now that
Aldo was in the custody of renegades. Ann Landers, farewell,
Heloise, horoscope, so long it's been good to know you. All
of Harris's energies now were directed at Aldo Moro, at the
drama of European shores. "A screech of tires," he read to
Elsie, to the children, to whoever would listen, "a sudden
confusion, a car crash." He said, "Oh, boy, listen to this: 'A
burst of gunfire filled the quiet air of via Fani. The car carrying
President Moro careened out of control. All five bodyguards
lay dead, in pools of blood and shattered glass. The President
was dragged from his car and thrust into one of the attackers'
cars. Two cars sped away in separate directions.'" He looked
up. The glow on his face might have been rapture. "Have you
ever heard of anything so wonderful? Leroy, you're old enough
to appreciate this. Isn't it great? Wouldn't you have just loved

to be there when those guns went off, when that car careened out of control? Can't you just hear it now? Rat-a-tat-tat, screech, oh, man. Oh, I know I would, you bet I would have loved to be there. I can't believe I missed it. I miss everything. That's what you get, being born in the South. Nothing ever happens. Just a bunch of rednecks is all we have in the South. But Italy! Oh, Leroy, you appreciate this, don't you, the cradle of civilization, violent decay, sweet romance, you see what I'm getting at here, don't you, son, I'm not alone in this, am I, I'm not just an oddball here, am I, Leroy?"

Leroy wanted to assure his uncle that he was not a solitary oddball, that in a cottage just across the llama pasture lived a pair of oddballs who were in an entirely separate league, that Uncle Harris had nothing to worry about if he ever needed the company of other lunatics. The thing was, Leroy was beginning fully to appreciate the value of such nuttiness. He couldn't explain it, any more than he could explain the existence of swamp elves, but there they were, there everything was, even the violence, the drama, the fall of heroes, the romance of foreign shores. All of it made sense in some insane way. Maybe when he was older he would understand, maybe understanding was irrelevant. It was no wonder that his mother had fallen in love with Uncle Harris.

And in love with him she surely seemed to be now, more than ever. She looked at him with new eyes, even less critical eyes than those that were attracted to Harris in the first place.

Aldo Moro changed everything. If the obits and horoscope and the execution of Gary Gilmore had sparked little interest in her, leaving her with mere physical attraction, then nothing could have suited Elsie so well as the kidnapping of Aldo Moro. Now she had got it, every fiber of her being seemed to announce. Now she was fully in tune. Grog rations, puppet shows, secret kisses, these were the preliminaries. Now she was ripe for possibilities beyond anything she had previously given serious thought to. Harris had sown the seed, the harvest was due. She became as interested in Aldo Moro as Harris was. Her interest was not merely a tagalong to Harris's lead. Leroy watched her assume the lead position. Her interest became stronger and weirder than even Harris's. Each day after this first day she jerked the papers out of Harris's hands before he could open them. She tore through, devouring each word, analyzing each photograph, calling the newspaper office to complain of various things, a paragraph omitted from the story off the AP wire that she had picked up out of another paper. Everything else became less important to Elsie than Aldo Moro. Molly moped about the house, sucking her thumb and wetting her training pants. Elsie scarcely noticed. Aldo, Aldo, Aldo—she seemed to think only of Aldo. She spoke his name to herself at the kitchen sink. She watched the television news every time it came on.

The words themselves, via Fani, the Red Brigade, the ruling party, even the name Aldo Moro—had there ever been so beautiful a name? she asked Leroy one day—"It rolls from the tongue," she said. "Such a romantic language, Italian. Such a beautiful language." This went on for days.

Elsie's interest outlasted Harris's. Harris had gone back to Miss Manners and the cryptogram.

"Isn't Italian just the most beautiful language in the world, Harris?" she said.

He looked up from the sports page. He snapped the paper once and then folded it. He was wearing his favorite Hawaiian shirt. He scratched his head. He said, "Well, yeah, I guess so—"

Leroy wondered if his mama didn't need a good fast backwards drive through the mud in an oversized car to calm her down some.

"What a wonderful man he must have been," she said, "this Aldo Moro, what a handsome man, to have so melodious a name." Elsie could think of nothing else but this. It was all she could talk about. She could not get enough of it. Leroy followed her around, he didn't know why. He was as entranced by his mother's transformation as she was by Aldo Moro. She told him things she thought, revealed her fantasies, and yet she did not have to do so. Leroy knew them already, seemed to know her thoughts as they came into her head, almost to read her mind. Elsie imagined tuneful voices, speaking in sorrowful Italian. She imagined violent words, also in Italian, no less beautiful. She imagined dark eyes and raven hair, spaghetti cooking on an iron stove, fruit vendors, good shoes, silk suits, she wasn't sure what else. Leroy could have been wrong about some of this. He wished he knew more about Italy so that access to his mama's sweet imaginings might not suffer these imaginative bumps.

It didn't matter, to Leroy or to Elsie. He knew in broad outline anyway the secrets of her private heart. She whispered the name of Aldo Moro. She fell in love with him. She imagined that she was his wife. She wrote his name a hundred times on a sheet of lined paper. She wrote her own name, then, as if she shared his name, Elsie Moro—Elsie didn't quite fit, didn't sound quite right, unless you whispered it in Elsie's own silent fantastic version of the Italian language, an accent of sorts, with a faint echo of *mamma mia* somewhere in the background. Leroy creepy-crawled. He found her diary hidden away in a drawer she thought he did not know about. He imagined her thoughts, her feelings. He saw that she had written the names with an unaccustomed slant in her handwriting, so that she might believe she had written in Italian. He knew that in her imagination she could speak Italian, and in her dreams.

The fear grew in Leroy's heart.

One morning Elsie told Leroy one of her dreams. She said she saw an image of Aldo Moro in an attic room of the farmhouse where she lived, with its steeply sloped eaves for a roof. The room she described sounded just like Harris's room. She said this was the way she imagined Aldo, in horrible captivity. He was chained to a chair. He was tragic and handsome. He was at the mercy of whoever wanted to abuse him, use him, in whatever way they wanted.

Leroy said, "Did he look anything like Uncle Harris?"

His mama looked at him quizzically for a moment, then her eyes seemed to lose focus. She seemed to have forgotten Leroy was standing there. She turned and seemed literally to drift away from him on a current of air.

Later she saw a photograph in the newspaper in which Aldo Moro looked almost the same as in her fantasy. Leroy looked at the photo. He did look a little like Harris, older, of course, handsome, with dark, dark eyes. Leroy heard her whisper, "Aldo, Aldo." He saw her hold the index finger of her hand in a certain way, finger out, thumb crooked. He saw her pretend to thrust something into her purse. Leroy understood the meaning of this game. In her fantasy Elsie carried a pistol. She was Aldo's kidnapper, his wife, and his bodyguard. She was all things to Aldo Moro. Aldo Moro became almost a real person in their lives, that was the way Leroy thought of him. When he imagined his mama with Aldo, he imagined that she wore Italian-looking clothes and high heels. The clothes were a little vague in his mind, but black and sort of flowing. She wore dark glasses and scarves. He imagined secret meetings and intrigue. He imagined blazing pistols, grateful kisses. Probably his mama imagined these things, too. Probably she ached for this lost man, alone somewhere among enemies. Leroy knew that at night she wept into her pillow, prayed for his safety. Leroy himself also wept and prayed. No one knew where they had taken him, the papers said. Where was the ransom note? Where were the political demands?

Later they all learned that Aldo's wife was named Noretta. Leroy imagined that his mama thought of herself by that name. Maybe she pretended Noretta was the Italian word for Elsie, anything seemed possible to Leroy.

Elsie said, "Nobody knows where he is, nobody who loves him. But he's somewhere. Right now, right this very minute, he's *somewhere*."

Leroy looked at his daddy for an answer. Anyone with the right response to this riddle would surely win his mama's true and eternal love.

Swami Don said, "Well, sure, Elsie. Of course he's *somewhere*."

She said, "But don't you *see*? He's in some particular place. He's outdoors. He's indoors. In a chair. A bed. A forest glen."

Molly said, "He's going doodies."

Leroy said, "Forest glen?"

Laurie said, "Oh shut up, Leroy."

Leroy said, "You shut up."

Laurie said, "Do you want me to slap the shit out of you?"

Elsie said, "He knows whether it is raining or if the sun is shining."

She looked at them with pleading in her eyes. The tragic Noretta had begun to appear on the television news each night begging for her husband's life.

Leroy's daddy said, "Everybody's got to be *somewhere*, Elsie."

Harris said, "It's too bad, you know, that there's not a private bathroom in the attic."

12

There was a hillside with a steep face sloping down into a ravine that might once have been an old riverbed. The ravine cut along the edge of a deep woods. If you walked far enough into the woods you would come to the river. The sky was clear, the sun was bright. Swami Don was thinking of this as he and Leroy stood at the kitchen sink together. He was also thinking of the day he got shot, the clear wide skies of brilliant blue, the sweet smell of cordite in his nostrils, the little slap dance he did with his hand against his face as the shotgun blast spun him dizzily in a circle on his toes and caused his hand to leap up to his mouth.

Later his Old Pappy had said, "You know, it's a shame you didn't work your mouth into an O right about then. It would have made one of them loud pops, like you hear in a skilled hambone demonstration."

Swami Don was still lying on the white sheets in the county

hospital when Old Pappy said this. He was drugged and sleepy.

He said, "Hambone?"

His Old Pappy was sitting in a plastic chair beside the child's bed. He started a slow, desultory hambone: hand to leg, up to his chest, slap slap slap hambone. Swami Don watched and listened through a haze of gentle drugs. Hambone, hambone, have you heard, his Old Pappy sang. He slapped his hand from leg to chest, leg to chest, doubling now on the leg, holding his mouth in an O and popping that, like a cork being pulled from a champagne bottle, hambone. The tempo of the hambone rhythm picked up. Papa gonna buy me a mawkin bird. Hambone, hambone, hambone. Swami Don had drifted off to sleep as his Old Pappy slapped his leg and chest and sang in an increasingly lively rhythm.

Swami Don looked at the little boy, his son, drying a plate with a dish towel. The days had lengthened, and though the hour was late the summer sky glowed with yellow light from the setting sun. They washed, they rinsed, they dried, they put away the supper dishes, breathed the steamy water, the detergent smell, noted their pruny hands.

Swami Don said, "You know, I've got an idea, Leroy."

He wiped off the sink with a wet dishrag.

Leroy gave him a look.

"Now don't say no until you've heard me out."

He laid down his dishrag and walked through the house.

Leroy saw what was coming. He watched his daddy as he

searched around for a key on his key chain and finally found the right one.

Swami Don went to a closet in the back of the house and unlocked the door and pushed back some winter coats in plastic bags. He lifted out a rifle and a box of ammunition from safe storage. The long barrel of the rifle he managed to keep pointed upward in a safe-seeming way. Leroy saw what was coming. The dreaded firearm safety demonstration.

He said, "No way. Forget it."

His daddy slipped the yellow pasteboard box of cartridges into his jacket pocket and propped the rifle against his hip so that he could jack the lever of the rifle and open its chamber to be sure it wasn't loaded.

Swami Don said, "Firearm safety."

Leroy said, "I'm not going to shoot that gun."

Swami Don said, "We'll take a few potshots. It'll be fun."

"It's not fun."

"Every boy ought to know something about—"

"Arrgh!"

"—firearm safety."

Leroy said, "You can't make me. I'm not going to do it."

"Leroy, please," his father said.

"It's too heavy," Leroy complained.

"Target practice, honey—"

"It hurts my ears. It kicks too hard."

The only time he had actually gone shooting with his father

he had pretended to get gunpowder in his eyes. He had walked around with his hands out in front of him for two days. He wouldn't go to school. He bumped into things, like a blind man in the comics.

Swami Don stood in the hallway with the gleaming rifle. He looked like a big wilted flower.

Even Leroy felt sorry for him.

Swami Don said, "It'll be fun. Come on. We'll find some, you know, tin cans."

He said this, but Leroy knew he had about broken him. His heart wasn't in it. He stood there with the rifle. He wiped off the rifle with a soft cloth. Leroy had won.

The problem was, the rifle was a thing of beauty. Leroy ached to look at it, it was so beautiful. He regretted that resisting firearm safety demonstrations was more important than shooting this magnificent weapon. It was a .30.30 lever-action Winchester with a ten-cartridge magazine and a steel ring with a leather thong depending from it on one side. It glistened, blue steel and walnut. The cartridges were gleaming copper jackets with lead bullets. Leroy loved everything about the rifle, its heft and balance, the fragrance of gun oil, sweet as peaches, the metallic clack of bullets, fed in or jacked out, the crack of gunfire in an open field. Once before, when his father was not watching, he had let the bullets roll out of his hands, off his fingers, like gold coins in a pirate's treasure. The rifle evoked the whole mythology of the Wild West, boots and spurs, ten-gallon hats, mesas and buttes and land lots of land under starry skies above, creaking leather saddles and stiff lariats.

Why Leroy would not go along with his father on firearm safety demonstrations was one of the mysteries of life. He longed to be his father's son.

While Leroy was standing around in the kitchen resisting the excursion with his father, Swami Don had given up and asked Laurie if she wanted to go shoot the rifle with him and she had said yes. They were already out the back door. Laurie was wearing a print cotton dress that struck her above the knees. She had on her yellow rubber boots.

Leroy walked through the house looking for them. He stood at the back door. He watched them walk across the yard together, to the gate in the fence, out into the pasture.

He called, "Wait!"

He banged out the screened door, down the steps. He chased along behind until he caught up.

Swami Don looked back. He said, "Did you change your mind?"

Laurie looked at Leroy without expression.

Leroy caught his breath quickly.

He said, "No."

Swami Don looked at him. "No?"

Leroy said, "I don't want to."

Laurie looked away.

Swami Don had been smiling. Now he stopped.

He said, "Oh. Well, all right then. We'll be back soon."

The two of them, father and daughter, turned and walked on in the direction they had been going.

Leroy stood and watched, just outside the pasture gate, as Laurie and Swami Don walked slowly away from him. Swami Don carried the beautiful rifle by his side in his good hand. Leroy trailed along behind.

Just then Leroy saw something he had never seen before. It was a wonder he noticed it at all, it was such a small thing. He saw Laurie reach up and take her father's hand. Not the hand that carried the rifle, of course. The other, the withered hand, the pale child-hand that hung lifeless, with curled fingers, by Swami Don's side. The two of them walked along in this way, Laurie and Swami Don, holding hands, like regular people. They might have been any loving father and daughter in the world. It was the first time Leroy had ever seen that history-paled-and-crumpled hand treated like a normal, real extension of his father's life. He realized how often he had seen his mother shun it, how often he had shunned it himself, in ways so small he himself had not noticed.

Leroy took off running. He ran and chased.

He cried out, "Wait! Wait for me!"

Swami Don and Laurie stopped and looked. They let Leroy catch up. When he did, he was breathing hard.

When finally he could speak, he couldn't think of what to say. Even Leroy knew he looked foolish.

Laurie rolled her eyes.

Swami Don said, "Well, uh—"

There was not much else to say.

Eventually, when no one spoke, the three of them began their trek again, across the pasture in the direction of the ravine. Leroy walked a lonely step or two behind.

13

One afternoon down at Mr. Sweet's store, Leroy happened to be buying bubble gum when the New People showed up. Mr. Sweet was always glad to have company, you didn't have to buy anything. He seemed especially to like the New People. They came in to ask Mr. Sweet's advice on something. Mr. Sweet was in a talkative mood, so it took them a while to get around to what they wanted to say. Leroy noticed that the New People were dressed normally, jeans, a baseball cap, you wouldn't notice anything peculiar about them, except the way they talked. The New Guy had an expensive-looking camera around his neck as well, though this seemed natural enough. It was their speech that struck Leroy as strange. They seemed to talk a little different every time Leroy ran into them. In a way he liked the silent-movie version of them best of all. Well, he wasn't sure. He liked the British accent pretty well, too. Today more than ever the New

Guy seemed to be using his British accent. He could turn it on and off.

Mr. Sweet said, "Well, shoot, you ain't wearing your head-dress. I'm disappointed."

The New Lady noticed Leroy over by the gum and candy display. She said, "Ah! Le Roi, so good it eeze to see you." What language she was speaking Leroy wondered, but he really couldn't say.

He said, "Hey." He didn't turn around, though, he just kept looking at the gum. He wasn't sure how to act after their wild ride together. In a way, all he wanted to do was to hang around them. He felt safer with them than anywhere else. He realized this was an odd thing to be thinking.

The New Guy said, "Rah-ther, old chap, tallyho, all that, special occasions, what, the headdress, you sam, special occasions."

Leroy had to look now. He saw Mr. Sweet squinch up his eyes. He looked to Leroy like he wondered how the New Guy knew his name was Sam. Mr. Sweet said, "Used to be a Pentecostal Holiness preacher out near Notasulga had him a head-dress, too. Looked a lot like the one you had on in here one day last week. You ought to heard that man explain the Pentecost. Explained that sapsucker better'n I ever heard it. Y'all folks know anything about the Pentecost, do you? Are you religious people at all? I'll explain it to you sometime if you want me to, I got it committed to memory, it's easy once you get the hang of it. He said that headdress was just chicken feathers but that was okay it was for the Lord. He was near-bout seven feet tall, Pentecostal preacher, they usually short, is my experience, not no seven feet anyhow, nowhere near. His wife played the piano and the Dobro, real musical gal, you'd of liked her. Church in the Wildwood, which I always thought was Church in the Wildroot, like the hair tonic, she could make that Dobro talk, brother. Look like Jack Sprat's wife, gland problems, real pretty in the face, though. She could make that Dobro talk, you better believe it. Another lady fell out and started talking in tongues one night, Dobro done that to her. That's the power of the Dobro, in the right hands, that's the power of the Dobro, the way that preacher's wife could play. Preacher he said, 'See she don't swaller that tongue she's talking in.' He also said, 'She ain't got no panties on, so keep her legs together while the spirit moves her.' He could explain the Pentecost so you could understand it, any idiot could understand it once he got through explaining it to you. He didn't preach no hellfire, just only God's love for the least of these my brethren. Plus he run the road grader for the county, hard worker, every road stayed cleared—this was back before most of these roads got blacktopped. You could see the marks of a scraper blade gouged into the banks of every hillside around here, wherever you went. You'd look at them scraper gouges and you'd say, Now I understand the Pentecost. I said to him one time, 'How come you to wear a chicken-feather bonnet?' This was long time ago. I was just about the same age back then as this little shit-for-brains." He smiled and indicated Leroy with a jerk of his head. "Preacher he said, 'I got me a good deal on it. You won't get no better deal on a chicken-feather bonnet than I got on this here one.' I said, 'Did Jesus wear a warbonnet his ownself?' Preacher said, 'Not likely. They weren't as many chickens back then.' I said, 'Was they any banties?'"

Leroy knew which preacher Mr. Sweet was talking about. He had never met him, he'd been dead since before Leroy was born, but he knew who he was. This preacher had been a friend to Swami Don, Leroy's daddy, long time ago, but not as long as Mr. Sweet thought it was. Mr. Sweet was no good with dates. This preacher had helped Leroy's daddy after Old Pappy shot him. Then he helped him again after Old Mammy died. Preacher helped him and Harris get set up in the foster home with the captain and the belle. Preacher was easy to talk to, everybody said so. He was respectful and kind. He encouraged Swami Don to cry if he felt like it, didn't mean he was a sissy, told him to speak all his angry thoughts to him. He said he didn't want to risk getting Swami Don beat up or killed, but that if he ever felt safe enough to do it, he probably ought to tell his Old Pappy how much pain he felt, inside and outside. He ought to try to tell him he wished he'd been a little less careless with his life. Leroy had overheard his Daddy tell Uncle Harris that this preacher was the reason he was able to talk straight with Old Pappy later on, out at the halfway house, that night on the coast when Swami Don was a boy and needed somebody to talk to, when he woke up that night, scared, after Uncle Harris stole Hannah away from him. He gave the preacher all the credit in the world, he said. People still talked about that preacher, not just crazy old Mr. Sweet.

The New Guy said, "I say, have a listen, here, please, tell me what you think, advise me here, you sam. Just now the señorita and I were making our way along a road we'd not driven on before when we saw the most amazing thing, I think you'll agree, hot as blue blazes out there, don't you sam, still as a grave, what, scarcely enough air to breathe, all that, red dust kicking up behind the car, the señorita's hair was blown by the wind in a pretty way, you sam." He looked at his wife lovingly. Leroy noted that she was a señorita today, all right. She had on a wide-brimmed black hat with a round, flat top. He supposed she could be a señorita in that hat. A bullfighter, maybe. She smiled and leaned her head back and shook her hair, as if to demonstrate something, Leroy was not sure what.

She said, "Me I was say to zee señor I joos love zees Mee-see-see-pee of yours! Zee sky she pour over you like zee blue cascade."

Mr. Sweet narrowed his eyes. He wasn't sure he under-stood Spanish well enough to follow this part of the conversa-tion. That's what his expression told Leroy, who was thinking along similar lines.

As if to prove that he was no señor but a British lord, the New Guy pulled out a briar pipe and clenched it between his big white teeth. It was already filled with tobacco. He struck a large kitchen match and set it to the bowl of the pipe and sucked vigorously at the stem until the store was filled with fragrant, chocolaty-smelling puffs of pipe smoke. Leroy looked at the New Guy's long-fingered, slender hand casually gripped around the pipe's bowl. The New Guy said, "So, in any case, crossing the swale just now, a few meters down this particular road, you sam, I espied a devil of a piece of material. Photography, don't you see, cameras and all that, what. A homemade saw-rig with an old car hooked on for power. Marvelous! Know anything about that apparatus, Sweet? Any ideas? Know who that marvel belongs to? Think it would be all right for a chap to photograph? Eh? Eh, what, what?"

Mr. Sweet said, "Pitchers?"

The New Guy explained that he was a photographer. "An artist in film, you sam, black-and-white mainly, some color, no purist here, no prima donna, what." He was touring "the American South," as he said. He wanted to know everything about it.

The señorita said, "We only joos, how you say, arrive zees shores, and already I seemply sheever weez an unbearable seenz of life."

The New Guy said, "Oh, quite, straight to the mark, yes indeed."

Mr. Sweet said, "You know, you ain't fooling me none."

The New Guy said, "Dear me, bad luck, drat, quite rotten, my, my."

The señorita shook her head. She was very sad, Leroy could tell.

Mr. Sweet said, "I place that accent somewhere in the lower Delta. Yazoo City? Are y'all river rats?"

Nobody answered, but that was all right. Mr. Sweet locked up the store and they all went out together. The four of them crowded into Mr. Sweet's old GMC pickup with STP stickers on the bumper. They drove out the road where the New People said they'd seen the homemade saw-rig. They parked on the side of the road and piled out of the cab. The New Guy photographed the saw-rig. Then for the next couple of hours Mr. Sweet led them through barbed-wire fences and onto posted property. He showed them a low spot in the hills where a fresh spring muddied the earth. He was old and he had that built-up shoe but he could still walk on uneven ground pretty well. Every now and then the New Guy had to hold Mr. Sweet's arm. Mr. Sweet led them past clearings where a fragrance of mint leaves was all they could smell. He took them to an abandoned barn where he got them to help him pull away a tangle of vines on an exterior wall to show them an enormous sign that said DRINK MILK. The words were spelled out in a million Coca-Cola bottle caps nailed to the wood. He took them down to the branch of a creek Leroy had never known existed. He showed them deer tracks. He showed them a sign, out in the middle of the creek, that said NO WALKING ON THE WATER. He showed them a bee-tree and stuck in his hand, in a deep hollow in the trunk, and pulled out a dripping honeycomb. Bees crawled all over his arm and face and did not sting him. He showed them a tiny graveyard in the briar patch where the headstones were all of wood. He said, "This here's my daddy. Over yonder's my granddaddy. Like to burned up every motorcar in town gittin over them two." He showed them a small lake, a waterfall that fed it, a beaver dam in the middle. They saw a beaver swimming in the stream, big as a yearling calf. They walked deep, deep into the woods until Leroy believed Mr. Sweet was lost and ashamed to admit it, or mentally unbalanced and unable to know how lost they'd become.

They came into a space where the trees were strange and low, unlike any of the other trees nearby. These trees had been planted. It was an ancient abandoned apple orchard. The limbs swagged to the ground, freighted with ripe red apples that would never be harvested. Mr. Sweet picked up a few of the ripe apples from underneath the tree and handed them around. They stood in the leaf-stained sunlight. The señorita bit into an apple. It cracked like a gunshot. They all ate. Juice both sweet and tart flooded Leroy's mouth. He had never tasted such an apple, such an amazing piece of fruit.

Mr. Sweet led them out of the hills and back to the road. They walked the long walk back to the pickup. Mr. Sweet said, "In Jewish Shavuot, Passover was sort of a party. It was the end of the grain harvest. This was in Palestine. Pentecost wasn't nothing special back then. It was more of just a calendar day. Somebody might say, 'When did y'all have that last baby?' Or 'When did you get your new wringer washing machine?' if you had one, whatever you wanted to ask about, it didn't matter, and you might say, 'Well, let's see, shit, honey, when was that, back around Pentecost? Or was it when we were farming shares for the rich motherfucker that owns the company store?'"

14

That day they went out with Swami Don and the rifle Leroy may have been the first to notice the colorless mound far out in front of them in the pasture grass, though it was Laurie who tugged at her daddy's small hand and stopped walking. They all stopped. They squinted their eyes in the sun to see better. Swami Don was carrying the rifle in his good hand. Leroy watched him give the rifle a small shake. Leroy had thought the rise of gray in the pasture was an anthill, fire ants. He had seen them before, many times. The large size of the mound, the color of the earth, had seemed the same. Fire ants excavated such places in the pasture, like miners, bringing deep earth to the surface. Children at play learned to avoid them, Leroy sure had. This was not an antbed, though, and Laurie had been first to sense this. Right away Leroy knew she was right, though he was still unsure what he was looking at.

Leroy's daddy said, "Uh-oh." They stopped and looked and

didn't say anything else for now. Leroy was beginning to understand what lay out in front of them. The plan had been to walk on out to the outer reaches of the llama farm to take some target practice with Swami Don's rifle. The day was bright blue, Elsie was back at the kitchen table with a pair of school scissors and a squeeze bottle of Elmer's glue, clipping articles on Aldo Moro out of newspapers and magazines and putting them in a scrapbook she'd started. Molly was content to stay with her, but Laurie had leaped up and put on her yellow rubber boots as soon as she saw her daddy go to the closet where the rifle was kept. Rifle fire and ringing ears and a bruised shoulder must have seemed a better way to spend an afternoon than with Aldo. Target practice was a thing Swami Don enjoyed as well. He was always interested in firearm safety—the accident had taught him the importance of it. There was that place in the deep woods where a ravine cut along the edge of the woods and where if you walked far enough you would come to the river. This was the spot where Swami Don always took the rifle to shoot. It was safe, there was a wide clear area, perfect visibility, and a steep clay wall on the other side of the ravine where no bullet could ricochet. Swami Don never used the rifle to kill anything. He shot it a few times a year, kept it well cleaned and oiled. He claimed he kept it around to prevent packs of wild dogs from damaging the llama herd—a pack could take down a weak animal, and sometimes they did, it was true—but really the rifle was just for fun, Leroy knew, everybody seemed to know this.

When there were wild dogs on the loose, Swami Don only always shored up his fences and kept the younger and weaker animals near the barn.

They started to walk again and finally reached the mound in the pasture where the three of them stopped and stood together, Leroy and Laurie clumped up close to their daddy. It was a llama, sure enough. It was dead, one of the baby llamas, the youngest animal in the herd, in fact. The rough earthen-colored fur riffled in the wind. The llama had begun to stiffen, the legs straight out, the lips curled up slightly to show the sweet bucked teeth. The young animal had had its throat torn out. One of the haunches had been gnawed away. The three of them just stood there above the little body.

After a minute Leroy watched his daddy look up toward the woods. He seemed to be looking deep into the shade. He was looking for dogs. The first thing he said was to comfort the children. He said, "It didn't suffer. Dogs make quick work." Leroy looked at Laurie and saw that she believed none of this. Laurie touched the dead llama with the toe of her yellow boot. He said, "We're safe. They don't attack humans. Not three of us together, anyway." He gave the rifle another little shake. Leroy stared at the animal's teeth. He was about to ask whether they could bury the animal when all of a sudden Laurie gave the llama a solid kick in the side. Leroy looked at her, he was shocked, he almost told her no, then decided he'd better keep his mouth shut. Laurie's face showed no emotion. She seemed to be testing the reality of something, the animal itself, its death, something about her own life and death.

He realized there were things he probably didn't understand. She frightened him with her hard way of seeing things. He stayed quiet. He looked again at the little beast. The llamas fur was coarse and stiff. The imprint of Laurie's boot toe stayed in the hide. Dust motes rose from it.

Swami Don said, "We'll have to drag it outside the fence. Maybe out to the ravine." They kept standing there. No one moved. He said, "No sense inviting the rest of the pack in here to finish up." They would have to cross the fence, of course, but firearm safety was always first in Swami Don's mind, everyone knew this. Leroy watched his daddy unload the rifle. It was a little tricky with just one hand, but Swami Don made easy work of it. He propped the rifle butt on his hip for support. He jacked the lever ten times, jacka jacka jacka, and the brass cartridges flew out the side to the ground until no more shells came out. Laurie gathered them up. When it was empty, Swami Don flipped the rifle out and grabbed it solidly by the curve in the stock and held it out to inspect the chamber. No shells, it was unloaded, he seemed satisfied. He left the chamber open. He said, "Well, I guess we better get busy."

They were about to cross the fence when Leroy thought of the story of the day his daddy took a load of number six shot in the arm, his Old Pappy's shotgun, as they crossed a fence like this one. Swami Don propped the carbine against the strands of wire. He pointed down the fence to an open place where the dogs had gotten through. A post had rotted, the fence had sagged. He said, "That's my fault. Later on I'll come back on the tractor. I'll bring the wire stretcher and some of that new wire in the barn."

Laurie said, "Let me help."

Leroy looked at her. At first he thought she meant she wanted to help with repairing the fence. Then he realized she was talking about the dead animal. Leroy kept watching. He didn't say anything. He hung back. He was a little scared of the death, he realized. The llama's head had flopped to one side and looked a little like Old Pappy the day he died and Leroy revived him. He wondered whether the dead llama could be revived. He imagined, for one bizarre instant, placing his lips upon the llama's lips and breathing life into the mutilated beast. Leroy imagined that he was responsible for all the suffering in the world. Swami Don stepped past Leroy and took the animal's foreleg in his good hand. He dragged the llama over to the fence and slung it underneath the bottom strand of wire to the other side. The animal was not large, about the size of a small goat, with a longer neck and longer legs. Swami Don took a breath. He was a big man and you could see he didn't relish crawling between the strands of barbed wire. He moved slowly. He lifted one wire with his hand and put his foot on a lower strand. He stretched the two wires apart to step through. You could see he didn't want to do this. For some reason he was resisting throwing this dead little innocent beast in a pit.

Suddenly Laurie said, "I'll do it." Both Leroy and his daddy stood frozen at the fence and watched her. She pushed right past both of them, right up to the dead llama. Expertly she tucked the skirt of her dress into the top elastic of her underpants and scooted under the fence wire, through the opening that Swami Don had made. She moved nimbly, even in rubber boots.

Swami Don stood up straight and took his foot off the barbed wire. She was already on the other side. He said, "Laurie, no—"

Leroy couldn't move, he only watched. His sister amazed and frightened him, she was unpredictable. She lived in a world without dreams. He saw Laurie stoop down to the dead animal and take the flint-hard little hoof in her hand, a back leg. She gave it a tug and it moved easily, it slid along the Johnson grass. He watched his daddy allow this, he did not understand why. He watched again as Laurie started to drag the llama through the grass, and as Swami Don only stood and watched as well, though he must have known better. Leroy looked across the fence and watched his sister dragging the llama along behind her. She seemed strong. She moved at a good clip. She was dragging the dead beast out toward the woods, to the ravine, where it would not attract more dogs into the pasture. She was doing this thing that by rights was Leroy's daddy's job to do. Maybe it was not, maybe this was Laurie's job, somehow, maybe his daddy knew this.

Swami Don called, "Are you sure—?"

Laurie smiled back in their direction and kept moving. She moved so swiftly and put such distance between them Leroy could scarcely see her against the trees. Her yellow boots were the last of her to disappear into the trees. She was completely out of sight now. Swami Don hollered to her, or into the woods anyway, "Just keep going straight, honey. You'll see the ravine. You'll come to it."

They waited.

Leroy said, "I was thinking of Old Pappy. In the attic."

Swami Don looked at him.

"Why did he poison himself?"

Swami Don picked up the rifle. He looked at it, put it back against the fence. He looked again out into the woods. He didn't answer. They kept standing and waiting, looking out toward the ravine. They heard Laurie's voice coming from the deep shade.

She called, "I see it. I see the ravine. I'm almost there."

Swami Don called, "Don't get blood on your dress."

The wild dog was still out there, of course, the one that had killed the baby llama. It was out there somewhere. This was a thought that Swami Don seemed to have forgotten until this moment. Leroy hadn't thought of it either, until he saw panic sweep into his daddy's face. He felt the same panic sweep through his own heart like a bad rain. He felt dizzy with fear. He heard a clatter behind him. He looked back and saw woodland creatures, fourteen or fifteen of them, the weird flightless birds of Mississippi called swamp elves, two-legged, three-toed beasts with long necks and wide, wild innocent eyes, strange beasts no more than a foot tall, running from a willow shade behind them across open ground in the direction of the trees. In an instant they were gone.

Swami Don cried, "Laurie! Come back now. Laurie! Answer me!"

Leroy thought about a man's putting his daughter at this kind of risk. He thought his daddy was, in a way, just like Old Pappy. He almost said this. He imagined Laurie then, in the woods, on the lip of the ravine. He wanted to imagine that she stopped there, looked gently on the dead animal at her feet. He wanted to believe that she stroked the strange ears of the creature, felt their coarse velvet. He wanted to hear her voice speak a benediction of gentle words, a prayer, a naming of the animal, a memory of its life in a pasture pulling grass with its teeth, its small voice in the singing of llamas, morning and evening with the mature beasts. But when he tried to imagine these things he saw instead the cold glare she had given him at the New People's gate when she had seen Molly's underpants in her boot. He saw her grim and serious at her work of hauling the llama by its glasslike hooves, taking a deep breath, then slinging the animal like a sack of flour off the cliff and into the rough trench down below. He saw blood on her hands. He heard the wilderness ring with a sound like bells, and knew she heard none of this. She made no judgments, so far as Leroy could tell. She embraced what was real, made it her own, even cruelty.

Swami Don called out again, took the rifle from the fence. He tried to prop it between his legs and dropped it to the ground. He picked the rifle up, very clumsy. His withered arm bounced this way and that. His infirmity was more obvious to Leroy than ever before. He fumbled in his pocket for cartridges. His pocket might as well have been sewn shut. He couldn't get his big hand in. Leroy could hear the shells clicking in there, but his daddy couldn't reach them. Swami Don tried to force his hand into the pocket. He pushed so hard the pocket ripped at the seam. It didn't matter to Swami Don. He jammed his hand in and pulled out the box of cartridges. The yellow pasteboard gleamed in the sunlight. He flipped open the box top with his thumb and when he did the box slipped out of his hand and fell against his knee before it hit the ground. Bullets spilled out everywhere. The brass casings looked ancient somehow on the grass, like teeth, prehistoric and inscrutable. Leroy watched in amazement. He watched his daddy kneel down and pick up some of the spilled bullets. He looked toward the woods, then his daddy looked out into the woods as well. Swami Don fumbled with the bullets and the carbine in the same hand, trying to get the rifle loaded, and as he did he dropped all the bullets again. Just then Laurie came running out of the woods, waving and smiling. Her boots were yellow as sunshine. Both Leroy and Swami Don stood and watched her. Her dress was still tucked into her underpants. Her skinny legs and bony knees gleamed like ivory. She raced up to the fence, grinning like a monkey.

Swami Don said, "Laurie, thank God."

She untucked her dress and showed him the printed cloth. She held out her hands and showed him her hands, too. She said, "No blood!"

Leroy said nothing, there was no need. Leroy thought he might as well have been a figure painted onto the scenery of these two people's lives.

After a while they walked along the fence, the three of them. The pasture was golden in the sunlight. Leroy trailed behind. They stopped and talked, Swami Don asked Laurie questions, she answered them, then they walked again. They came to the spot in the fence where the dog had entered the pasture and stood regarding it for a while. The hole was very large, so they talked about this for a while. It was a wonder the whole pack hadn't strolled through, Swami Don said. Leroy could tell that his daddy was disgusted with himself for allowing such a thing to happen. A herd of llamas, milkers and all, could be destroyed overnight, Swami Don said, mostly to himself. He said, "It looks like I've got some work ahead of me."

Laurie said, "Can we shoot?"

"Shoot?"

She said, "Before you have to mend the fence?"

Swami Don looked up at the sun. It was not late. There was still time to shoot. Leroy hoped his daddy would say, No, we've had enough excitement for one day, something like that. It was true, really. Leroy had had enough excitement. He was sick of excitement, if you wanted Leroy's opinion.

Swami Don said, "It's loud, you know. It hurts your ears."

Laurie said, "I know."

He said, "It kicks."

She said, "It's okay."

He jiggled the rifle in his hand.

"I guess we could get off a couple of rounds."

She said, "Can I load it?"

Swami Don seemed pleased.

"I guess that would be all right."

Swami Don gave her instructions and she filled the magazine.

"That's it," he said. "Now crank the shell into the chamber."

Leroy didn't say anything, he just felt like being quiet for now, for some reason. He stayed quiet for the whole long walk through the woods to the place where his daddy liked to go to shoot.

They were standing in a clearing along the ravine. Behind them lay the woods and pasture and fence. In front of them was the deep cut through the wilderness. Swami Don explained again that this was the safest place to shoot, the ravine had steep soft banks, there was no chance of a ricochet, a stray bullet. They looked a long distance down to the bottom. They talked about what they might shoot at. Leroy said it was okay with him if Laurie wanted to go first, go right ahead.

Laurie's target was a two-liter plastic bottle, Coke, Diet Coke, something, the label was faded. People were always throwing trash down this ravine. Swami Don moved up close to her side, helped her hold the gun. He told Leroy, "You stand right there, son, that's good, no sudden movements, stay well behind the shooter, you know all this stuff by heart, don't you?" He showed Laurie how to line up the notch on the rear sight with the raised front sight at the end of the barrel. Leroy was eaten up with envy, yet he stood apart. It wasn't only envy he felt. He was always filled with wonder in the presence of his sister. It was no different this time, it was more wonderful in fact. She looked beautiful and strange holding this gleaming, rich-wooded, sweet-smelling rifle. She looked dangerous, and Leroy loved this about her. Laurie was holding the rifle to her shoulder. "I've got it," she whispered. "I can see the front sight."

"Excellent," Swami Don said, almost whispering himself. "All right now, line both of them up with the Coke bottle, your target, you know."

Laurie automatically took a deep breath and exhaled evenly, without being told.

Swami Don said, "Can you see it?"

Leroy watched him adjust her elbow slightly.

What happened next caught Leroy by surprise. A sudden shock of sound, a violent crack, seemed to strike him in the face, that's how unexpected Laurie's first shot was. From the look of wide-eyed surprise on his face, Leroy's daddy was no less astonished. The wilderness clattered. Birds startled from the trees. A rabbit sprang from the brush. An echo as crisp as a thunderclap smacked the three of them square in the face, two slaps in one second, like a forehand and a backhand. The echo was already back from the opposite face of the ravine. The gunshot and the echo seemed simultaneous sounds. The fire from the barrel and the ringing in their ears were simultaneous.

For what seemed like a long time, then, the sound of the shot, and its echo, traveled away from them. They seemed to diminish in size, as if into the distance. They became a distant rumble, a memory, a prayer. They seemed to reach the river and catch a current and glide away on the moving stream.

Leroy blinked his eyes. He opened his jaw to click open his ear passages. His daddy did the same.

Laurie brought the rifle down from her shoulder. She shucked out the spent shell and sent a live round into the chamber. The three of them looked down into the ravine. The plastic bottle was split wide open. It was hardly recognizable. It lay several feet farther down the gully from where it had been. Swami Don turned to Laurie. Probably he was going to congratulate her. Good shot, maybe he was going to say. Or maybe he would have scolded her mildly for firing without first letting him know, waiting for the go-ahead. "From now on, give me a signal of some kind, okay." Maybe that was what he would have said, if there had been an opportunity. Or maybe he just then noticed what Laurie had already seen, what Leroy would take another couple of seconds to pick up on. The pack of wild dogs that had been sleeping in a camouflage of wild brush and cane, far down the length of the ravine, now roused itself at the sound of the gunshot. The dogs milled about, anxious and nervous, seven or eight of them, on the lip of a gravel bar. One of these dogs had killed the llama. Maybe Swami Don only meant to say, You see there, see what I mean, this is proof of the need for good fences, didn't I tell you, didn't I say I had work to do before the end of this day? He didn't say any of this, though. He didn't say anything. He didn't get a chance. Just before he might have spoken one of these fatherly thoughts, both Swami Don and Leroy witnessed something completely unexpected. This was the most amazing thing either of them had ever seen. They watched as Laurie took a deep breath, her second in this brief space. A second time they watched her exhale. A second time, too, the wilderness exploded with gunfire. Laurie had aimed and squeezed the trigger.

When Leroy heard that shot, even before he understood that one of the dogs had crumpled and lay dead on a spit of the gravel bar, whole worlds, some of them not yet even a part of his experience, opened wide to him, the white and red of the fair fleet limbs of gods, the steel shields of their eyes, the pomp and peacocks, the sun's disk crescent over a hill at dawn, the aura, the halo of lightning as it strikes a pine tree and ten gallons of pine sap boil up out of the trunk. The pack was scattering. The dogs ran every which way at once. They ran up the ravine, down the ravine, into the brush, the cane, around the bend, out of sight. The dog that lay dead was a big shepherd-looking creature. A bright red gash was visible in its side, even at this distance.

There was nothing to say. No one could think of anything. Leroy sure couldn't. They stood around together until the wilderness seemed to calm down again. The clatter of their hearts was not so loud. All the birds had flown. The swamp elves had all run away, like tiny ostriches. No one could have said whether they could still hear the distant river.

One of the dogs was dead. The baby llama was dead. Old Pappy was dead. Leroy watched Swami Don take the rifle from Laurie and unload it. He cranked the lever and kicked out all the shells, live and spent. Laurie gathered them all up and put them into a pocket of her dress. Swami Don carried the rifle. The three of them made their way in silence, back across the pasture, in the direction of their house.

Many years later, after he was all grown up and had gone away to college, Leroy read a story in *Ficciones* by the writer J. L. Borges. In it a character recalls a detective story he once read in which there was an inexplicable murder in the first pages, a slow investigation in the middle ones, and then a solution in the end. After the mystery had been solved, the speaker says that he then noticed a sentence he had paid no attention to before. The sentence is, "Everybody believed that the two chess players had met by chance." This sentence makes clear that the solution by the detective in the story is the wrong one. Then the perplexed reader rereads the misleading chapters and finds *another* solution, the right one.

Just as Swami Don, Laurie, and Leroy reentered the yard from the pasture they saw Elsie rush from the house, out the back door. She was waving something above her head. She was calling, "Donald! Donald!" Leroy stopped walking and looked, they all did. Leroy's mama ran in their direction, out of the house, down the path, clumsy, wild, distraught, as if with grief. She stopped. Leroy knew that she could have been an actress in a movie. She stood with her legs apart, her arms outstretched, in extravagant feeling.

She called out to her husband, "Only of love, my darling, do I want to talk. Only of you, whom I love, will always love, of the gratitude I owe you, of the inexpressible joy you gave me. I only want your hands to hold, the embrace of your strong arms. Disasters will follow disasters. Blood will always spill. And always only you will I love."

For one moment, shining, fleeting, Leroy believed in silken dreams, their sweetness more ruby-throated than prayer, their efficacy more pure than geology. He loved his mother, he loved his father and sisters, the llamas and dogs and Old Pappy, even death, in the odorous apple, the song of cardinals, the red of poppies. Leroy saw the streets of a perfect town, its spotted trees, the dull lozenges of its paint and hardware store, a reverberant sun upon greenhouses, a long windowless hospital wall bright with fresh whitewash. For one moment he believed in true love, which had once been his parents' to own and had come back fully.

The key sentence in Borges's story is translated "Everybody believed that the two chess players had met by chance." The key sentence in Leroy's mama's outpouring was, "I only want your hands to hold, the embrace of your strong arms."

Hands? Arms? Two of each?

The thing Elsie had been waving above her head was one of Harris's newspapers, a late edition maybe, or maybe it was a page from her scrapbook. In it was published a letter from Aldo Moro to his wife, Noretta. These romantic words upon Elsie's lips were the last Aldo Moro would ever speak, with tongue or pen. *Always only you will I love.*

"Did it kick?" Leroy would later ask Laurie about the rifle.

"Yes."

"Did it hurt?"

"I liked it."

"I kiss you. I hold you, my dearest," Leroy's mama concluded, speaking from the memorized letter, there on the path that led into the pasture. "Oh, I kiss you."

15

"Hope this is okay," the New Guy was saying with a bright smile on that warm, clear evening when the New People stopped by for a visit. Leroy had seen them walking up the path toward the house and he followed along behind them. He saw his mama see them, too, and watched her get up from the wicker rocker and open the screened door and invite the two of them up on the porch. Leroy came inside, too, trailing along behind. Leroy's daddy was already home from work. He was all cleaned up and had finished supper and was sitting out in the breeze in his khakis and sockfeet. He stood up from the glider and made sure his shirt was buttoned up and his belly wasn't showing from beneath it and came to the screened door to greet the New People, along with Elsie. Laurie and Molly were back in the house somewhere, so when they heard the commotion they came out and sneaked looks at the New People from around the doorjambs. The New Guy was saying that he and his wife had begun to know the children, especially Leroy here, he said—he said this with a firm, confident wink in Leroy's direction—"We had a nice trek together one afternoon with Mr. Sweet," he went on, and so now he thought it was high time to get to know the children's parents as well. "Hope an impromptu visit like this is okay with everyone, not an intrusion." Leroy listened. The New Guy did not say you sam. He was not British, and not in costume, did not seem strange at all. He wore casual clothes, jeans, shirt, sneakers. Both of them did. His wife was not a señorita. The New Guy passed some object he'd been holding to Leroy's daddy's hand. "Not at all," Leroy's mama was saying, "please come in, I haven't been much of a neighbor, I'm afraid."

Swami Don did not react right away—he had stood up and come to the door, all right, so he was not impolite, but once he was there he seemed incapable of anything else, he didn't actually speak to the guests, only stood and looked at them as if he had been taken completely by surprise. In fact, Leroy realized he had been taken by surprise. He'd been handed something, which he'd taken in his one good hand, and now seemed to have concentrated all his attention on this object, so there was no energy left over for anything else, even the smallest of conversation. He held the object he'd been given, he regarded it—Leroy would have said suspiciously if he could have thought of the right word. It was something contained in a brown paper bag.

"Well, let's see," Elsie said to Swami Don. She meant the

small gift he had just received. "Don't keep us in suspense. What is it?"

Laurie sat down on the glider. Leroy sat beside her. He wanted to get a good view of everything. Their arms touched, they sat so close. Leroy watched as his daddy realized he was holding something foreign in his good hand. It seemed not to have been handed to him but simply to have appeared there, as if by magic. It had come into his hand in a moment of confusion, during introductions. Leroy realized his daddy had missed the introductions, too. He might as well have been a sleepwalker. He had accepted the bag, whatever it was, automatically. He looked slowly down at the bag and could see now that it was a bottle of wine. Except for grog rations, this was the first alcohol to make its way into this house. It was the first time Swami Don had ever held a bottle of liquor in his hand. Leroy watched him closely. He stood holding the wine bottle by the neck like a chicken ready to be slaughtered for supper.

"And as long as we're making these introductions," the New Guy went on saying, "well, let's do them right, make it formal, get them out of the way." Leroy had never seen so bright a smile. He watched as the New Guy extended his hand in Swami Don's direction to be shaken. He spoke his name and the name of his wife, but the words made no impression on Leroy. He might as well have said, "We are the New People." He did say, "At your service, sir."

Leroy knew that an extended hand meant a handshake. And

he knew that with his daddy a handshake was impossible. He watched his daddy stare at the New Guy's hand as if it might be a snake. Swami Don was still holding the bottle of wine like a chicken by the throat. A few times over the years Leroy had seen a hand stuck out at his daddy in this way, at church maybe, at a PTA meeting when there was a new teacher, or down at Mr. Sweet's store. Usually the other person caught on quickly that Swami Don had no hand suitable for shaking and so the extended hand just went away and no one mentioned it. Once or twice he had managed a successful left-handed grasp. In this case, though, he was holding the wine bottle. No left-hand grasp was possible. There was no free hand. Leroy also realized his daddy could not speak, he could only stare. He had no skills to explain his situation. The New Guy had not yet realized that Swami Don's arm was withered and useless. He kept holding his hand out expectantly. The smile stayed bright.

In the confusion there must have seemed only one thing to do. Leroy watched the twisting of his daddy's face as this conclusion seemed to be reached. Leroy knew it was a mistake, what was about to happen, but there was nothing he could do to stop it. He watched as his daddy maneuvered his good left arm, the hand with the wine bottle in it, until that hand was under his tiny right wrist. Leroy watched him lift the lifeless arm with the other arm. He watched him extend his useless, pale baby-hand straight out to be shaken. Leroy looked at the New Guy. He must have caught on by now, he had to have. But no, he had not. He still did not know that the hand in front of him could not be shaken. He did not understand at all the extent of Swami Don's confusion and ineptitude. Abruptly then, in a manly way, the New Guy seized the diminutive hand in front of him in his own and gave it so hard and ringing a handshake he might have been trying to tear it off and throw it out the window. The wine bottle dangled wildly below the handshake like a clapper in a wildly clanging bell. Bells seemed actually to be clanging in Leroy's mind and heart as he watched.

The moment went on forever, it seemed to Leroy, but it had to end eventually. Eventually the New Guy would have to see what he had done. The knowledge came to him too late. He was already in midhandshake, pumping away. He was slinging Swami Don's hand this way and that, every which way. What a handshake it was. It was surely a world-record handshake. No hand was ever shaken so thoroughly as this. Even good hands, real hands, unmaimed and unmutilated hands, would have had a hard time withstanding this handshake. It went on and on, even after it was clear what had happened, what a mistake had been made. Even now that he knew what he was doing, the New Guy seemed unable to stop. Handshakes have a momentum, their own life, they are unmanageable once they are set free. He shook and shook and shook and shook, already embarrassed and remorseful, and yet unable to stop shaking, pumping, ringing. At last he did stop. At last he dropped the hand, more than dropped it, slung it away from him like something hot. The hand seemed now to take flight it was cast away with such force. It seemed to Leroy to spin out into the air like a Frisbee, it seemed to hang suspended. The hand became a great bird hanging on a column of air. Actually, it was still propped upon Swami Don's good hand.

For a moment then no one moved, no one spoke. Elsie was a deer caught in the headlights. She could not move. Finally she did move. The New Guy said, "Oh! I'm sorry, I—" Elsie took the bottle from Swami Don. She smiled. She seemed calm. She said, "Here, honey, I'll take that." She stripped the paper bag away from the bottle and held the bottle up to look at it. She was smiling. To Leroy she seemed to have done this every day of her life. Leroy's daddy's face was a mask. The others smiled and chatted, but he seemed unable to say anything at all. The New Lady produced a knife with a corkscrew in the handle and expertly uncorked the bottle. Elsie went into the kitchen and came back with four glasses with Peter Pan figures on them. She said, "Okay, who's Captain Hook and who's Tinker Bell?" The New Guy said, "Ah yes, that would be us." The New Lady said, "Wherever did you *find* these?" Leroy's mama said, "Aisle 3." When everyone laughed, Leroy knew this was a fine day for Elsie Dearman.

The New Guy poured wine for everyone. He lifted his glass for a toast. "To our beginning," he said. Everybody clinked glasses. Leroy kept his eyes on his daddy, who did not raise his glass for the toast. He seemed unaware of the presence of anyone else on the porch. The wine had hypnotized him. Leroy watched as Swami Don looked down at the glass of wine in his hand. He watched as Swami Don failed to clink with the others. He watched him hold it to his face. Swami Don looked into the purple liquid as if it were a magic well. He looked like a man contemplating three wishes. He stuck his nose deep inside the glass.

The New Guy sipped from the rim of his glass and noticed Swami Don at his strange ritual.

The New Guy said, "Fruity?"

Swami Don kept on breathing the fragrance of the wine. He looked up. He said, "What?"

The New Guy said, "Would you say it has a fruity smell?"

Leroy watched his daddy put his nose back into the peanut butter jar.

"Flowers," he said. "It smells like flowers."

The New Lady said, "Excellent."

The New Guy said, "Why did I take a class when I am living next door to an expert?"

Next Elsie put her glass to her lips. She paused. Leroy knew that this was the first time she would have ever tasted alcohol. She had never even sipped from Uncle Harris's glass at grog rations. He watched as she tilted the glass. The wine slid up the side of the glass and into her mouth. He watched his mama taste alcohol for the first time. He watched her hold it in her mouth for several seconds. He watched her swallow. She brought the glass down then and Leroy watched her face and saw what happened inside her as the wine went down. He saw a perfect inner warmth radiate throughout her whole self. He saw a network of countless invisible hot wires hurled out through her body from a single perfect source of heat. He watched everything. He could read all this in the small pleasure of her hooded eyes, the skin about her mouth. He believed that everything had suddenly changed, he was not sure why. He believed—though he could only sense this at some vague core—that some enormous new thing was about to happen, maybe even to himself. He looked back at his daddy, who watched Elsie even more closely than Leroy did. Swami Don looked as if he expected to see horns pop out from his wife's forehead and a tail with a spear-point unfurl from the base of her spine. She said, "Mm." She put her jar down on the table. She was Wendy. She said, "Flowers," nodding, thoughtful. "Yes, flowers is right." Swami Don nodded with her, the flowers of death, yes. "Fruity, too," she said, with a small smile in the New People's direction. "The forbidden fruit that leads to the grave," Leroy heard his daddy suddenly say without meaning to do so. Swami Don let out an abrupt little scream. Leroy thought Swami Don would be humiliated, but he was not. He did not know he had screamed and the others paid no attention, or took this to be a joke. Elsie was not finished. She said, "Nutty." The New Lady broke into tiny applause, literally, and startled Leroy. She said, "Oh, my, that was impressive." Elsie took another sip, a gulp actually. She said, "It's like holding acorns in my mouth."

The afternoon lengthened toward evening. The grown-ups sat and talked about many things. The children stayed put, they were allowed to stay near so long as they were quiet. Molly wandered in and out. For a while Elsie kept saying, "Do you need to sit on the potty, honey? Let mama know, okay? Don't forget." Then she finally gave up and let Molly wander around without pestering her. She kept on sipping at her wine. Swami Don could not take his eyes off Elsie as she drank the wine. Leroy realized they were talking about the lightning that had started to strike the house this summer. No one could really explain the lightning, Leroy's mama was saying. The New Guy said, "I imagined I saw what looked like a fire snake sliding down the roof and into the window." Elsie said, "You should be inside the house when that happens." He said, "I'm waiting for my engraved invitation!" Everyone laughed a little at this. It was a party. It was better than grog rations. It was too bad Uncle Harris was out tonight.

Elsie had two glasses of wine, or was it three? Leroy watched his daddy watch her. "Do you hear a buzzing sound?" Elsie asked. Everyone listened. Well, maybe, they agreed, they weren't sure. There might be a buzzing sound. Leroy listened and heard nothing. He was certain his daddy heard nothing. Elsie touched her lips over and over. "Are your lips numb?" she said.

The New Guy produced a second bottle of wine from somewhere. Everyone seemed pleased at this. The New Lady went to work with her corkscrew.

Everyone was surprised when Laurie spoke up. She had been so quiet.

She said, "May I have a glass of wine, please?"

No one was more surprised than Leroy. He looked at her. Laurie had asked for wine as if it were the most natural request on earth. He realized there was a great deal he would never understand about Laurie. The New Guy said, "In Argentina parents use water to dilute the wine for their children." Argentina sounded to Leroy like a subject his daddy might be interested in talking about, but Leroy was wrong about that. Swami Don didn't even hear the word *Argentina*. The New Guy had scarcely got the words out of his mouth when Swami Don said, "*No.*" His tone was very sharp. Leroy's insides jumped a little. He had never heard his daddy speak quite like this. Swami Don said, "You get out of here, Laurie. Right now." The New Guy said, "I'm sorry, old man, I didn't mean to—" Swami Don looked at him fiercely and caused him to stop whatever he was about to say. He said, "Our children don't drink."

Laurie slipped immediately from her chair and spun around and left the room. Leroy heard her say, "God." Everyone heard her. It infuriated Swami Don. The house seemed to explode. The noise of his daddy's voice filled every small space. Suddenly Swami Don was almost screaming. It was the most unexpected thing Leroy could have imagined. Swami Don shouted, "You come right back here this minute, young lady." Laurie kept walking away, right off the porch. Elsie said,

"Donald, please." Leroy could tell that his mama was shocked, too, though she managed to seem calm enough. Anyone would have seemed calm next to Leroy's daddy. He leapt up out of his chair. He said, "Laurie! I mean it!" He chased after her, he ran from the porch and into the house. He said, "You get yourself right back here!" His withered arm was going in circles he was so excited, it looked like a pinwheel. Elsie said, "Donald, calm down, please, you're acting like a maniac." She looked at the New People as if in appeal. Swami Don had caught up with Laurie at the back of the house.

From one of the farther rooms, then, everyone heard the sound of a smack. It sounded like a gunshot. No one could believe what they were hearing, least of all Leroy. Swami Don was spanking Laurie on her bare legs. Leroy's daddy had never spanked anyone in his life. They heard another smack. Laurie was screaming. Angry words reached the porch. Swami Don was saying, "Don't you *ever*—" And then another smack, and more screaming.

The New Guy said, "Elsie, I feel terrible." His wife said, "Maybe we'd better go. We know about family fights, believe me."

Molly came into the room. She said, "Why is Daddy hitting Laurie?" She looked ready to cry. She had wet her pants again.

When Elsie rose from her chair she tottered a little. Leroy watched her steady herself with one hand against the wall. She stood for a few seconds as if her legs had gone numb. She recovered her balance. Leroy watched as she lifted her glass and drained what was left down her throat. Then she picked up another glass, the full glass Swami Don had set down, and drank it as well. She said, "Don't leave." She was speaking to the New People. They stayed put. They weren't going anywhere. Leroy followed his mama off the porch and into the house. He followed her through the living room and down the hall.

Laurie was in her bedroom, huddled up at the head of her bed as far as she could wedge herself, against the pillows. Leroy watched his mama pick Laurie up from the bed, whimpering and sucking her thumb. Leroy stood outside the door, insinuated there. Swami Don was standing in the little bedroom too, holding his withered hand in his good hand. He was rubbing the back of it with his huge thumb. His face seemed very pale. He looked as though he had seen something that scared him. He said to Elsie, "I'm sorry— I told Laurie I was sorry—" Leroy heard his mama say, "Shut your fucking mouth." Her voice was a deadly whisper. He heard her say, "Every time you look at that hand, yes, that one, the only real hand you've got, I want you to remember that it's the hand that beat this child." She turned with Laurie in her arms. Leroy scooted out of the doorway to keep out of her way. Swami Don was bouncing the tiny hand in the big one. He said, "Elsie, please—" She was not listening. She went back out onto the porch, carrying Laurie with her, red-eyed and quivery-lipped. Leroy tagged along behind. He wanted to say something—to Laurie, to his mama, his daddy, he didn't know who, and couldn't think of anything to say anyway.

The company on the porch was very quiet for a while. Leroy took Molly into the living room and pulled off her wet underpants and wiped off her bottom with a damp cloth, the way he'd seen his mama do. He poked through a little pine dresser in the girls' room and took out a dry pair and helped Molly put them on. He went back out on the porch then and sat on the glider. Molly sat beside him and sucked her thumb. For a while nothing at all was said. The grown-ups just sat and drank wine for a while. Swami Don didn't come back outside. When the glasses were empty, the New Guy poured another glass of wine for everyone. The bottle clinking against the rims of the glasses seemed loud now. The gurgle of wine from the bottle sounded like a river. Leroy watched his mama pick up her glass. They all picked up glasses, but there were no more toasts. At last Elsie put the glass to her mouth and drank. They all drank, all of them, slowly. They sat and drank without speaking. Laurie stayed on Elsie's lap. Molly moved to Leroy's lap. No one seemed to care where Swami Don was. At last Elsie held the wine to Laurie's lips. She said, "Just a taste." She allowed her to sip from the rim. Laurie drank a little of the wine and made a face. Elsie said, "Do you like it?" Laurie said, "No." Elsie said, "Want a little more?" Laurie said, "Okay." Fireflies lit up the yard. The redness in the west deepened to purple, then darkness. The New People said they'd like to make love in Elsie's attic someday during a lightning storm. Elsie cried a little and said she and Donald had never even thought of doing that in a lightning storm. The New Lady said, "There, there." The New People told Elsie they'd had a son murdered. "He was fourteen," the New Lady said. Then they cried a little. They told Elsie the night they got the call about the murder—the boy was spending the night with a friend—they were watching a pornographic video.

"This is the happiest day of my life," Elsie said. It was a special night, all right, Leroy just knew it was.

16

Twirling camp was to be held each morning on the high school football field in the village, weather permitting, Leroy's mama said, reading from the church bulletin. Leroy sat on the sofa in the living room and watched her read. She looked up from the page to see that he and his sisters were listening. Her voice was very enthusiastic. Baton twirling was one of several suggested wholesome summer activities for children of the parish, she told them. "It sounds to me like the most fun of all. 'Fun and fellowship for all,'" Elsie read. Leroy squinted his eyes. What was going on here? "Now doesn't that sound interesting?" his mama said. "Wouldn't you say that sounds like fun, everybody?"

Leroy was suspicious. His mama and daddy were scarcely speaking after the night with the New People. Something in the tone of his mama's voice told him—well, he wasn't sure what it told him. Why was she suddenly in such a good mood, why was she figuring out wholesome activities?

"Twirling lessons for girls ages three through ten," she read. She looked up again. "Well, what do you think?" she said. "Sounds like fun, doesn't it? Don't you agree that this sounds like an excellent summer activity? It sure sounds like fun to me, baton twirling."

Uncle Harris was there as well. He was equally enthusiastic about twirling. He was nodding his head, he was agreeing with everything. In fact, he chimed right in. He said he had met the young woman who would be in charge of the camp. He said she was great, a really super gal. "An excellent twirler in her own right," he said. The twirling teacher, he told everyone, was a high school girl named Ruby Rae. "A very high-quality baton twirler," Uncle Harris went on. "Professional, actually. They don't come any better than Ruby Rae. You'll see. You'll like her," he promised. "Scout's honor. Give you my word." He gave Leroy a special wink. "She's pretty!" he said.

Okay, so Leroy was right, this was a setup. He said, "Twirling is for girls."

Elsie said, "Now don't be a sourpuss, Leroy. Keep an open mind, will you please? I just hope you will please try and keep an open mind about this summer activity with fun and fellowship for all. Will you do at least that much for me? It's good exercise, too, it says so right here."

He said, "Twirling is for girls."

She said, "Not necessarily."

Harris said, "There are plenty of boy twirlers. Sure. The Ole Miss marching band had a couple of boy twirlers, if I remember correctly. Nothing wrong with boy baton twirlers."

Leroy said, "It's for girls. It says so right there, three through ten. I'm a boy. I'm twelve. I'm not doing it."

"We'll just ask if boys might be included as well," Elsie said. "Special dispensation, you know? It can't hurt to ask. Will it hurt anything to ask, Harris?"

"Not a thing. I give you my word."

"See, Leroy? Uncle Harris knows all about these things. Asking never hurt anybody, now did it?"

This deal had already been done. There was no use arguing, really. Something told Leroy that special permission had already been granted, he was already signed up. All his mama had to do was convince him to go along with it. What a gyp. Wholesome summer activities had already been set in motion. What a total gyp.

He said, "I'm not twirling."

Elsie became irritated with him now. She said, "Well, believe you me, no one is going to beg you to enjoy summer fun and fellowship, Leroy. This is a privilege, not a chore, young man. Maybe if you would look at the nice things I try to do for you as a privilege for a change, and not such of a chore, you might not be quite so negative about every single solitary thing I suggest. Back me up here, Harris, if you don't mind."

Uncle Harris was wearing one of his Hawaiian shirts, with

a ukulele print. "Absolutely," he said. "Your mama is absolutely right. It's not a chore, not a bit, it's more of a golden
opportunity."

"In fact," his mama went on, "the instructor might not even
let you twirl anyway. Even if you did want to. So just don't go
and get your cart before the horse, young man. So okay, that's
it, then, no twirling for Leroy. Leroy's not going to be coop-
erative, count Leroy out. That's fine, Leroy, your sisters can
have all the fun and fellowship themselves, I guess you'll just
have to miss out on everything."

Leroy said, "I'm not twirling."

Elsie said, "Go get in Uncle Harris's car. Leroy, you'll have
to come along with us for now, whether you twirl or not."

"I'm not twirling."

"Would you please stop repeating that one single expression
about one million times until I'm ready to pull my hair out,
Leroy, if you don't mind, would you do that for me please?"

Uncle Harris burned rubber when they hit the pavement.
He gunned it. The car skidded briefly out of control and then
straightened itself on the road. They went tearing down the
highway. Harris held up his hand and shouted above the
engine noise, "Twirl, twirl, twirl!"

Leroy looked at his mama. She looked very pretty in the
seat next to Uncle Harris with the warm wind in her hair. He
hated to admit it, but she did.

Leroy looked around the backseat, what passed for a backseat, the little space behind the real seats where they were

crammed in. His sisters were holding silver batons with rubber tips, but there was no baton for Leroy.

He said, "There's only two batons."

You had to shout to be heard with the top down. Elsie and Harris gave each other a look.

Elsie turned a little in her seat and said, "You're not twirling, remember?"

They drove on. Elsie looked forward and ignored Leroy.

Molly had a junior-sized baton, silvery with rubber bulbs at either end. Hers was a smaller version of the model Laurie held. They were nice-looking instruments, Leroy had to admit that. Molly was content. She was almost always contented.

It was Laurie, though, who understood the meaning of the baton. She held it as if it were some sacred thing, Excalibur or the Holy Grail, a relic of the True Cross, you would think so, from the look on her face, about which an aura had formed. Leroy was unaccustomed to seeing his sister so vulnerable, so nakedly in love and purely affected and unable to hide the fullness of her feeling. She stroked the baton with her fingers. It might have been a pet. She put her nose to the larger bulb at the end and breathed its fragrance of new rubber. She laid her small tongue upon it. She closed her eyes and savored the treasure in her hands.

Leroy immediately knew that she was right. He hated to admit it, but she was. He had never seen a baton so close, stood in such intimate propinquity to one. He had given not one moment's thought to a baton before now, and yet now that it was here before him he could see nothing else, could not deny that it was a beautiful object, like art he might almost have been grown-up enough to think, truly beautiful, its perfect shape, its admirable heft, its miracle of balance and form, the scarcely perceptible million indentations in the bright rod that gave its holder the confidence of skid-free traction even on a summer's day and with sweaty palms.

The little car went zooming down the road toward the village.

Leroy said, "Let me see that thing."

Laurie said, "Fuck you."

Leroy looked at his sister. Who was this child?

Elsie and Uncle Harris could hear nothing in the front seat of the convertible.

Then Laurie held out the baton as if to hand it over to Leroy. She said, "You can touch it."

Leroy would have preferred resisting the temptation, he believed he would have been a better person if he could have said fuck you right back to Laurie, but he could not, he knew he could not. He understood the hopelessness of any such competition with Laurie. And anyway, he had to feel the baton beneath his hand, this wand of silver and rubber. It was irresistible to him. He reached out. He touched it. He ran his hand along its length. He felt the subtle indentations in the shaft. He saw the glistening of sunlight upon its surfaces. He touched the rubber bulbs at either end, the greater and the lesser ones. He looked up at Laurie and her hard eyes gave him further permission. He bent down his head and smelled the baton, shaft and bulbs, as his sister had done. He tasted it with his tongue. Lightly he bit it with his teeth. Laurie was kind to him, for once in her life. She did not snatch the baton away, did not make fun. She allowed Leroy to linger there, in this weird worship.

For the only time in his life Leroy wanted to renounce himself, his whole identity, and to be a girl, to share this moment with his sister in a way that as a boy he could not, to commune more closely than even now he did, though it was hard to imagine how a moment could have been more intimate. For the first time in his life he thought that there might be something wrong, something sinful and irredeemable, about being born into the world a male child and not female.

He had not been wrong about the baton. Its perfection was real, all right. No one could deny its perfection. More than merely real or perfect, the baton was magic. There seemed little doubt of this now. It held invisible powers. Its entrance into his life signaled changes that would stay with him in perpetuity, blessing or curse, he did not know, or even care really, so strong was its power to charm and change him. The power of it throbbed into his own body like electrical drums. It vibrated through his hand and up his arm and into his heart, where it made its imprint, a thumbprint and more than a thumbprint, a mark that might as well have been an image of Leroy's own DNA upon his soul.

In this baton lay the universe, it seemed to Leroy, its every secret and all beauty. Leroy wanted to twirl. He didn't care what he had said before, he renounced every belief he had ever held, every assertion he had ever made. He didn't mind the humiliation of changing his mind, of chasing a girl's dream. The baton was the living bone of him. Twirling suddenly lay at the marrow. He wanted to be a twirler, longed to be one, deep down. Somewhere near the beginning of the universe he already was a twirler. Twirling was his identity, his life's core. I am a twirler, he thought, whispered, prayed, as if in a foreign tongue to enhance the mystery, *Ich bin ein Twirler*. With no baton of his own—his mama had suspected she would lose this battle and Leroy's daddy had convinced her they should see how the conversation worked out before spending the extra money—Leroy was empty, worthless, he was nothing. With his own baton he would be complete, only then.

His heart ached, his soul, to possess a baton, to twirl and twirl and twirl and twirl, endlessly, through infinite space and time, until the purest part of his very self became known to him, and to all the universe. Twirl, he had to twirl, for God's holy sake, I twirl, therefore I am!

The problem was that at the same time he knew these things he also fully understood why his mama had begun to manipulate the three of them into attending this camp. He knew it had little to do with wholesome summer activities, as she pretended. Fun and fellowship were only a peripheral motive. This whole setup had entirely to do with Harris, with herself and Harris. It had to do with getting the children out of the house. It was all about the kissing that Leroy had seen. And probably more than kissing. He thought of his mama in a western vest, he hoped it had buttons. He was alert suddenly to just how much more there was on this earth for a man and woman to share in secret beyond the act of a kiss. It was awful how deep a secret could be, how deep a betrayal could go. Leroy had seen them kiss, so that much was clear, undeniable and real. He had looked at the naked pictures in the magazines beside his uncle's bed, and so nakedness was real as well, bodies of unthinkable and painful beauty. Beneath her clothing Leroy's mama was no less naked than the demented lady. He began to suspect that his mama might already have done this thing, whatever it was, with Harris, this sex he had begun to hear about. He was driven for the first time in his life to consider the death of his sisters, and his own death. He stood at the beginning of knowing such things, knowing also that the means by which he was accustomed to comprehending the world were merely inadequate in the extreme.

Then he laid eyes upon Ruby Rae. He saw her as soon as they arrived at the school football field. Harris pulled the car into the school parking lot. The gravel crunched beneath the tires as he pulled to a stop near the fence. All of them struggled out of the car, children and adults, and walked in the direction of several other persons milling about, parents and children, all girls of course. Then, there she was, the person

Uncle Harris had said was pretty, the professional-grade twirler Ruby Rae.

All right, it was settled, then. It didn't matter any longer what he was doing here. Everything was changed, pride meant nothing. Secret agendas were irrelevant. Destiny was made. Leroy would twirl. The earth's twirling on its axis was not a greater certainty than this. When he first laid eyes on her Leroy knew that Ruby Rae was the final answer to all doubt on every subject. Ruby Rae was every twelve-year-old boy's most private dream of heaven. She was beautiful. She was other-worldly. She was the most beautiful vision ever to have been visited upon human eyes, or even upon a twelve-year-old boy's imagination, as richly textured as that. Leroy's reverence for the baton suddenly paled and disappeared in the sunlight of sexual need first felt. He ached, his entire body like a bad tooth ached simply to look at her. He loved his mama in a way he had never loved her before. He loved the women in Harris's magazines. He loved his sisters, and all the women of the world. He loved Miss Alberta, who taught Mississippi history. He loved Rosalynn Carter. He knew why people wanted to kiss, even in sin and betrayal. He knew now that he could forgive anything, anything at all, for a woman's love.

He would have died to kiss Ruby Rae. Gladly would he have given his life for a single kiss, though he was not even sure he would know how to kiss if he had the chance. Only once would have been enough. A single kiss would suffice, pure as snow. Or maybe not. Maybe he would have to have two kisses. Or about a million. Maybe there were other things to want that he didn't know about. He wondered whether his Uncle Harris had felt this feeling, longing, urgency, for his mama, and she for him. He believed they did. This explained so much. It explained everything. No guilt of betrayal was too great to resist the urgency of this need, once felt.

Leroy began to fear that he had said too much, complained too vigorously, that they would not let him twirl. Was this possible? That he had actually talked himself out of this opportunity for a complete personality? They hadn't bought him a baton. That was a bad sign. Those things were expensive, Leroy knew that. Had he lost his chance? It was conceivable that Leroy had gone too far, had trusted too much that the world would not take from him what suddenly he understood he could not well live without. He would do anything to repair the damage, anything. He would beg. He would cast his lot with the swine herd of little girls around him, those who had showed up for this thing, this camp, which he was certain now only he understood. He cared not a whit what a sissy this would make of him, prove him to be. Nothing else mattered any longer. He had no regard for himself at all, no memory even of any values he had held in this world before he saw the baton and the girl, or for any life beyond the sexuality of the young woman standing before him and his family on the green table of land, the football field, in a purple leotard, casually speaking to parents and, as if unconsciously, slowly twirling her own baton in a desultory, heartbreaking way.

Her legs were long, her hips were slim, her lips were full, her hair she wore in an auburn braid to her waist. Those dear qualities of beauty were not all, not even in fact a fraction, of what broke this child's heart. Ruby Rae's breasts were by far the most beautiful breasts on this or any other planet. Why is it a child loves breasts? Not just beautiful, visible there beneath the leotard, they were huge. They were as big as watermelons. He would never pass another watermelon in a supermarket without whispering her name. He would never pass a roadside fruit stand without thinking of batons.

17

The night before twirling camp—or maybe another night, later on, Leroy could never remember which— a call came in from Security at the sporting goods plant out on Old Wire Road, close to Fateville. Could Swami Don fill in on short notice, the caller had wanted to know, they had a guard out on sick call and needed a substitute. Leroy listened to his daddy talking on the phone. Swami Don said okay, sure, that sounded fine, the late shift, all right, they could count on him, no problem. Leroy watched then as Swami Don made a second quick call and heard his daddy speak in low tones—he couldn't tell what he was saying—then hang up. Swami Don came into the bedroom and told Elsie he was working tonight.

Leroy's mama was cool to Swami Don, she was still mad about Laurie's spanking, and maybe about some other things as well. Still, she helped him lay out his uniform, the sleek gray trousers with a stripe of a darker gray down each leg, the military-style webbed belt and buckle, the plain-toed shoes polished to a fare-thee-well, the starched khaki shirt and slim tie. Leroy watched it all. No matter what kind of mood Elsie was in, this uniform always seemed to soften her, Leroy noticed. Swami Don never unknotted the tie so he wouldn't have to struggle to retie it each time with only one hand. Elsie offered to tie it for him, said it would look better freshly tied, but he said, "Aw, no, no thanks." The chocolate brown nylon jacket with a silver badge, the jaunty hat, cowboy-style— Swami Don looked very different in his guard uniform, everybody who ever saw him dressed in it said so. It was the only time Leroy ever noticed how handsome a man his daddy really was.

Seeing him dressed in the uniform, it's a wonder Elsie didn't catch on to what was going on. It was a wonder Leroy hadn't understood what the second phone call meant. In the uniform Swami Don looked nothing like the dumb-moose dad, the cripple, the steady guy, Farmer Jim, which were the ways Elsie, and Leroy, too, were accustomed to thinking of him. The issue of his crippled arm disappeared altogether when he was dressed in uniform, along with all his other customary identities. In this uniform everything you knew about Swami Don seemed to fall away, as if those things had been the costume and this were the real person, unmasked. Leroy had a hard time thinking such thoughts, they were so foreign to him, but he knew the truth of them anyway. Even Swami Don saw the difference, Leroy could look at him and see this, the way he stood, everything. He watched his daddy regard himself in the mirror on the back of his bedroom door and you could tell Swami Don was quite astounded by the person he saw. Elsie saw it, too, this difference. Whenever he wore the uniform she said, "Don't you look handsome tonight." She even said it on this night, when she was scarcely speaking otherwise.

It was a long time before anybody found out what went on later. Leroy was already in bed, though he was not asleep. He heard the engine of the pickup turn over and start. He imagined his daddy's cowboy hat on the seat beside him. He saw a reflection of the headlights turn on and heard the truck pull out of the drive and head out down the lane. Autumnlike air swept in through the open window of the pickup on Swami Don's drive through the hills. By this time Leroy had already closed his eyes. He was already dreaming. The wind ruffled Swami Don's tie and blew his hair over his forehead and into his eyes. The quick call he had made, when Leroy was hanging around trying to listen, was to the Indian girl who worked at the factory. Some of this would come out later. There would be noisy fights between Swami Don and Elsie. There would be fierce, quiet conversations. The phone call was something the two of them had planned, Swami Don and the Indian maiden, next time he got called in for the dog shift. The breeze through the window brought into his nostrils the fragrances of cedar and mown hay from beyond the roadside. Swami Don wondered whether this was what the world smelled like to a liar. He wondered what those small lies, the things he'd withheld from Elsie all along, throughout their marriage, had to do with this larger one.

There was no moon that night, the storm clouds were gathering, so he kept his strong left hand firm upon the wheel. Over time Leroy grew uncertain how much of this he knew to be true and how much he had imagined. The road was a winding one, newly surfaced and smooth but with no lines yet painted to mark the center or the edges. The darkness seemed very deep. Swami Don kept leaning over the steering wheel, peering out at the roadway bathed in yellow light. He was trying to assure himself that what he saw was only a roadbed, only the headlights, the graveled berm, a few other cars along the way, road signs, shadows. He couldn't believe a person raised Pentecostal could do what he was about to do. Or maybe it was only Leroy himself, later on, who would have a hard time believing the events of this night could have happened.

Later, Swami Don could not have described the motel where he stayed for two hours before work that night. Not the parking lot, the name of the inn, the key he must have used to open the door. Was there an ashtray, a Bible, a matchbook? Was there a desk, a television set, telephone? There must have been a window, drapes, a picture on the wall. He was not sure. He couldn't remember. There had to have been drapes, they were well hidden in there.

There was a bed, of course. That he was sure of. The Indian woman named Roxanne had sat naked propped against the pillows. And a chair, too, there was a soft chair. He remembered sitting down when they first checked in, so yes, there was definitely a chair of some kind.

The rain had begun, was lashing the streets, the parking lot, outside the motel room. There was thunder in the hills, probably above his own house.

There was a mirror in the room, he remembered seeing himself. Most of these things he remembered much later, after Elsie knew, after even Leroy knew about some parts of that day. The details eventually came back some. Roxanne was only a girl, really, nineteen years old, she told him. When he first noticed her at the factory, as he was making his rounds of the key stations with the leather-cased clock slung over his shoulder, she smiled at him. Her straight white teeth in that dark face brightened dark corners all around. He gave a casual, left-handed salute from the brim of his hat and even winked. He knew for certain he had never before winked at anybody in his entire life. And that salute—where did it come from?

Roxanne worked in Screw Machine. She fed long brass rods into seven machines, breech and feeder and threader. The noise was unbelievable, a constant high-pitched squeal. She poured sweet-smelling oil over the action, to cool the metal. At the other end of the machines screws by the thousands clattered out of a chute and piled up in metal bins, a different-sized screw from each machine. Brass shavings piled up all around, like spun gold.

Roxanne was not beautiful. Though her hair was long and blue-black, it was bundled up under a hair net to keep it free of the machinery. Beneath the dark rust color of her skin lay a pallor, not of sickness, only a bone-weariness, the product of constant noise, the brutal hours of the graveyard shift, the strain of whatever life she lived beyond these factory walls. Her face was pitted in several places with scars that must have been left by chicken pox or acne. She was not fat but not shapely either, with a wide, flat butt and sturdy legs. She wore earplugs to protect her hearing from the incessant din of the machinery.

To Swami Don she was the most fascinating, the most exciting woman he had ever seen. She looked nothing like Elsie, or like Hannah, whom he also thought were beautiful. Roxanne's particular beauty, if that was what it was to be called, was electric. The sharp shock of coming upon her in the factory, even when he expected to see her, caused him to remember the wonderful terrors of first love. The exotic copper color of her flesh, the high cheekbones, the bright smile, her amazing youth! He imagined her hair net to be a beaded band, crafted by old squaws sitting together in a circle of light by the fire. It was a full headdress, made of the feathers of eagles. The screw machine key, which she carried on a string around her neck, he imagined to be a necklace made of squash blossoms. He thought of his own passing youth, of his daughters and son, who seemed always so unhappy these days. He wondered if he was the cause of their unhappiness. He wondered what his own sad youth and dead mother and inept father had to do with tonight, with his children's lives. He imagined drums and horses and spears and paint.

Conversation was almost impossible in Screw Machine. Once in a while Roxanne took out one of the oil-filled earplugs when Swami Don was on his rounds and waited for him to come near. He stopped and they shouted greetings and pleasant words into one another's ear.

Other times they talked in the break room over coffee. She told him she was Creek, a full-blood. She came from Oklahoma, had moved east to try to make a break with the past, start a new life. She said she didn't want to end up smoking cigarettes and shooting pool and drinking Blue Ribbons out of long-neck bottles in an Indian bar. She pronounced the word *Indian* as In-din.

He told her he was married and in love with his wife and didn't think his wife loved him. He said he thought his wife wished she could make a new start. He said he thought she would probably be happier with somebody else. He told her about his arm, the accident when he was a child, how his hand flew up and slapped him in the face.

She told him a few things about herself, too. She said, "I'm moving up in the world."

He said, "Mississippi doesn't seem like much of a step up from Oklahoma."

They smiled, maybe sadly. This was when they started talking about maybe going to bed together. They touched hands sometimes. That was about all, for a while. When he stood close to her sometimes she would lean against him so that he could feel her breast briefly against his arm.

She said, "It won't be the first time I been with a married man."

Swami Don was shocked, but he said nothing.

She said, "Or a one-armed man neither, come to think of it," and both of them laughed.

A few times, in the first light of dawn, after their shifts were finished and Swami Don had made his last round of the warehouse and plant and had raised the American flag on the flagpole in front of the factory, they stood in the parking lot among the parked cars and kissed. After work they usually sat for a while in his pickup and mostly talked.

Once when they were kissing he held her breast for a while in his good hand. They agreed to meet at a motel near the plant. He said he would call next time he filled in. That's when they would do it.

She said, "If you change your mind, that's all right."

He'd said, "I was brought up, you know, pretty strict."

She said, "If you call, you call. If you don't, you don't."

He met her in the motel parking lot. He handed over the money to the person at the front desk. He opened the door to the room for her and followed her inside.

For a moment they only stood and held one another, just inside the door. They kissed a couple of times and stepped apart. Swami Don was trembling.

Roxanne began to undress.

Swami Don knew almost right away that he would never go through with what they'd planned. When he looked into the mirror and saw himself, that's when he knew for sure.

He said, "Uh, Roxanne—maybe you'd better not." Take off her clothes, he meant.

She had her back to him when he spoke. She'd just taken off her shirt and bra. She paused for a moment, didn't move or turn around. She laid the bra on the end of the bed next to her shirt and sat down on the edge of the bed and went on undressing. Each boot she pushed off with the toe of the opposite foot. The boots were worn and cracked with tooled swirls engraved in the leather, the heels were run down. She unhitched the silver buckle of a tooled-leather belt and pulled her pants down over her feet and laid the pants out with the other articles of clothing. She took off her underpants, which Swami Don noticed were new and still had a tag on them. She was fully naked now.

Across the hills the lightning was flashing, the thunder rumbled outside the motel walls. Swami Don thought of his wife and children asleep in their beds, of Leroy, his strange and distant son. He saw in the mirror that he was still wearing his rolled-brim cowboy hat. He took off the hat and held it in his hands.

He said, "I can't, Roxanne. I'm sorry."

Roxanne still didn't speak. She turned and pulled back the covers of the bed. He saw her fully naked now. The bush of black hair between her legs was as dense as a jungle. It seemed to grow out of control, from hip to hip. Her nipples were so dark they seemed black. She propped both pillows together against the headboard and got into bed and sat leaning back against them.

She said, "I know you love your wife."

Swami Don sat in a chair across from her and laid his hat on the floor beside him.

"It's not that," he said. "I'd probably do it anyway, if it was only that."

Roxanne was patient, requiring little. She kept on sitting there, in the bed, with her legs stretched out.

She said, "What's your wife's name?"

He didn't look straight at her at first. Then he did.

He said, "Elsie."

Her head moved up and down, only slightly.

She said, "Elsie."

"Yes."

She sucked her teeth in a quiet way.

She said, "Ain't that a cow's name?"

He said, "Are you angry with me?"

She took one of the pillows from behind her back and put it in her lap and folded her hands and laid them on the pillow. She seemed very young.

"Borden's, yes," he said, finally.

"Right. Right."

"'Milk from contented cows.'" He shrugged, unhappily.

"I thought I remembered that."

"Except my Elsie's not so contented."

Roxanne lifted her breasts in her palms and set them comfortably on the pillow.

She said, "Anyway." She said, "I guess we agree on one thing."

Swami Don looked at her.

She said, "She's a cow."

They both laughed, sadly.

Swami Don said, "Well—"

She said, "I should talk, with this set of jugs."

He said, "You're beautiful."

She shook her head.

"No way."

She reached to the foot of the bed and snagged her bra and put it on.

She said, "I'm saving up my money."

Swami Don didn't ask what she was saving for.

He said, "It's this uniform."

She just sat there, in her bra. She unfolded and then folded her hands again.

He said, "I can't explain it."

Roxanne said, "You don't have to explain it—"

He shook his head. "I'm not sure."

She grabbed her shirt and swung her legs over the side of the bed and started to dress.

She said, "Listen to that thunder."

He looked out at the flashes of light in the distance.

"*Somebody's* taking a pounding." She looked at him. She said, "Didn't mean to make no pun."

She pulled on her boots and stood to check herself in the mirror. She turned and sat at the foot of the bed and leaned in toward Swami Don, with her forearms resting on her thighs like a man.

She said, "Okay, listen. I'm going to enlighten you about some stuff most folks don't know about me, so get ready, here it comes. You're a pretty good-looking boy, buckaroo. Gimp arm and all. I seen plenty worse. I fucked most of them. Took money for it sometimes. Plenty of times. And me just nineteen years old. Drugs for payment, other times. Sometimes I did it for nothing at all. Not even the common courtesy of their name. I knowed that, afterwards, I'd probably go back to the trailer park with a dose, or the crabs. I didn't care. Didn't make no difference to me. Just so I didn't have to be by myself. And take a good look at me, while you're at it. Do you really believe I'm nineteen? If I'm nineteen years old I'm also the king of Norway and a virgin. I'm twenty-eight years old, cowboy. This is where I'm at, right here, and this is what I'm doing, right now. The hair net and the smock I wear in the plant, to keep from getting sucked into one of them machines, ain't exactly the uniform that fully expresses my inner self, like you seem to be trying to tell me about that monkey suit you're wearing. And it strikes me as the complete and living end that a semi-fucked-out bitch like myself would get a job in a factory running an apparatus called a screw machine.

Don't that one just take the cake, for real? Somebody must of
seen my resume, put me right on the floor. 'Put that one in
Screw Machine, hell, make her the foreman.' So next time
you're praying for true love, buckskin, you tell whoever it is
you're praying to that Roxanne said go fuck hisself. Except my
real name ain't even Roxanne, it's Darla, and if I begin to
sound bitter, you can start your philosophical and psycholog-
ical analysis of me and the universe with the drunk squaw-slut
who give me birth and saddled me with that stupid name, my
mama. I'd trade Darla for Elsie any day of the week, believe
it. Elsie is an excellent name compared to Darla. Are you
beginning to get the drift of what I'm saying? I ain't going to
bother mentioning the abortions and the child, a little boy,
that the welfare took away from me and put in foster care. Let
me spell it out for you. I got no business being here, in this
motel, in this room, with you. To me, you're dangerous as
poison. I could fall in love with you. I'm already in love with
you. I been in love with you since the minute I first seen you.
I been dreaming about you all my life. You didn't know I was
a romantic fool, did you? Well, I am, sure as shit, romantic
right down to the bone. When I imagine the perfect life, you
want to know what I think about? I think about being married
to you, sleeping beside you on the farm, milking them goddamn llamas you told me about. What the fuck is a llama anyway? It ain't nothing like an ostrich, is it? There's ostriches all
over the goddamn state of Miss'ippi, have you noticed that?
Sumbitches run wild. You don't need no uniform to make me

fall in love with you. You don't need that bad-ass cowboy hat and nightstick and badges. You could wear a grass skirt and a bolo tie and, to me, you'd still be the world's most perfect man. It's wrote all over you. If your ungrateful cow of a wife ever takes off and leaves you, well, fuck it, Jack, you're still ahead of the game, you've still got a good life, because you are who you are, can't nothing change that, can't nobody take it away. All right, end of confession, end of sermon. We got to go to work, we got to get out of here, see. But just let me tell you this one thing first, one more thing. I'm lucky, too. You didn't know that, did you? You thought I was just somebody you could fuck or not fuck, depending on how your uniform fit you right at that particular moment, depending on whether you felt like shedding the perfect outward expression of your innermost self and getting yourself a piece of pussy or not. That's what you thunk, wasn't it, asshole? Well, that's where you're mistaken, see. I'm here to tell you, I'm a lucky woman. I'm bitter, all right, so be it, and I'm resentful, ain't got over that yet neither. And I still fall in love with the ones I can't have, I'm addicted to romance, ain't that the shits. Don't romance just chap your fucking ass? But I'm out of Oklahoma, partner. That's victory, right there. It ain't no small thing. I had the courage to get out, leave it behind. The brown state, that's how I think of it, Oklahoma. Treeless as the fucking moon. Home of Oral Roberts University and Roman Nose State Park. I come from there to here, to Miss'ippi, see, the Magnolia State, all the way out here to this green paradise with its awful reputation, and I'm happy. I'm a lucky girl. If you ain't from Oklahoma, you don't know what I mean. You might not think it's a big deal—Oklahoma, Miss'ippi, take your pick, you might be thinking. But take my word for it, there ain't no comparison. Another thing I'm lucky about. I'm out of the business, you know, peddling pussy. Two years, I ain't bartered or sold. That's another big deal for me. It's like a world's record, a personal best. You might take it for granted, but I don't, not me. Three, I'm off of everything, all substances, and I mean everything, boy, smack, crank, perks, blow, rock, no needles, whiskey, beer, grass, nothing. I go to them meetings. I went to one before I come here tonight. I don't even drink none of them piss-tasting Coors Lights, God's revenge on the cowboys and Indians, a western curse. I got friends now, too, I got a good-paying job with a job description that makes me laugh sometimes, on my better days, Screw Machine. Nobody but you knows my name is Darla. I got a letter from the welfare in Oklahoma City, talking about letting my little boy come live with me on a trial basis. Scares me to death, but that's all right. Scared ain't the worst thing I ever been. And one of these days, if I live long enough, I'm finally going to get around to forgiving my crazy-ass mama, too, for what she never meant to do anyway. Everything will happen in its turn. First things first, like they say in them church basements. I ain't saying my life is perfect, or even good. It ain't worth a shit by most standards I can think of. I ain't what you call fully evolved or nothing. Forgiving God for putting me in Oklahoma, for example, is going to take a little longer. I ain't sure they got enough steps in that goddamn program to cover Oklahoma. They might need to add a couple more."

Swami Don moved from his chair and sat beside her on the foot of the bed. He leaned into her body, his face in her black hair. Her hair smelled like baby shampoo. She kissed him at the corner of his mouth and moved away.

She said, "I don't think so, cowpoke."

He said, "We could punch in a little late."

She leaned back from him to see him clearly.

She said, "It ain't no crime to be selfish, but it ain't a good way to finish this nice conversation we're having neither."

Swami Don thought of Darla's child somewhere, her son, a thousand miles away, in a tract house in a treeless landscape beneath the western moon, a little boy asleep in a kind stranger's bed, as his brother, Harris, had once been, as he himself had been. He wondered about that child's future, the betrayal he was yet to commit or endure.

They left the motel room together and walked out in the direction of their cars. The rain was falling hard. His family was at home getting struck by lightning, probably.

The two of them stood in the shelter of the motel eaves, watching the sheeting rain before making a dash for the parking lot.

Darla said, "Eventually there ain't nothing to do but make a run for it."

Lightning flashed in the distance.

She said, "Book!"

They took off, laughing, running, rain pouring down their necks. They splashed through the parking lot, veering off this way and that, he one way, she the other, in the direction of their separate cars.

Above the sound of the rain and thunder, Swami Don heard the fine, profane twang of her wonderful voice—he thought of her only as Roxanne. She would never be Darla to him again. He was unable to make out what she said through the rain and wind. He jumped in the pickup and waited to see her headlights come up. When he saw her pull out of the parking lot he aimed the nose of the pickup in the direction of her tail-lights, through the storm.

Later that night, as he made his rounds with the clock, he saw her feeding brass rods into the number three machine. She noticed him and waved. She was smiling. The machines were running full power, all of them at once, and the noise was too loud to talk, so he didn't get a chance to ask her what she'd said in the parking lot. He picked up a straw broom, which he found leaning up against the number seven, and with it swept up the brass shavings, like spun gold, all over the floor around her work space. He dumped them into a barrel that was already filled to the top.

She mouthed, "Thank you," above the racket of the machines.

He mouthed, "I love you!"

Her face brightened and she laughed.

Leroy's daddy was a happy man.

18

Uncle Harris's little car pulled away from twirling lessons, down the road, leaving Leroy behind and in love. Uncle Harris pressed the button of his amazing car horn—ah-ooga! and the strains of "Dixie" and fields of cotton!—as he sped away, carrying with him the sounds of bright laughter on the summer air. Deep somewhere in the heart of him Leroy understood many things for which he had no words just then. He understood that love is a hopeless dream, that it is seldom what it seems but only evil done in a holy name, he understood, at least in this dark, unlighted place of his knowing, darker than mere instinct or intuition, that no good ever comes of love but only pain, or from what we call first love anyway. Dimly he perceived the life draining and inevitability of disappointment and heartbreak, the constant pain of surprise at the shattering of illusion. He knew he and his sisters had been dumped here so that his mama and uncle might have privacy to kiss.

And yet this mattered not at all, none of it, not a whit, to Leroy Dearman. Nothing could have mattered less. It did not matter that there was no chance on earth that this girl, already a woman, could ever feel for him what he felt for her, that if there should ever be such a chance it would signal pathology, not hope. It did not matter that he had just committed himself to baton twirling, the pure purview of girls and sissies, and had even briefly longed to be a girl himself and denied, through self-loathing, a gender he had been cursed through accident to own. He was in love. Nothing else mattered but love, the hopeless pursuit of it and inevitable loss of what was before not even imagined.

He followed the others. He tagged along behind Ruby Rae and her multitudinous entourage of female twirling disciples, miserable wretch that he was, the only boy in this bright procession—baton twirling being too sissified a pursuit even for the well-known sissies of his school and the Episcopal church. This didn't matter either, not in any way that would cause him to turn back, to change his mind.

He followed behind this beautiful girl, this Ruby Rae with the magical name, to the end zone, beneath the goal posts, morose and quiet among the giggling and the chatter. He was a living portrait titled *Lost Hope*. He knew the depth of his moral failure at wanting what he wanted, at going to these humiliating lengths in pursuit of mere proximity to a person who could not love him. If their ages were reversed he would be a stalker. And worst of all, Leroy knew this: he knew he was the only child in this company of children, no matter their sex, who had made the commitment to become a twirler without having a baton. He was in love, no one could have denied it, for even this absurdity made no difference to Leroy.

Later, or maybe even in this moment, Leroy knew that he owed much to his mother, to his Uncle Harris. He wanted to give them the credit they deserved. They were exactly like him, for one thing. He could look at himself in these unproductive dangerous moments of his own life, stepping off a cliff of some kind for a hopeless dream, and see the urgency of their own need, their kisses behind the refrigerator, their harmful fantasies built upon alcohol and paper umbrellas. He looked at them and saw himself, he looked at himself and saw them, and these merged identities taught him something he had not known before or even suspected a need of. For a long time he was not even sure of its name. It was something of forgiveness, of remission of sin, of relaxation of the general requirement of perfection in others and the self.

They made mistakes, obviously, his mother, his uncle, his dumb-moose father who stumbled clueless through their lives, but in this moment they were pure and true, all of them. Through neglect, somehow, they were perfect parents, Harris a perfect uncle to Leroy, exactly when he believed he needed them most. When Harris and his mama saw Leroy see

Ruby Rae and fall in humiliating love with her, and later when his father saw the same, Leroy's face aflush with testosterone, and animal groanings speaking in his blood, they understood the depths of his need and chose to neglect rather than to smother him. With a word any one of them could have destroyed him, with a single knowing smirk, one misplaced joke or teasing elbow to the ribs. Any small thing that placed excessive or improper emphasis on what was already, in Leroy's heart, excessive and improper, despite all its necessity, would have made returning to his parents' home an impossible burden.

They did nothing of the kind. They did not make secret gestures of intimacy between one another, either, no special glances, no casual touching. For whatever reasons, the two of them understood the vulnerable position he occupied. For this Leroy vowed forever to be grateful, despite what was to happen later.

"I'll twirl," he had said.

He did not look at them when he said this, he could look at no one but Ruby Rae.

His mother said, simply, "You'll have a good time."

Ruby Rae stood on a step stool of the kind bandleaders use, with her baton in one hand. She waved both her arms above her head, like a tree swaying in the wind. This seemed to be a well-known majorette signal of some type. She blew hard on a steel whistle to get attention, to call order to the throng of children.

Uncle Harris had said, "If, later on, you find out you don't like it—"

"I like it," Leroy replied.

Ruby Rae's leotard was purple. Little was concealed. Ruby Rae picked up a megaphone from the ground beside the step stool. She spoke through it, though there was no real need.

She said, "Okay, listen up, twirlers!"

Leroy stood in a clump with the others on the field. He looked straight into the barrel of the megaphone, the wide funnel-opening that led through darkness to the narrower end and its unsolved mysteries.

Deep inside the cylinder he could see her lips, Ruby Rae's perfect mouth. He imagined himself small enough to crawl inside the megaphone, down its beautiful tunnel, headfirst. He imagined himself coming to its mouth, the smaller hole that emptied out of the pipe, her tongue, her teeth, her red lips. He imagined himself nestled there, inside the safe barrel, his earnest self, his face pressed against the smaller opening so that his lips rested against Ruby Rae's lips. She could not speak or sleep or breathe without kissing Leroy. He was her master and her slave.

Ruby Rae shouted through the megaphone, "Let's see those batons, twirlers! Show me your batons!"

At this command, all the twirlers, except Leroy, of course, held their batons high. He cut his eyes from side to side, watching the batons in hideous envy. His sisters, everyone held up batons, everyone but himself. They shook the batons above their heads, they celebrated their batons in joy beneath the laughing sky. Leroy was impotent, spiritually bereft, help-less, with no baton.

A few girls made inexpert attempts to twirl. In the brilliant sun the batons became many elongated mirrors, casting golden rays back into the blue heavens.

Ruby Rae said, "All *right!*"

In all, there were perhaps twenty-five or thirty children, Leroy and many elementary-school girls of all ages and sizes and shapes. Even one of the midget children showed up, whose parents worked on a transient construction crew and lived in the trailer park outside of town. No one had expected the midget, who carried a half-sized baton, like Molly's. Other unexpected children were in attendance as well. The entire Quong family seemed to have signed up, Chinese children whose father owned the butcher shop in Fateville, and a cou-ple of black children as well whose parents taught at Valley Hill Community College nearby. Mifanwy Moser was there, a girl with a flipper where one of her hands should have been. She allowed Leroy to half believe that twirling might be an activity his father and he might someday share. He imagined becoming skilled and teaching Swami Don many things. One arm was no handicap for a twirler, if Mifanwy was any indica-tion. Leroy tried to believe this.

All of the other children had brought batons, of course. He tried also to believe that his not having a baton might prove no handicap either.

Ruby Rae put everyone into lines—"files," she called them —in accordance with some principle of age or height or something or other, which Leroy never understood. He stood at the front of his file, scant feet from Ruby Rae, for whom his heart was breaking. She instructed the new twirlers in the uses and history and construction of the modern baton. Leroy had not expected this somehow, this "educational component" of twirling, as Ruby Rae called what she was doing.

"The experiential component will come later," she said.

She named the parts of the modern baton, shaft and bulb and butt. She explained weight and balance and recent improvements in materials and workmanship. She spoke knowledgeably of the historical relationship, largely misunderstood, she said, between twirling and juggling. She hypothesized a relationship to rain-making and knife-throwing and spear-chucking. Her voice became passionate. Leroy blinked his eyes. She traced the baton to the days of ancient Greece and the original Olympic games. And then, out of deference to the Quongs, Leroy supposed, she traced twirling to China as well, and then to Africa and cannibalism, and cited many sources to prove that the first baton was a human bone.

Leroy looked around him to see whether anyone else had noticed that twirling lessons had taken a bizarre detour. No one seemed affected. They scratched their noses, dropped their batons, pulled their leotards out of their butt cheeks. Who could tell what Laurie was thinking, now or ever. She wore her accustomed ironic smile.

Ruby Rae mentioned many famous twirlers, modern and ancient. She touched upon the baton as a phallic symbol, and its appearance in cave drawings, baton twirling in the Bible, and batons found in crashed spaceships from alien planets in galaxies far away.

Sweat beaded upon her forehead and upper lip, formed a chevron between her breasts, their impossible beauty, moons at the pits of her slender arms. Every child upon that green field, the youngest to the eldest, in every file beneath the Mississippi sun, every race and sex of them, fell in love that day with Ruby Rae. Each had her own reasons. Testosterone was no requirement for love of Ruby Rae.

Nor apparently did it concern any one of them, except possibly Leroy, for whom it made no difference anyway, that Ruby Rae was completely out of her mind. She was mad, despite her youth and beauty. Not at all did anyone seem bothered by this incomprehensible lecture. Nor did it matter that not one word she was saying was true, even if they could have understood it.

Leroy more than any other was stricken, of course, male child that he was, and old enough to perceive, however dimly, his sexual future and the preferences of a lifetime, Leroy who had already given over his whole heart, and as it turned out far more than his mere heart, to the love of Ruby Rae, even before he stepped out of his Uncle Harris's car.

Despite whatever else might be said of Ruby Rae's mental disturbances, the girl could twirl. No one could ever have denied it, least of all Leroy. She was impressive. She could twirl like an angel. You never saw such twirling in your life. She could have gone professional any day. Uncle Harris was right. Her great beauty and blatant sexuality were part of her appeal, no doubt, but sex appeal was not all of her talent. Ruby Rae was not merely another set of titanic boobs, she was an artist. To watch her twirl was to hear music and poetry, to become the dancer in the dance.

She had an orderly agenda. Right after her bizarre and sweaty lecture she began a twirling demonstration, the things the children would need to know to begin.

"First, the basics," she said. "Before you learn to walk, first you have to learn to crawl, don't you?"

The children nodded silently. Leroy nodded along with the rest.

"Well, *don't* you?" she teased.

"Yes, ma'am," they said in unison.

Ruby Rae cupped a playful hand to her ear, as if she might be deaf.

The children called out in loud voices, "Yes, ma'am!" Leroy shouted loudest of all.

"Well, all *right,* then," Ruby Rae smiled.

She clenched her beautiful fist and pulled her elbow to her side to show her enthusiasm.

She showed her students how to hold the baton.

"Make a fist," she said. "Like you're going to punch some-body."

Everyone held their baton in a fist, as Ruby Rae demonstrated—everyone but Leroy, of course, who had no actual baton, though he also made a fist and held out his hand as if it clutched this instrument. He performed every function as if he were holding a baton.

"Keep holding it," she instructed.

The children held on, Leroy as well.

"Now back and forth," she said.

She twisted her baton back and forth until it gleamed.

"Twist those wrists and don't let go!" she called through the megaphone. "Back and forth! Let's see it!"

Thirty batons flashed in the sun, this way, that way. Leroy twisted his wrist along with the others, though he produced no flashes of light, since he held no actual baton.

Next, the basic roll. Ruby Rae was marching them through the fundamentals. This was a simple, one-handed technique that began with the baton lying flat in the outstretched palm. She demonstrated. All the little girls held their batons in their hands in the same way. Leroy held out his empty palm. He imagined a well-balanced baton to be lying in it. Ruby Rae showed them then how the baton was manipulated with the thumb so that it rolled completely off the palm and around the hand and back into the palm again.

"Ta-dahhhh!" Ruby Rae exclaimed, as she completed her demonstration of the technique.

All the children there on the field tried the same maneuver. Some succeeded, some did not. Many batons dropped to the ground.

One baton did not drop. One baton stayed firm, made the loop. The invisible baton in Leroy's palm became a perfection of the maneuver. It made an easy circuit of his hand, first lying still, then propelled by the thumb, over, careful, over and around, and at the end it fell expertly into place in his palm again, a perfectly executed basic roll. Life was easier, his burden was lighter, Leroy was at home with his invisible baton.

Ruby Rae covered every imaginable facet of baton twirling. She called this "an overview" of what was to come in later sessions.

When she had finished all the one-handed techniques, she said in her prettiest way, "Now let me tell you something I'll bet you all forgot."

Forgot? Could they have forgotten something? Leroy couldn't believe there was something he had forgotten. He had done everything perfectly, followed every instruction. Well, he had forgotten his baton, but she didn't mean that, did she? She seemed to mean something else. The children listened intently for the solution to this mystery: what could they have forgotten? Leroy could not imagine. Tell us, Ruby Rae, what did we forget?

She said, "I'll bet each and every one of you forgot that you have—*two hands!*"

As she said this she expertly flipped her baton from her right hand to her left and began a series of basic rolls. The children applauded and laughed with joy. Two hands! Of course! They had forgotten that they had two hands. This was

Ruby Rae's means of demonstrating the important fact that everything they had just learned about one-handed baton manipulation applied equally to the other hand, left or right, whichever they had left out the first time around. Immediately each twirler-child in this company of children flipped her baton to the recessive hand and attempted a version of the same roll they had so recently learned.

Ruby Rae was a wonderful teacher. Everyone had to agree. The twirlers were not excellent twirlers yet, of course. How could they be expected to be experts at this point? The amateur nature of their endeavors was immediately apparent when thirty batons fell to the ground. No one could perform the operation in the weaker hand. There were no ambidextrous twirlers here just yet. Batons clattered everywhere, helter-skelter, crisscross, and bass-ackwards upon the turf grass. Literally everyone had dropped their baton.

Not everyone. All but one. One baton held firm. Leroy's left-handed roll was ideal, not a bobble, not a flaw, grace itself, the envy of many. Once again, as with his very first perfectly executed right-hand roll, Leroy stepped out in front of the pack. He was peerless among twirlers, right hand, left hand, it made no difference to Leroy. He was not showing off, he was good, he felt it.

When Leroy was finished and certain that it was a perfect maneuver, he held his imaginary baton high, in triumph, he pumped his arm, up and down, up and down, yes, yes, yes, in a kind of power salute. He brought his knees up high to his chest in an exaggeration of in-place running. *I'm number one, I'm number one, I'm number one*. Maybe he was showing off. Maybe here was a time in life when self-appreciation was no sin, when celebration was only celebration. Move over, you clumsy little baton-dropping pissants, long live the king of twirlers, twirler-deaths to the many.

Or had Leroy spoken too soon? Something, he was unsure what, nagged at the corner of his vision. The midget girl? One of the many weird Quong sisters? He looked about him, a critical glance, ostensibly to survey and judge the destruction in his wake, and yet for the first time uncertain. He saw his nemesis. It was Mifanwy Moser, the fat girl with the flipper where her left hand should have been. She had not dropped her baton. She was still twirling. She was twirling with her flipper. Her flipper was the key to success. Around and around her flipper flew the baton, it looked like a propeller. The flipper was an admirable thing. Ruby Rae applauded her, and then so did everyone else. Even Leroy applauded her. There was no denying her superiority, her magic with a baton. Unskilled in the right-handed roll, as clumsy as all the other baton-clumsy little twerps, Mifanwy Moser had an advantage in her flipper almost as great as that of an invisible baton, greater when you factored in the obvious truth that Leroy was not twirling at all, only jacking himself off in a moment of lost sanity induced by a rush of pure testosterone to the brain.

One little girl wept, "No fair, Mifanwy's got a flipper!"

• • •

The day of twirling was one of many beauties and miracles, it seemed to Leroy. Lightly he tripped through the details of many two-handed techniques, the crossover, the pump, the over-the-shoulder, behind-the-back, slide-and-sleeve, and any number of combination moves, the pump-and-roll combo, for example, and many more. All the variations of the toss as well, basic, spin, and combo, and the many techniques by which the baton is then caught, or received. The double toss, the twist, the so-called jack-in-the-box, the so-called suicide maneuver, and the infamous flaming baton trick, its many combination forms, though without fire for now, for safety purposes today.

Leroy watched Ruby Rae, he was impressed by her, and because his baton was imaginary he was able to attempt all of these maneuvers himself. Despite the momentary setback of cold water dashed upon his enthusiasm by Mifanwy and her flipper, he found himself successful at many of them. Even Mifanwy could not compare.

Eventually shadows shortened on the field. The session was coming to an end. Cars started to pull into the school's driveway and to park along the fence that separated the football field from the rest of the school property. These were the children's parents, of course, coming to retrieve their twirlers at session's end. Twirling camp was finished for the day.

The sun above was hot as blue blazes. The twirling children were, for the most part, too young to sweat, though Ruby Rae was not. She was drenched. Even her hair was quite wet and stuck, as if plastered, to her scalp.

She was not tired, though. She was in wonderful physical shape, and cheerful and bright as she said good-bye to each child and shook hands with many of the parents.

Leroy looked into the parking lot and was pleased to see his father's pickup parked out there, not Harris's car. It meant a great deal to Leroy that this new activity was approved by his father, whom he knew had no ulterior motives in getting him out of the house. Swami Don was sitting alone in the cab of his truck. When Leroy saw him he waved and watched him open the door and step out, headed onto the field.

Leroy had now been in the presence of the admirable Ruby Rae for an entire morning, one of the strangest, most glorious mornings of his life. As his father walked in the direction of the end zone, Leroy was saying good-bye to his instructor and she was telling him how courageous and admirable a person he was, to have risked the embarrassment of being teased for being the only boy, and especially to have taken such a serious interest in twirling without even the advantage of a baton.

Leroy wanted to say how grateful he was to her for having breasts, and to tell her that he loved her and would die for one of her kisses, and to say how truly easy a choice humiliation had been, no risk at all really, under such remarkable tutelage as her own. He wanted with all his heart to reach out—indeed he was terrified he would do so—and touch her body with his hand and explain that he had had many erections but never one so painful as this, even in Uncle Harris's room with the magazines, never one that endured for so long, through time and heat and stressful activity.

If Leroy could have successfully spoken any of these words, however regrettable their expression might have been, he would have done so, but he could not. He could say nothing. No actual words would come from his mouth. He stood in silence, it was all he could do. For once in his life Leroy understood his father's discomfort on this earth and loved him for his faults.

Leroy looked at his father, in fact. Ruby Rae's enormous sexuality could not have been lost even on Swami Don, and yet Swami Don was dignified and articulate as he spoke with her. He seemed unmoved by her beauty. He apologized to Ruby Rae for Leroy's not being prepared with the proper twirling equipment. He explained that no one had dreamed a young man like Leroy would have taken such an interest in twirling and that he himself had to take responsibility for Leroy's being batonless, that the boy's mother and uncle had offered to buy him a baton at Dollarhide's music store but that Swami Don had been the one to advise them to take a "wait-and-see approach," and now, doggone it, he learns the boy has talent and finds out Dollarhide's is all sold out of batons and will not get any more in from the distributor for another ten days or two weeks. He said he wanted to stress that this mistake of the boy's parents should not be held against Leroy, it wasn't Leroy's fault.

Leroy had never seen his father in quite this light. He felt well loved, well protected, a part of this family for the first time in a long while. He was able to forget Ruby Rae long enough even to bring the conversation around to his sisters, for whom he felt such pride. Seeing them there with him he felt such hope that his mama's secret kisses did not mean the disintegration of all things important to him.

Laurie had enjoyed the morning, she said. Things had gone pretty well for her. She had felt successful with a few of the baton moves she had learned. She proved herself to be a nimble child, and dexterous, as skilled with a majorette's baton as with a high-powered rifle. She chattered briefly to Swami Don about what she had done. She asked whether he would buy Leroy a baton of his own so that he would not have to pretend to twirl but could be like everyone else.

Leroy was grateful for her concern but felt uncomfortable with the reminder that he had only been pretending, though it didn't seem to register with Swami Don how truly ridiculous this was and so did not dampen his enthusiasm for Leroy's participation.

Molly was tired and cranky. She had spent much of the morning playing in the dirt under a shade tree on the school grounds. She said she liked it okay, the twirling, but it was too long.

Then this odd day began to take its oddest turn. There were times in Leroy's life, in the succeeding years, when he thought back upon these remarkable hours and half wondered whether such events as he remembered could actually have occurred. Some of them must have been exaggerated in memory, the strange twirling flipper of Mifanwy Moser, and much else, perhaps. And yet surely every important portion of the memory was true, Leroy was certain that it was so.

One needed only to stand in the company of Ruby Rae for a single morning to appreciate how fully her mind's circuits had been blown by twirling, or to understand the unfathomable depths of her own needs and compulsions as manifested in her relationship to her baton. She was, Leroy would say years later, a good girl, hardworking and ambitious, hopeful, sweet to a fault, the kind of girl her parents must have admired, must have driven her to become, and yet Leroy—even Leroy, lovesick swain that he was—was beginning to understand that something was not quite right here, that there was chaos behind the sweaty and perfect lashes of Ruby Rae's eyes, that Ruby Rae might quite possibly be a dangerous person.

These details of their immediate universe Leroy's father did not pick up on, no parent would have, it was not possible to see so much at once. It was remarkable enough that Leroy, who in his heart had already declared himself Ruby Rae's devoted slave, could have detected the flaw, or felt some intuition of it, enough anyway to remember years later.

Ruby Rae was too much the perfection of everything a parent wanted his or her own misfit child to turn out like, too much of what the parents had never been themselves and had wanted to be, all those years ago, when the world was new and they themselves were the misfit child. The disguise of her manners and talent was made complete and impenetrable to detection by her inestimable beauty, whose brightness would have prevented any parent from noticing something amiss behind that brilliance, some mental instability, her excessive emphasis upon control and all of beauty's perfections, all of needs' fulfillments. But that body, those impossible comets that preceded her, constituted darkness visible beneath purple leotards, and it blocked from all parental view any flaw, however obvious or great.

Ruby Rae gave Swami Don strong assurances that Leroy had done well today, had showed exceptional promise as a twirler, that he had, in fact, been a leader. She commented again upon his courage in the face of gender alienation, his willingness to take risks. She insisted she was confident that with an actual baton in his hand Leroy could have made even greater strides than he had already done.

She placed her hand upon Leroy's shoulder as she spoke these words of praise and encouragement. The warmth of her fingers infused every fiber of the child with sexual longing. She was Graf von Zeppelin, she was Hindenburg. She told Leroy's father that she believed his boy had been born to twirl.

If Leroy had ever doubted his father's love, in this moment that doubt was erased. No man could have shown such pride in a child as he showed now. The radiance of his face, his coun-

tenance, could have expressed nothing but the perfection of a
father's love, no matter how imperfect the father. He believed
every word Ruby Rae was saying. He believed Leroy had been
born to twirl. He offered to do anything, anything at all, to
acquire a baton for his son's use. He would get one right away.
What was the point of wasting time, his son deserved it, deserved the best. He would take a day off, he would drive to
Jackson, or Memphis. Didn't Ruby Rae imagine there were
batons in Memphis, they must have plenty of batons in big
cities, mustn't they? He seemed frantic to rescue this moment, how could he solve this problem? There must be a
solution.

For Leroy there was a moment of clarity. Suddenly it
seemed possible that he was not talented at all, that he had not
been born to twirl, that no one on earth, not even Ruby Rae,
could successfully predict anything about twirling talent by
observing a boy pretending to hold a baton. Could she have
heard banjo music if he had been strumming the kitchen
broom? Leroy understood now that this was impossible, that
Ruby Rae had some other agenda, some other plan for him
that had nothing whatsoever to do with baton twirling.

Whatever happened to Leroy, for better or for worse, after
this moment, he believed would be no one's fault but his own.
He alone, he believed, stood in a position to understand the
nature and intensity of all their various needs. He knew something was wrong here, he had the power to prevent it, and he

did nothing at all. He was willing to pay any price for the favor of another day, another moment, in the presence of this beautiful girl. So he believed in the innocent depths of his youthful heart.

19

The simple solution to Leroy's problem was for Leroy to borrow one of her batons, Ruby Rae said. And why not? She had lots of batons, plenty, dozens. Didn't that seem like the best idea? No waiting, no substitutions. She had a closet full of batons, some of them scarcely used. She told him that later on she would be happy to consider selling Leroy a used baton, if he wanted one of his own. Unless of course Leroy and Swami Don didn't like her batons. Unless they thought they could find a better baton someplace else. Mr. Dollarhide's weren't the best batons available, if they wanted Ruby Rae's private opinion on the subject, but it was up to them, it was their decision, whatever they decided was fine.

What Leroy began to understand was that Ruby Rae wanted something. Just what he was unsure, and cared not at all.

Swami Don must have heard something strange in the conversation as well. Though her voice was calm, expressive, sincere, and her body a powerful expression of confidence, there was some great tension in her, some concealed pain or fear radiating outward from a depth, through the fingers of her hands. Not the nails, which were the blunt-tipped, well-manicured nails of a young athlete, a person interested in her appearance and physical well-being, but her hands.

For all her youth and beauty, the hand upon Leroy's shoulder seemed the hand of an old woman. Leroy noticed this, his daddy must have noticed it, too. The fingers were long, the knuckles were prominent, every tendon was visible. Blue veins showed through the skin, which seemed pale and thin. They were bony fingers, the fingers of a hag-witch in the movies. By looking at her hands and not at more obvious parts of her physical self Swami Don must have seen Ruby Rae, the sad, long history of her heart, the humanity of her, the terrified little girl in the body of a woman. He must have seen even her thoughts, the constant question in her heart: which one of my selves is real, the visible or invisible, the self that aches alone or the self that every man admires and becomes changed by, woman and child occupying the same space, the cosmic discrepancy, the balance-dance upon the razor's edge? And yet even seeing so much Swami Don could not have seen the dangers implicit in her pain, an oversight for which Leroy knew his father would always blame himself.

Looking back on this day, Leroy never really understood how Ruby Rae accomplished so much, how she managed to convince Swami Don that it was a good idea for Leroy not to get into the truck with his father and go home, as any sane father and son would have done, but for Leroy to go home instead with Ruby Rae. It seemed impossible that even as she stood vulnerable before them, her hands a map of her troubled heart, that she could have exerted so much control. Why on earth did Swami Don not say, simply, sensibly, "Well, gee, thanks, but I've got a better idea, why don't you just bring the baton to practice tomorrow morning? He won't be needing it before then, now will he, no need to inconvenience everybody"? Why didn't he say, "You go on in your car, Ruby Rae, and me and Leroy, we'll follow you in the truck, he can just scoot in the house and grab a baton and we'll be out of your way directly"? There were at least a half dozen other sane things he might have said, including "No thank you." Looking back, anyone in his right mind would have known this. What Swami Don said in fact—and it was exactly what Leroy had wanted him to say, prayed to the bizarre heavens that he would say—was the opposite of sanity. It made no sense at all. Swami Don agreed that Leroy should go home with Ruby Rae, do as she suggested, choose a baton, take his time choosing, not be rushed, handle each one until just the right baton surfaced, and she would drop him off at the house.

Swami Don said, "Well—"

Ruby Rae said, "I'll tell you what. Let Leroy hop in my car, just like the extra-special little grown-up that he is, all by himself, let him ride to my house, make his choice—I promise you it will be a good one!—and then and only then, and not one second before, I'll drive him out to the farm myself. You'll see. Leroy can give me directions. Can't you, Leroy? You don't mind doing that, do you? What do you say, Mr. Dearman, how about it, any objections?"

He said, "Well, uh, okay, uh, yeah, I guess that would be all right."

Even Ruby Rae must have been astonished for a moment at the hydroelectric power, the nuclear energy, of her sexuality, though every day since the onset of puberty she must have employed this power in some fashion, must have been aware of the atomic potential of her breasts, must have hauled them out of bed each morning in the knowledge that they held such strange powers over the affairs of men. Somewhere near the center of him, Swami Don must have known that this plan of hers was ridiculous, a stupid idea, but he agreed anyway that Leroy should have the right baton.

"Try not to be too long, though," he said, weakly. "Don't overstay your welcome, son. And well, you know—"

He said good-bye to Leroy.

"Bye now, have a nice time. I'm proud of you, your being such a good baton twirler and all. So okay, see you at home. You won't have any trouble finding the place, Ruby Rae. Leroy here can show you the turnoff, can't you, Leroy? You know where the turnoff is, don't you? Okay, so long, I'll see y'all later."

Leroy never asked nor tried to imagine his mother's re-

sponse when Swami Don drove the old pickup into the yard
that afternoon without Leroy, with only Laurie and Molly in
the cab, and told her that Ruby Rae had taken Leroy home
with her because he was such an excellent twirler, that she
wanted him to choose the perfect baton for his twirling needs.

"He was good," Leroy one day would imagine his father
telling his mother. "An excellent twirler. A leader in his class."

He imagined Laurie trying to keep a straight face.

He imagined his mother's puzzlement. A leader in his class?
With no baton? Maybe this conversation took place during
grog rations. Maybe she was simply glad to have Leroy out
from underfoot. Maybe the conversation never took place at
all.

The reason Ruby Rae took Leroy home with her was for sex.
She parked in the driveway beneath a basketball hoop and the
two of them got out of the car. Ruby Rae's parents' home was
a comfortable bungalow with dormers and red-painted wood
shingles for siding and a weathered slate roof. On one side of
the house was a red-stained deck with a gas grill and comfortable deck furniture, including a table with a big striped
umbrella. The yard was shaded by pecan and walnut trees. A
redbud and a dogwood were in full leaf. Ruby Rae's parents
were not at home, as Ruby Rae had seemed to know before
she and Leroy arrived. She did not call out to them when the
two of them entered the house with a key she retrieved from
a bird feeder on the porch.

The house was cool and spacious. On the floors lay enormous Oriental rugs with brilliant designs of peacocks and dragons. The floors themselves were covered with large Spanish tiles. Oil paintings of a modern and original sort hung on the walls. There was a low hum of central air-conditioning. Leroy and Ruby Rae had exchanged not one word between them on the drive from the school grounds to her home.

Leroy looked around the room. He said, "Where are the batons?"

Ruby Rae held her hair up off her neck and fanned herself with her hand.

She said, "Are you hot? I'm about to burn up."

Leroy followed her through the front rooms and into the kitchen. There was a note on the refrigerator door that Leroy didn't have time to read.

Ruby Rae read it hurriedly and said, "Huh."

She opened the refrigerator and took out a full pitcher of lemonade that her mother or father apparently had left for her. She took two glasses out of a cabinet and scooped ice into each of them from an ice bin in the freezer and poured two glasses of lemonade.

Leroy said, "Thank you."

She took the lid off the top of a yellow cookie jar in the shape of a scrunched-up rabbit and signaled Leroy to help himself. He reached in and took out a peanut butter cookie, his favorite kind. He bit into it.

She said, "Yummy, right?"

Leroy said, "It's okay."

They sat on tall bar stools at the kitchen counter and sipped their lemonade and chewed their cookies. Ruby Rae was right, Leroy had not realized how uncomfortably hot and humid the day had become, how good the air-conditioning felt. They had been out in the sun for a long time. Leroy felt very tired, suddenly, as he began to cool off.

Ruby Rae said, "I don't know about you, but I *smell.*" She raised her arm and stuck her nose into her armpit. "Whew!" She did the same with the other armpit.

Leroy must have felt something in this moment, fear, erotic need, he could not say, then or years later when he remembered.

Ruby Rae said, "I'm going to pop in the shower for a sec, okay? That okay with you?" She said, "Okay, Leroy?"

"Okay."

What Ruby Rae did with him was wrong, Leroy knew this then, knows it now. He does not in his memory romanticize this day, or minimize its consequences, does not pretend to have escaped suffering gravely the effects of what happened. Many disasters of his life, bad choices, bad behavior, were controlled by this moment. But those conclusions stood nowhere near to Leroy's heart. He focused entirely on the girl, her flesh, her outlandish nakedness. This was the first time Leroy had ever seen a real naked girl, except to change Molly's diaper. This was entirely different from the pictures in Uncle Harris's magazines. Entirely different.

Out of the kitchen, wordless now, and down the hallway of this sparkling house, Leroy's feet sinking like animal paws in the pine-needle cushion of the forest floor, soundless, into the pile of a thick and tightly woven carpet, to a gleaming bathroom Leroy followed Ruby Rae, as he knew he was meant to do. He had no will of his own, but if he had been in possession of any power of will whatsoever, Leroy felt sure that he would have done exactly what he was doing. Nothing could have stopped him.

If he could have seen the future, the spectacular ruin, the unhappiness of years, the wreckage, the obsessions and their concurrent resultant debilitations, still he would have chosen what was now chosen for him, this trek, this incredible journey down the hall behind the beautiful Ruby Rae.

She entered the bathroom. Leroy looked past her, he saw the porcelain, he saw the framed artwork on the walls, he saw a bouquet of fresh flowers on a shelf beneath a window. He stopped at the door as she stepped inside and switched on lights as bright as an airport runway and stood before the mirror that hung above the vanity. The two of them, Ruby Rae and Leroy—she with her eyes in the mirror, he with his naked eyes, a metaphor whose application had never seemed so just—watched Ruby Rae peel herself out of the leotard.

Only for an instant could he watch the real person of her.

He averted his eyes. The pain of her beauty, unfiltered, was intolerable. He watched instead her image in the mirror, a practice that provided only small relief.

First one shoulder, and then the next, she pulled the garment away from her flesh and bared her chest. The great boulders of her breasts avalanched free of the blessed nylon that had held them. The sound they made was like thunder as they rolled forth. They were large enough to have their own weather. He imagined lightning crashing around them and striking his house. He saw fireballs emerge from their chimneys. He watched them glowing through the eternity of his life.

What could he do, what could he say, in this moment that required so much?

He said, "Tits."

Ruby Rae smiled into the mirror. Leroy was stone, he was the petrified man, he was the entire petrified forest. He could only just retain consciousness.

She turned from the mirror and faced him.

He said, "Knockers."

He said, "Hair."

Later on, down at the New People's cottage where Leroy would start to visit regularly after this day, the New Guy would tell Leroy that pornography is a dangerous pursuit, for the woman is objectified. He was referring to the video he was watching after his son was murdered. He said, "When the breast appears the woman disappears."

Ruby Rae disappeared, only her sexuality remained. For a child it was as true in life as in pornography. He could not see her. Leroy could not consider his own objectification for the blinding light of Ruby Rae's nakedness, into which all the peoples of the earth were swallowed up. She stood before Leroy entirely naked. The soft space between her legs socked him in the stomach like a punch. It was her nakedness only that Leroy could see.

She did not delay, or parade about, this was not a striptease. She stepped into the shower and turned on the water and adjusted the direction of the nozzle and the temperature and force of the stream. She stood beneath the falling spray and turned her face up to receive it. She took a bar of soap from a soap dish and lathered herself fully, then turned herself slowly beneath the nozzle to rinse away all the suds. The hair between her legs flattened out in the water and formed a little curl down at the bottom.

She turned off the water and stepped out onto a bath mat. She took a heavy white towel from a rack and dried herself vigorously, like an athlete.

She snapped Leroy playfully with the towel.

He giggled, despite himself. It was the driest, the saddest of giggles.

Afterwards, when they had risen from the snowy sheets, Leroy looked around on the floor for his clothes and put them on. He buttoned his shirt. He pulled on his socks, tied his sneakers. Ruby Rae dressed, too, and they got ready to go out to the car. She lent him a good baton, which he carried with him out to the car and held on his lap all the way home. When she let him off at his house she gave him a peck on the cheek.

She said, "Don't tell, okay?"

The sound from his throat was almost laughter, almost a wail.

20

Next morning when the girls were jumping into their daddy's pickup with their batons, Leroy followed them out into the yard and said he wasn't going.

Swami Don said, "Not going?"

He said, "I don't want to go anymore."

Swami Don scratched his armpit.

He said, "Ever? You don't ever want to twirl?"

Leroy didn't answer. He looked like he might cry.

Swami Don said, "You liked it so much, you were so good at it."

Tears flowed out of Leroy's eyes, he couldn't stop them.

Swami Don knelt down to speak to him.

He said, "Did somebody tease you? Did anybody call you a sissy?"

Leroy just stood there with the tears.

Elsie came out in the yard then.

She said, "Don't be late for twirling."

Swami Don said, "Well, you'll have to return Ruby Rae's baton, I guess."

Leroy said, "You."

Swami Don looked at Elsie.

"He says he doesn't want to twirl."

She said, "Oh, of course he's going to twirl, don't be silly."

Just then a thing happened that changed everything.

Leroy began to scream. He screamed and screamed and screamed and screamed. No words at first, just screaming.

Elsie and Swami Don could only stand and stare.

They said, "What on earth?"

Molly wet her pants. Laurie stood with wide eyes.

Leroy began to call them names. He said, "Goddamn, fuck, motherfucker, shit, piss, cunt, cock, death, corpse, suicide, murder, blood, cadaver, cigarette." He didn't know where these names came from. He ran inside the house screaming. The girls were crying. Swami Don tried to comfort them. Elsie ran after Leroy.

He was tearing the curtains down from the window. He turned over a table and spilled all its contents. He grabbed a knife off a kitchen counter and threw it across the room and hit the door and broke off the tip.

Laurie had come inside now. She was hysterical with tears. She thought he had thrown the knife at her.

Leroy flailed about, he swung his arms, his fists, he showed his teeth like an animal. Elsie was afraid of him.

What has happened, what has happened to our family? Elsie and Swami Don asked this, with broken hearts.

Eventually the incident ended. It had seemed to go on forever, and then it stopped. Everyone was left dazed. The adults spoke calming words. They put the best face on things. The children were held, petted, calmed down, given assurances. They were taken to separate rooms, separate beds.

Everyone was most worried about Leroy. All the children were pampered that day, but Leroy especially. No one knew what to say, which questions to ask. Later they went over and over the details. Leroy calmed down and cried for a long time. He slept. He was allowed to prop up against two pillows in Elsie and Swami Don's bed for the rest of the day. They brought him ginger ale and comic books.

They kept saying, "Are you all right, honey? Are you all right?"

Uncle Harris brought down his oscillating fan and plugged it in for him. He did a few puppet tricks, but Leroy wouldn't smile.

It happened so suddenly, they said. He was doing so well. He seemed to really take to twirling. The teacher said he was a leader, they said. He just fell apart. He just completely lost it. What on earth could have caused him to act like that? What was that all about, what on earth got into that boy?

Elsie said, "Maybe it was the heat."

Harris said, "Maybe it was, maybe it—" Well, Harris couldn't even guess.

Swami Don said, "There's no point in making him twirl, I guess. I guess we better let him stay home."

21

The slow summer crept on. Leroy sat silent at the dinner table each night. He picked at his food. He played alone. He seemed to forget that he had sisters. Sometimes he only lay on the glider and stared. Other times he cried easily. On his worst days he screamed at Molly. Elsie felt Leroy's head often with her hand to check for a fever. She would say, "Feeling a little better today, sweetheart?"

The llamas were fed and milked and brushed. Their long hair was sold to rope makers. The excrement was shoveled and loaded for fertilizer and fuel. Zoos around the state sometimes called. Stud fees were collected. A few times wealthy persons around the country bought a llama for a pet and that paid for a whole year's expenses for the farm. Evenings fireflies came out and shined their strange cold light about the yard and fields. Figs ripened on the trees. A storm or two still rolled in, the house was struck a few times by lightning. Fireballs rolled through the house. Harris told exciting tales of what happened in the attic when the fire was dancing. The tractor started up each morning with a *whoosh* with Swami Don riding in its saddle and crept out into the fields. Wild dogs yipped within hearing some nights, far out in the trees. Two dogs got into the pasture, but Swami Don managed to get the young llamas rounded up and out of harm's way.

Harris slept late most days and took long walks. He went into the village and drank coffee with men he knew. He read newspapers and talked on the telephone, which by now he had had installed in the attic. His phone bill was tremendous. He had started to call Hannah, his wife, down on the coast. He ate like a horse. Elsie asked him if he could contribute a little to household expenses.

Harris said, "Are you suggesting that I am a freeloader?"

She said, "Harris, I'm just asking whether you could share some expenses, for heaven's sake."

He said, "I see. I see exactly what you're saying."

He went into the attic and stayed there for three days. Nobody even saw him come down to go to the bathroom. He didn't seem to eat, either. He watched a little TV—he had gotten the television hooked up by now as well.

Swami Don told Elsie, "Maybe you were a little harsh."

Elsie said, "I just don't think I was."

Eventually she gave in and apologized.

She told Harris, "I've been so tense lately, I don't know why."

Harris said he was not one to hold a grudge.

Elsie allowed herself an alcoholic drink each day now, with Harris in the evening. Sometimes she had to lie down on the couch for a while afterwards and take a nap with the TV on, while Swami Don went on to bed without her.

Leroy watched all this as if he were watching someone else's life, maybe a movie. When some days had passed and he was certain he would not have to see Ruby Rae again he began to feel a little better. He started to get out of the house a little. He walked down to the New People's cottage and visited with them one day. After that he went back every day, for a little while at least. They didn't seem quite so crazy when you saw them every day. One day he and the New Guy went down into a far field to feed pine siskins, small yellow birds, in a patch of sunflowers. The New Guy was dressed in a purple smoking jacket with satin lapels and a broad-brimmed white straw hat that he called a "boater." Each day there seemed to be some new costume, a pirate's bandana and eye patch, a three-cornered hat, a tall silvery crown and rubber boots, a policeman's badge. He had a sailor's suit, with thirteen-button trousers, and a fireman's helmet. His wife carried a boomerang on a leather sling or wore a one-piece swimsuit and a banner across her chest that said Miss Argentina. She painted her face with white makeup and drew lines out from her eyes as if she were surprised.

Leroy said, "Why do you play dress-up?"

The New Lady said, "Hm. I never really thought of it."

She outfitted a costume wardrobe for Leroy. This was a large pasteboard box that she filled with old clothes of various sorts—dresses, hats, high heels, a tuxedo jacket with narrow lapels, men's shoes, purses, shirts, a church fan, a pair of seersucker pants, several pairs of old eyeglasses. She placed in the box the huge pair of wings she had used in grief therapy, in the Crown Victoria. She also put in a rusty baton with the larger bulb missing. Leroy avoided the baton. He didn't know what to make of the wings, though he liked them. There were other articles of clothing as well. When the notion struck him he went to the box and put together an outfit. Once it was a floral print dress and size-thirteen wing-tip shoes and a Mennonite bonnet. He added the wings at the last minute. He walked slowly in his unsmiling, melancholy way through the house. He stopped by the door of the New Guy's room. The New Guy looked up. "Very attractive," he said, and went back to whatever he was doing. Another day Leroy was dressed in full drag, with lipstick and makeup and a wig. Once or twice he spent the night with them. Elsie and Swami Don let him do whatever he wanted these days. The New People made up a trundle bed and gave him two pillows just for himself.

One day on a walk a huge armadillo scurried past him in its slow-motion way. Leroy looked at its armor plating, the bone-encased tail. He leaned down and took the animal by the tail. It was a tug of war. The animal pulled and Leroy hung on. The armadillo began digging in the loam. Leroy kept hanging on. He was not a big boy. The armadillo could pull him along. The armadillo kept digging. Dirt flew into Leroy's face, through the armadillo's little legs. The armadillo was going underground. Leroy lay down on his stomach and allowed himself to be pulled along. The armadillo was taking Leroy down with him. That was all right with Leroy. Being buried alive was just fine with Leroy. The New Guy pried Leroy's hands free from the steel cable–like tail. The armadillo disappeared beneath the loam.

22

The lights were out on account of a storm that was pounding the house with lightning and hail and so Elsie had to be careful on the stairway not to fall. The only light was the illumination of the fireballs that were rolling everywhere. Leroy was spending the night on the New People's rollaway, so he didn't learn about his mother's movements in her house until later that night. By then things had taken a pretty dramatic turn, but now it was only Elsie, who had just pulled down the trapdoor in the ceiling by its rope. She crept up and up the ladder, step by step, in the direction of Harris's room. The house was struck by a strong bolt. Gremlins of charged ions in many sizes, many shapes, danced near her. Lightning banged on the roof, let me in, let me in. Elsie knew that the house must look spectacular to anyone watching from outside; it was taking an unusual pounding. This night, in fact, someone *was* watching from outside the house, three persons, across the llama pasture. Leroy, of course, was one of them, along with the New People. They were watching the storm from the New People's cottage, just as his mama was making this climb up the stairs and through the ceiling. Thunder cracked like the heavy couplings of metal boxcars in a train yard. Fireballs rolled through, in many shapes. Leroy watched a fireball in the shape of Santa Claus dance along the rain gutters and pop in through an open window, and by the time Elsie saw it, inside the house, it had broken into a thousand scampering elves with little hammers and saws and workbenches.

At the beginning of the storm, Elsie had been sitting at home alone. Swami Don was at the factory again. Harris had said he had some calls to make. The girls had gone to bed early and were already sound asleep. Even Molly no longer woke up at the sound of heavy thunder. The clatter of the falling rain began as a heaviness upon the shingles above Elsie and in the leaves of the trees and on the tin roofs of the outbuildings. It was hypnotic now. Later Elsie thought of blaming the sound of the rain for what she had it in her mind to do. Next, thunder in the distance, and flashes of lightning across the western swamp, in the direction of the river. She felt restless, she didn't know why. She liked being alone usually, but tonight something seemed missing. She wanted something, it was hard to say what. She picked up a magazine, thumbed through a few pages, and put it down again. She started to turn on the television and then remembered there was no electricity. The house hadn't actually received a direct hit yet, but the electricity had gone off anyway. The storm kept up its pounding, rain at first mainly, the lightning remained at some distance. She walked to the porch and looked out. She couldn't see anything much, vague outlines of farm buildings. The llamas were safe in their barn. She could see the New People's cottage and knew that Leroy was there, her poor melancholy boy. Darkness had fallen some time ago, tinged with yellow. She moved restlessly, here and there, about the porch. She picked up a couple of Harris's newspapers and folded them and set them on a low table. She swatted a couple of flies against the screen. She came inside and closed the south windows against the rain and found a dirty undershirt of Swami Don's and wiped moisture off the windowsill with it and tossed the undershirt in the hamper. She snapped on the TV again and remembered again about the electrical outage. There was a generator in the barn, if Swami Don were here to get it running. She sat on the couch and picked up a book and tried to read in the dim light and gave that up, too.

She put the book down. Maybe she was hungry, she thought. Maybe that was it. There did seem to be a sort of emptiness that needed filling, if she could just find the right thing to fill it with. She went to the refrigerator. The light was out when she opened the refrigerator door, but she felt cool air when she bent close to look inside. She took a flashlight out of a kitchen drawer and shined it into the refrigerator. A cold peach cobbler was there. No, she didn't think she wanted that.

That was not quite what she wanted. She kept looking, directing the beam on object after object on the shelves. A leftover stew in a Tupperware dish, Lord no. Milk, canned fruit cocktail, no. Then she noticed a bottle of port wine standing near the back of the first shelf. Harris had bought it for grog rations some time ago. It had been sitting open for a while. She took it out of the refrigerator and set it on the kitchen counter, icy cold, almost full. This might do the trick, this might be just what she was looking for. She took out the cork and laid it on the kitchen table. She took a glass down from the cupboard and tilted the bottle against it and poured the syrupy wine. She had stopped using peanut butter jars, she had proper wine glasses now.

The rain outside was steady. She listened to it as she poured the wine. The lightning was coming closer. She lifted the glass to her lips.

As she drank, a warmth spread through her limbs and into her cheeks.

A heavy bolt struck the house and sent a shaggy basketball-sized fireball down the chimney, onto the hearth. It wallowed about, then broke up and dissipated. The phone gave an abrupt one-bell ring, so it was probably gone now, too, just like the electricity.

She took the flashlight and walked out onto the porch with it and turned the beam toward the llama shed. She didn't know what she was looking for. The llamas were all right. They didn't need any comforting in a storm. Elsie went back in the house. She had never realized how sweet port wine was. It was sweet enough to make you sick. She looked at the bottle and noticed that it was empty. Well, how did that happen? she wondered. How could the bottle already be empty? It was almost full when she took it from the refrigerator. Man, this was some storm, she was thinking. The storm was pounding the living crap out of her house. She was sitting in the dark. She was afraid she was going to throw up, the wine had been so sweet. The house was struck again. A fireball as big as an orangutan leapt in the window and walked around on its hind feet and pounded its chest. She felt like she'd eaten a bag of sugar.

She rubbed her face in both her hands. She rubbed it really good and then opened her eyes wide. She was pretty sure she was going to throw up. She didn't want to but she might have to. She would wait a little longer. She would just wait and see. Take a wait-and-see approach. What did "wait-and-see approach" mean? she wondered. She would just have to wait and see, she supposed. She would practice positive thinking. Then she wouldn't have to throw up, she might not, it might work, you couldn't tell. No throwing-upping. Up. Whatever.

She heard something. What was that she heard? It wasn't the storm. She listened. She heard it again. Oh, yeah. She knew what it was now. She recognized it. It was that message. It was the message from her heart. It said *I want I want I want I want.*

She looked at the wine bottle. It was not only empty but

there were two of them. Two wine bottles, empty ones. She looked around the room. Two television sets. What do you know about that? She thought about what it means when you say "what about that."

She hauled her head around and put one hand over one eye. She took it down. There were two, uh— Two something else, who cared, fuck it. She was sick of all this two shit.

She stood up. She didn't quite make it the first time. She flopped back on the couch. One more time. One more stand-up. She stood up again, hauled herself up. Made it. Okay. Okay, standing up. Maybe that was the other two thing. Two stand-ups. Standing-uppings. Two of them.

She took a couple of unsteady steps. No problem. No big hairy problem. Deal. Whatever.

She took off her clothes. That's the whole problem with clothes, she was thinking. Eventually you got to take them off. She threw her dress on the floor. She tried to kick her underpants off her foot. She weaved about in one spot for a while. She looked like a Weebly-Wobbly somebody had just punched.

Lightning struck the house and unsealed all the dill pickles. Now see, that's the problem with lightning, it makes you think of pickles. Why did she have to think of dill pickles? Oh God, she was so sick. She noticed that her underpants were still hooked around her ankle, so she kicked at them a few more times.

She staggered out into the hall and steadied herself. She reached up and took the rope and pulled down the trapdoor of the attic. This was about when Santa and the elves popped in, who cares. She put her naked foot on the first step.

Lightning struck the house again. Fireballs scattered like a covey of quail.

She started up the attic steps. She knew now what she wanted, she could decipher the encoded message from her heart. She wanted to have sex with Harris in the attic during the lightning storm. That's what she was going to do, that was the answer to the question, what was the question? She was getting all mixed up. She rose up through the trapdoor into his room like a mermaid rising from the sea. She appeared before Harris in her nakedness.

Leroy and the New People had been standing at the back door looking out at the clouds, heavy and low and tinted with a color of apple-green, as the storm blew in. The wind was high in the trees, shaking the brittle branches of the pecans and walnuts and tossing the willows and the chinaberries. The wind whistled in the eaves. Thunder came rumbling across the lowlands.

The New Lady said, "Come into the bedroom."

Leroy and the New Guy followed her. She said she had an idea, no costumes required.

She opened the bedroom curtains wide and turned off all the lights. She looked out the window, they all did. The lightning lit up the pasture with golden light. The window looked out upon Leroy's house. She said, "We can watch the storm."

The house seemed far away and sweet, like an old memory, a photograph you suddenly come upon unexpectedly. Leroy had never seen his house struck except from inside. The three of them stretched out across the bed on their stomachs. They lay on the taut-stretched tidy quilt and propped their chins in their hands. Leroy suddenly knew that he had been given many gifts.

The rain had already begun to fall, slowly at first, and then very hard. It pounded like great hammers upon the roof. It poured in sheets over the rims of the flooded gutters, fell through the trees, filling up the fields. The ditches flooded with water and flowed swiftly. The windward slope of the ravine, where they had shot the rifle, crumbled under the weight of the rain and became mud and slid, a chaos of erosion, into the channel below. Small birds were washed from the tree limbs, llamas bleated, small animals—raccoons and nutria and possums and swamp elves—were flushed from their dens, their lodgings in tree stumps, their warm nests in the cane, and were tumbled along, head over heels, upon the flood. Or so they must have been, so alive, so vivid, was Leroy's imagination in this safe place, with his chin in his hands, lying between his friends Hudson and Eve, watching the home of his birth as if on a television screen.

The lightning flashed. Leroy's house shone like a ghost ship on an illuminated sea. What they had been waiting for finally happened. A leader stroke hit the lightning rod, straight on.

A ball of fire as large as a manatee danced upon the chimney's rim and then dove like an otter down the flue.

One said, "Oh my."

The other said, "Impressive."

The pounding began in earnest now. The storm was going at full tilt. The world was rocking. With each flash of golden voltage Leroy's house appeared suddenly out of the darkness, then sank back into it again.

One said, "Shall I make some popcorn?"

The other said, "Oh, don't leave."

Harris was talking on the phone in the dark when he saw a dark form rise up through the floor of his room. News of this part of the storm came to Leroy the next day. It was the easiest part of all to learn the details of. Harris couldn't stop talking about it, he wouldn't shut up, he told it a dozen times, always indignant. Swami Don said if it was all the same to Harris he'd rather not hear it again. It was his wife, after all, who was drunk and naked. He was the cuckold here, so you know, Harris, if you don't have anything substantial to add, how about just not telling this again, in fact, shut up, if you don't mind my saying so. Harris couldn't shut up. He seemed halfway to blame Swami Don for what had happened, for being away, for having a wife who was a lush. He didn't know who he was blaming, he hardly knew what he was saying, all he knew was he was mortified, indignant, what on earth was going on, what was the world coming to, I thought I knew you, Elsie, what did you imagine a few kisses behind the refrigerator meant, for God's sake? All this was later, after all hell had broken loose in other ways as well.

A flash of lightning showed Harris it was Elsie rising through his floor. He said, "Elsie, my God! You scared me half to death."

She came toward him. Another flash showed him that she was naked.

He sat straight up in bed and clutched at his sheet. He said, "Whoa! Hold on a minute. Stop right where you are." He was speaking to Elsie, of course, but he also seemed to be saying the same words, with maybe a different meaning, to the person he was talking to on the phone, the person on the other end of the line. The telephone was not out of service after all.

Elsie did not stop. She had no intention of stopping. She walked right into the room. She staggered a little. She sat on the edge of Harris's bed. The lightning struck. Harris said, "Elsie, get your crazy ass out of my room, I mean it."

Elsie saw now that Harris was on the phone. She had not noticed this before. She had not noticed much of anything. Now she saw in the flash of light what the darkness had hidden. Harris was holding the telephone in one hand and holding himself in the other. Hannah was on the other end of the line. Elsie had never known about phone sex before, but the minute she saw it she recognized it for what it was, it was inescapable, it could be nothing else. He said, "Get the hell

out of this attic, right now, I mean it, good-bye!" Into the telephone he said, "Are you still there, are you still there, honey,
can you wait?"

Harris, later, even told this part, told whoever would listen, told Leroy, little Molly, everybody. He said Hannah said,
"Oh baby, oh God, oh my God—" Harris said, "Honey, baby,
whoa, sweetheart, could you hold the, ah, like line for a
minute?" Lightning filled the room with fireballs. He covered
the receiver with his hand. He said, "Elsie, leave right now
or I will kill you, I mean this." Elsie stood up from the bed.
She was beginning to understand something important. Harris said, "I'm back, honey, here I am, wait for me, can you
wait—"

Elsie was beginning to understand what was wrong with
Leroy. She knew suddenly, as if in a flash, what was wrong
with her son. She leapt up from the bed. She staggered into
Harris's table and knocked it over. She limped across the floor
and finally found her feet again. She bolted from the attic,
down the stairs, out of the house, into the storm. The rain hit
her solidly in the face. Immediately she was drenched. She
was weaving, she staggered, she kept on. She ran into the pasture, past the sleeping llamas. She was still naked, she stepped
on things, she didn't know what. She was running in the direction of the New People's cottage. She was so sick. She puked
as she ran, blah, port wine blowing off to the side of her, the
hard rain washing her clean. She saw the light in the New People's window. She splashed through puddles, she stepped in

shit. She leapt the cattle gap. The rain poured, the lightning flashed. She stood at the New People's bedroom window.

This was when what had been going on in his house started to become clear to Leroy. His mama appeared in the window from the darkness like a monster in the movies. Inside the cottage, all three people on the bed startled like children. They hadn't seen her coming. It took everyone a minute to understand who she was, what she was. She stood in the rain desperate and naked. They looked at her. She looked like a chicken washed out of the henhouse with a fire hose. The New Lady jumped up from the bed and grabbed a robe from a hook on the closet door to wrap Elsie in. She ran to the back door with the robe. Leroy left the bed, too. He didn't know where he was going. He was filled with rage and confusion. He ran in circles for a minute. He ran to the big box he called his wardrobe. He flung costumes everywhere until he found what he was looking for. He took out the damaged, rusted baton the New Lady had put there in case he ever needed it. He needed it tonight, for some reason.

The New People rescued Leroy's mama from the storm, they dried her with towels, they dressed her in the robe, sat her at the kitchen table, they started a pot of coffee. Now that he had the old baton, Leroy ran past all three of them, he might have made a sound like *whizzzz*, right out the back door, into the rain. Lightning was cracking, the air was filled with nitrogen. He almost slipped on the slick porch but he kept his feet, he was nimble as a llama, the rocks in the driveway did not pierce his feet. He screamed, "I hate you, I hate you, I hate you!" The others came out onto the porch, they called for him: "Leroy! Come back!" His feet had wings, he ran and ran, he sailed across the cattle gap, he flew through mud and shit, the air crackled, electrical daylight, his hair stood on end. Elsie screamed, tried to follow him, but the New People restrained her.

Lightning struck the baton.

Elsie watched her son light up like a bulb. Later she told Leroy these things, which he did not remember. Flames rose from his hair, flashed out like torches from his heels. All of his dark history was suddenly bathed in light. Ruby Rae was revealed.

For a moment after the spiderweb-thin filament of light hit the raised baton, Leroy did not fall. He became transfixed, a bright image in stasis of a child marching in a single-member band to some private silent music, twirling in the crackling air. He was surrounded by a blue halo. A part of this he did remember, later on. He remembered what it sounded like. A high-pitched ringing filled his ears. He remembered what it smelled like. A light like a nuclear flash irradiated from his flesh, which was set on fire and quickly extinguished by the rain. He breathed the odor of his flesh's charring. It was not a good smell, not like barbecue, it was like rubber, like hair, like garbage. The lightning streaked straight through the baton, straight through his whole body, it found its way into the ground by his right heel, which blazed up. He wished he could remember that part, when he walked on a column of flame.

23

Rapidly now the days seemed to grow shorter and not so hot as they had been. Earlier and earlier in the afternoons the llamas' sweet cries came from the pasture to say good night to the sun. The summer storms decreased as well, were not so violent or so frequent as they had been for three months, and the wind was not so high. Autumn seemed a tamer season than the summer had been. The air grew crisp, fruit ripened on the trees, the summer crops finished up and the fall crops went in, turnips and potatoes and peanuts. Leroy came out of the hospital with bulky white bandages and many bottles of solution for treating his burns. Doctors kept a careful eye on him and decided no skin grafts were needed. Each night Elsie bathed the bad places and soaked and replaced his bandages and taught him to peel away the smelly dead skin. Some days there was pain and he took a pill from one of the plastic bottles that came home from the hospital with him, and those days he took long naps. Pink new skin grew over the charred places on Leroy's hand and foot. Before he knew it, the bandages were off altogether, and this made Leroy happy. Leroy and Laurie started thinking about school starting. They described their teachers as Old Mrs. So and So, names they used to get themselves ready for all the time they'd have to spend away from home soon. Leroy was glad for school to start this year, but a little scared, too. It didn't seem possible that he was in the seventh grade already. He would be in a different building this year. He wouldn't get to see Laurie at recess. Uncle Harris was gone, no longer living in the attic, so Leroy was both happy and sad about that. Harris had moved out soon after the night when Leroy was struck by lightning. He seemed in a pretty big rush to go. You could tell he didn't want to have anything to do with Elsie for a while. Leroy knew about the things that had happened in the attic, it all came out, everybody knew. "Me and Hannah, we worked it out," Leroy heard Uncle Harris telling his daddy. "Having a telephone made all the difference. I want to thank you for the exclusive use of that telephone, Donny, it truly made all the difference." He said, "Actually, I'd have to leave anyway, Donny. You do understand my position here, don't you, I wouldn't want to seem ungrateful. It's like a nuthouse around here, you know. It's hard to get any rest. I don't mean to be critical, but Elsie is a little unbalanced, I'd say, you may have noticed, just a layman's opinion, I'm no psychiatrist, as you well know." Swami Don said he understood, he had no hard feelings, didn't hold a grudge, but yeah, it was probably better for Harris to leave now, it was time to go, but no, he didn't agree that there was anything wrong with Elsie, he just couldn't agree with Harris about that. Harris said, "I didn't mean a thing by those kisses, you know that." Swami Don said, "I know." They gave one another stiff hugs. There was no party when Harris left, Leroy hardly had a chance to say good-bye. Leroy was still a little sore at this time, he still had a low fever some days, so he didn't even get to walk out to the car with his uncle and watch him throw his carpetbag into the back and drive away. Harris did stop by Leroy's room, though, and fluffed up his pillows and mussed his hair and punched his arm a couple of times before he left. They said good-bye, that was about it. No big hugs or kisses. The leaves fell, and stalks of corn and sorghum and sugarcane turned golden brown in the fields. Wasps became noisy and sluggish in the eaves. The fireflies disappeared from the yard. The wind began to carry a chill.

Two more of the young llamas turned up dead in the pasture. This time it was pretty clear that Leroy's daddy had been mistaken when he said wild dogs make quick work, that the beasts didn't suffer. These had been run down, torn apart, anybody could tell these deaths took a while, they were not easy. Swami Don had never moved so slowly, had never seemed such a slow and clumsy beast himself. He wandered about the farm, aimless as a blind man. He was thinking, maybe praying. Leroy knew what this meant. His daddy had to admit that something had to be done, the dogs were on the move again, fall was the worst time for wild dogs around a farm. The dogs would have to be killed, the pack thinned out at least, in order for the llamas to have a chance at survival. Swami Don would have to do the killing himself, there was no other way. Leroy watched him, he knew he was coming to this decision, it was painful to watch.

Leroy watched his daddy take the rifle down from its safe place in the closet. He watched him sit out on the porch with it across his knees for a long time. He looked like a man preparing to go to his own death instead of somebody ready to do the natural work of caring for livestock. That night after the moon was up, Swami Don left the porch and made his way through the pasture to a rise where he could survey the hillscape and shallow valleys. He did this after Leroy had already gone to bed, but Leroy knew, listened carefully and heard him leave the house, heard the sound of the screened door closing. Later he heard his daddy tell these things, in sadness. At midnight Swami Don spotted a single wild dog, one skinny white old thing, with one brown ear. He could see this much, even so far away, in the bright moonlight. The dog put its nose into the wind, which was in Swami Don's favor. He felt sorry for the dog. He wanted to feed it. Another dog stepped from the brake and stood with its fur riffling in the wind. Then other dogs came out, frisky and nervous in the autumn air. They prowled and pranced at the edge of the pasture. Swami Don was nervous, he was licking his lips. The moon was high and white. The dogs grew calmer and began to bunch up. They scratched at fleas, licked a paw. Swami Don sat down with his back to a tree. He moved the Winchester with great care into position at his shoulder. The rifle was steadied on his knees. The leather thong hung down. The rifle began—that was how he told the story later—the rifle seemed to begin firing without him. Later he told everybody he couldn't remember beginning to pull the trigger. He shucked the lever of the carbine and fired again. He was surprised at his own agility, his swift recovery after each shot, firing, cocking, over and over, in his one-armed way. Brass casings leaped from the rifle and brushed his cheek as he fired. The crack of gunfire was startling in the nighttime wilderness. Two dogs fell and did not get up. The others scrambled, frantic, soundless, trying to become invisible in the moonlight, not even howling, not even those the bullets hit. Swami Don swung the barrel this way, that way, with amazing skill. Four dogs were dead. He stood up and walked until he had covered the distance from his ambush to the canebrake where the bloody dogs lay. Two of them lay there wounded, with their clear eyes open. Later Leroy's daddy said, "I put the rifle to each head and closed the eyes." About a quarter of the pack, maybe more, Swami Don thought. Not bad, not bad shooting for a one-armed man, he said he found himself thinking. He dragged the dogs to the ravine and flung them in. When he got back to the house, he didn't wash himself at the spigot where the children sometimes got a drink of water, he said it didn't seem right. He went to the old out-of-use cistern and dropped the zinc bucket to the bottom and drew it back, brimming, on the pulley and washed the blood away. He slipped back inside the house and got into his bed and said nothing at all to anyone that night, and maybe Leroy heard him in there crying, it was hard to tell.

The next day Leroy watched both his parents carefully. He watched his mama smooth flat the wrinkles in a comforter she had taken out of storage and put on the bed. He saw the cloth flatten beneath her hands. He watched as she turned the comforter back. She said, "I got too chilly last night." The ribbon at the throat of her gown was untied.

He heard his daddy say, "Six of them."

That was all for a while. She said, "I—well, I'm proud of you."

He said, "Don't say that, Elsie, please."

She said, "I am proud of you."

He said, "All right, Elsie, all right."

Leroy was sitting on the bed in his room trying to hear. They were quiet for a while. Leroy believed he could feel his daddy's shame through the walls.

He was surprised to hear his mama say, "I love you."

Swami Don said, "No you don't, Elsie. It's all right. It's nobody's fault."

She said, "Did they die right away? I mean, did they suffer?"

He said, "They were beautiful, Elsie. I've done something very wrong."

She said, "You haven't. You have not. Don't say that. It was necessary. I'm proud of you."

Leroy heard nothing else, he may have slept for a while. When he woke up a little later he heard them talking again.

His mama said, "Today I couldn't find the broom. I didn't really need it, I just didn't know where it was, and it was all I could think about."

Soon everybody noticed that there was no more lightning. One day they just realized they hadn't been struck for a while. They didn't remember exactly when this happened, the end of the lightning. For a time it was all they had thought of. After Leroy was struck they were alert to any threat of bad weather. At every cloud they cast a critical glance. Even when Elsie and Swami Don were not speaking to one another they would sometimes share a sentence or two after the weather report. They were not sure when they began to notice less. One day Elsie realized she had forgotten to watch the six-o'clock weather. She said, "Donald, I missed the weather. Are we expecting a storm?" "You know," he said, "I forgot to watch. I got busy out in the barn." Eventually they couldn't even have said when the last bad storm had passed through. The storms seemed far away, the summer seemed to have occurred in another life. Leroy's burns healed. On the surface there was little trace.

When Leroy felt like getting out again, he asked to go down to the New People's cottage for a visit. Both Elsie and Swami Don said no.

"Why not?"

Swami Don said, "Not right now."

Laurie had been sticking close to Leroy since the lightning struck him. She said, "When?"

Elsie said, "We'll see. Give us a little more time."

One day Laurie and Leroy stood on the edge of the field of sunflowers that the New Guy had planted. The flowers were six feet tall, large and yellow as tigers, with big sad faces and thick necks and sleepy drooping heads. The sunflowers faced the light at sunrise and then again at sunset. In this way they were like the llamas. Bumblebees the color of the flowers buzzed nearby, harmless and tuneful as tiny violins. Laurie and Leroy held sunflower seeds in their palms and small yellow birds flew near them, all around, pine siskins. The New Guy told them that if they did this each day, eventually the curious little creatures would eat from their hands.

School began. Laurie and Leroy walked together to the end of the lane and waited for the school bus. They sat together on the bus seat and jolted along toward town. They didn't say much. They watched out the window, the houses, a country store, the harvested fields. Acorns were everywhere underfoot. Some days they heard the high school marching band at practice and, if they were walking, they stopped for a while to listen. The band played "Let Me Call You Sweetheart" and

"Are You from Dixie?" and the national anthem. Afternoons, when the bus let them off and they had walked back up the graveled road, they stopped and visited for a while with the New People before walking the rest of the way to their own home. Leroy almost never took a costume from the wardrobe these days, though Laurie did. She always chose the same one, the angel's wings. She wore them around the house, or on walks, wherever they went. Sometimes the pine siskins would land on her wings and ride along. Leroy said, "You're the bird girl."

Once when they were visiting, the New Guy was sitting in a big cracked-leather chair in the front room of the cottage reading a magazine. The children saw him sit up straight in his seat, as if startled. He began to read aloud from the magazine. Everyone listened. The story began with an account of hikers tramping through a woodland. The hikers were happy and tired, making jokes and enjoying the scenery, the gum trees, a red fox, a bubbling spring. They began to smell something, sweet smelling, they thought at first, then realized it wasn't sweet at all, it was putrid. They found the body of a boy, rotted away and blanketed with flies. There were bullet wounds in the boy's head. The body looked like a mummy encased in green glass there were so many flies. A dusty ruffle of feathers could be heard in the tree branches overhead. When the story was finished you knew that one of the hikers walked along, out of the woods, carrying a guilty secret. This hiker thought the dead boy was beautiful and envied him and thought he'd like to die, too.

Leroy said, "That's not true, is it?"

The New Guy said, "No, it's not true."

Laurie said, "It might be true."

That night when Elsie tucked Laurie into bed, Leroy could hear what they were saying. Elsie said, "Did you have a nice visit with the New People?"

Laurie said, "Yes."

"Tell me about it."

She said, "If I didn't have Leroy—I don't know—I would die."

Elsie said, "Oh, Laurie."

They sat for a while and didn't say anything. Leroy was lying in his own bed picking at a scab on his heel. He kept listening. He heard his mama say, "Come here, sweetie." Maybe she pulled Laurie close and held her. Maybe Laurie wriggled away. He couldn't tell. He could hear them, though. He knew that he would never love anyone as much as he loved Laurie.

Laurie said, "Tell him."

Maybe Elsie looked at her. Leroy heard nothing for a while. Elsie said, "You mean Daddy? Tell him what?"

"I don't know."

"He has to tell me, too."

"I killed a dog."

"My God, Laurie."

Leroy listened for a while. They might have been crying, he wasn't sure.

Later he heard his mama say, "I don't know why I can't talk to him."

It took Leroy a while to understand this, but when Harris moved out, Elsie moved up into the attic. At first she slept downstairs for a while and tried to act like everything was all right, but then that got too hard and so she moved out of the bedroom and into the attic. Leroy's daddy even helped her. They were separated, Leroy supposed. He had heard that expression and now it made sense. They scarcely spoke as they worked at moving Elsie's things upstairs, rearranging the furniture, adding things, taking others away. The move took place over several days, that was why Leroy didn't catch on right away. You could say the move was elaborate, even. Elsie found a small sofa in a used-furniture store and picked up an oak library table at Goodwill and refinished it herself. The sofa pulled out into a large comfortable bed, which she used at night instead of Harris's cot. The cot was long gone, out in the loft of the barn, dismantled and stored away. A table lamp with a green shade cast friendly shadows through the room. Leroy watched his mama carry up the wicker rocker from the porch. Harris had left his small TV and there was the phone, which Elsie used to talk to the Evil Queen most days. She referred to the attic as her "apartment" and encouraged the children to "visit" with her. She kept a few things in a tiny

refrigerator, which she bought on credit at Sears. She liked to
keep a few bottles of Coke on hand to give them as special
treats sometimes. She had to share the regular bathroom,
downstairs, of course, but Leroy could see that that was not so
bad. After school started, she took on a few more hours a
week at her job in town and so Leroy didn't see much of her.
Sometimes no one was home when he and Laurie got off the
bus. Molly was staying half days in a nursery school in the village and had stopped wetting her pants altogether; it was odd
that no one could remember exactly when that happened.

Swami Don kept up with the farmwork. He looked more
like a convict than a farmer. Leroy had never seen anyone so
sad. He dragged himself around the farm. His work clothes
looked like a uniform. At meals he usually ate alone and he
looked like a condemned man. Elsie seemed furious at him for
being sad. One day she said, "If you just wouldn't look so
stricken. Why do you always have to look so stricken?" He just
looked at her. He couldn't think what to say. Leroy wouldn't
have known what to say either.

One day Swami Don and Elsie happened to be standing
in the kitchen at the same time. They usually avoided one
another at mealtimes. Leroy was sitting at the table eating a
peanut butter sandwich. Elsie was making herself a sandwich
as well. Swami Don opened the refrigerator and seemed to
forget they were not speaking and said, "Want a glass of milk
with your sandwich?" Elsie's face flushed and she said, "You
mopey son of a bitch." He didn't even turn around, just kept

staring into the refrigerator. He said, "Fuck you." She said, "How dare you." He took out a bottle of milk and got a glass down out of the cupboard. He said, "Shut your ugly mouth." The entire peanut butter sandwich seemed stuck to the top of Leroy's mouth.

Sometimes the children went up through the trapdoor at night and watched TV with Elsie. A few times Molly fell asleep on the sofa bed beside her and Elsie let her spend the night. Other nights Elsie stayed downstairs and sat on the sofa with a few pieces of mending or a book she was reading. These days seemed to Leroy almost like old times, almost normal. One night Elsie read an Ann Landers column to Swami Don before she realized this was not a thing she intended to do. Leroy watched to see if this would remind his daddy of Uncle Harris and make him angry, and it did not. Some days were not so bad.

The best day was when Leroy's daddy decided it would be a good thing for the children to have a pet. "Children need a dog," he said. "What's the point of living on a farm if you don't have a dog?" Everybody knew he was still feeling guilty about killing the wild dogs, they figured this was his way of making amends, but that was all right, nobody blamed him, and a dog did sound like a good idea, it was an excellent idea, even Elsie had to agree. Swami Don said he had heard about a place way out in the country where he could get a good dog, free, too, had all his shots, Mr. Sweet told him about it, drew him a map out to the place. He said, "Y'all go on out to the pickup if you want to go along," so all three children went flying out the door and jumped up in the cab and fought for the seat next to the window. Elsie surprised everybody by saying she thought she'd go along for the ride, too. She said she had never heard of this place they were going. Swami Don said, "It's way out in the boonies." She said, "Are you sure you can trust Mr. Sweet's map?" It was pretty crowded with five people in the cab of the pickup, but they managed. They all squeezed in. Leroy said he'd sit in the bed with the new dog on the way back, Laurie said she would, too. Swami Don said if they sat back there they couldn't stand up, they'd have to sit down the whole way back. Elsie took the window seat and Molly got to sit in her lap, so everybody was more or less satisfied as they pulled away from the house and down the lane.

They drove and drove and left the paved road for a gravel road and then another mile or more down a dirt road that ended in an old trailer park. Mr. Sweet's directions were pretty confusing, but Swami Don said he guessed this had to be the place. Mr. Sweet had neglected to mention anything about a trailer park. All the trailers were old and in pretty bad shape, but some had porches and carports made of green plastic sheeting. A couple had flowers planted along walkways. There was one plastic swimming pool for little kids, left over from last summer, with green scum on the water. Leroy looked at all this, and looked left and right for some sign of a dog, but couldn't see anything promising.

Elsie said, "Are you sure you got the directions right?"

Swami Don said, "Well, I'm not sure."

They drove very slow along a road through the trailer park until they saw a small crowd of men milling about. Swami Don pulled the truck over to the side of the lane and stopped. He said, "I guess this must be it." He and Elsie opened their doors and all five of them got out and looked over at the men. The men were looking at an ostrich. The ostrich was six feet tall and must have weighed two hundred pounds, it had to, it was a seriously big ostrich. Leroy watched it walking around with great big round eyes. Every now and then it stopped and ate a little corn from a wooden tub. Leroy trailed his mama and daddy up close enough to get a good look.

A man was saying, "It bit me, that's all I'm saying."

Another man was saying, "I ain't clear what you're trying to tell me."

"I'm trying to tell you it bit me."

"So you're saying this here ostrich bit you?"

"I could have been bad hurt."

"From an ostrich bite?"

"You never know."

"I never known this ostrich to bite."

"It sure bit me."

"I known him to kick."

They started walking back to the pickup.

Swami Don said, "That was something."

A woman in a housecoat called out the front door of one of

the trailers. She said, "Are y'all the ones Mr. Sweet sent out here for a dog? He won't hunt."

That day ended well, with everyone smiling and throwing sticks for the new dog. Leroy looked at his parents and wondered how long this would last.

The worst day was when Elsie figured out that Swami Don had had a girlfriend out at the sporting goods factory. Once this leaked out, Leroy didn't have to be quiet to hear. The words came through the walls in Dolby stereo. Deaf people from miles around heard all about the girlfriend at the factory. It got nasty, Leroy would have to admit. Up to that point it had been a pretty good day, too, before this information slipped out. Elsie and Swami Don had been trying to "communicate." That was the word Elsie used over and over these days. She was always "communicating." Some days Swami Don would forget and just want to "talk," but she always reminded him they weren't supposed to be talking, they were supposed to be communicating, anybody could just talk, that was the whole problem with their marriage, they'd always only just talked, never communicated, there was a difference, a big difference.

Leroy suspected the Evil Queen had come up with communicating. The Evil Queen was very modern. He could just hear the Evil Queen advising his mama to communicate. Elsie had been complaining to Swami Don that day that there was no romance in her life. That was the idea she was trying to communicate. Even to Leroy she sounded like a broken record. Leroy could tell that his daddy was getting irritated. He looked like he had heard about enough about how unromantic he was. He had had about enough of this communicating, it was starting to get on his nerves. Elsie kept on communicating, she didn't let up. That was why she was so infatuated with Aldo Moro, Elsie explained, the romance aspect. "The romance that I'm missing on this farm, that's why I'm always reaching out for more." That was why she—she kept this part vague—why she "did what she did" with Harris, was the way she put it that evening. Leroy could tell that Swami Don had communicated until he was blue in the face. One thing led to another. It was right after this that the Indian maiden problem started to unravel a little. At first Swami Don just said that she was a young woman at the plant, that was the way he communicated it, before he lost control of the situation. He kept it real vague. He hadn't meant to say anything about her at all. You could tell it slipped out. Elsie had complained that there was no romance in their lives and Swami Don said that there was so romance, there was plenty of romance in their lives if you just looked at it the right way, he'd talked all about it with this Indian maiden at the factory, Native American woman, he corrected himself, and she seemed to understand full well just how filled with romance their life was. "So I just wish you'd quit saying there's no romance," he communicated through clenched teeth.

Elsie said, "Indian maiden?"

He said, "Uh—"

"You've been discussing our private life with an Indian?"

He said, "Roxanne is not really the point, Elsie, the point is the romance in our life. Let's try to stick to the subject, if you don't mind. Anyway, I shouldn't have said Indian. I meant to say Native American. Roxanne says In-din, I realize, but—"

She said, "Roxanne?"

He said, "For example, the lightning. That's really the point I'm trying to make here. I'd like for you to understand what I'm getting at. The lightning striking us is romantic, see? See what I mean? I'm seeing the lightning in a more positive light than maybe you're seeing it. Roxanne sure agreed with me that it seemed romantic to her. You ought to hear her go on about lightning. About the llamas, too. Roxanne really understands romance, she sees it the same as me."

Elsie's voice had become quiet and steady, fierce, Leroy might have said if he could have thought of the right word. She said, "I see. And what else did you tell this Indian named Roxanne?"

"Well, I told her about the night you and me had to go out together to put the llamas in the sheds, remember? A storm caught us by surprise. Lightning had been arcing through the hills, the rain hadn't started up yet, and then all of a sudden it was right on top of us. We were running every whichaway, remember? We just about had the herd rounded up, everybody safe, when that tall cedar lit up. It just lit up. You couldn't have forgotten it, Elsie. The whole tree was surrounded in blue light. You said it looked like a blue halo. And remember the smell? The whole world smelled like it had turned into a cedar closet just then. Remember that smell, how we just stood and breathed it in, again and again? Red resin bubbled down the side of the tree like paint, it coursed along the trunk. Splinters hung in the air. Remember, we said the splinters looked like ruby-colored hummingbirds. Great dark slabs of bark flew away from the tree like crows. Cedar needles blazed up in flames. That was the most romantic moment of my life. I told her about that, I sure did."

"And this is what you told some Indian bitch? What does this Indian factory worker look like? Where did you do all this fancy talking? What's the name of that sleazy little motel near the plant, is that where you were? Is that where you got so poetic about lightning and llamas with an Indian? Lightning is not romantic, it's a curse. Lightning is the opposite of romance, you idiot. Even an Indian ought to know that. Roxanne, is that it, is Roxanne her name, is that what this romantic Indian who understands you so well calls herself? Well, that's fine, that's just great. What else did you do with this Indian, this so-called Roxanne person? How old is she, by the way?"

He told her everything, he couldn't seem to stop himself. Oklahoma, Creek nation, nineteen years old (that was the story!), black eyes, her hopes, her dreams, a son she loved that reminded him of himself. He left out the abortions and alcoholism and the welfare. He didn't tell her about the kisses, either, not right away, or about Roxanne getting naked. That would come later, when the screaming had reached a higher pitch. Elsie insulted him, he got madder, and then he told her that part as well. Leroy ran for cover. He put his hands over his ears, but he heard every word anyway.

She screamed, "You fucked an Indian? You spoke intimate secrets!? Did you tell her you loved her? *Do* you love her?"

"Elsie, stop calling her an Indian. It's—I don't know— I wish you would stop. And I didn't say I actually—"

She said, "That's pathetic, that's just pathetic."

He said, "The point is not really Roxanne anyway, it's lightning."

She said, "All right then, while your son was getting raped by a majorette and struck by lightning, you were spending our money on a motel where you could fuck a factory worker. Is this the true meaning of the lightning? Is this the romance you are speaking of?"

They moved into the bedroom and slammed the door— they must have realized Leroy was listening—but they were screaming so loud Leroy had no trouble hearing. His daddy was warming to the fight now. He was shouting as loud as Elsie. He said, "Does it matter to you one iota that over two thousand people in the United States last year were struck by lightning, that our son was lucky enough to be one of them?" Leroy could hear Swami Don pacing around in there behind the closed door. Swami Don said, "Does it matter that five hundred of those people died and he didn't? He'll carry that magnificent moment with him for the rest of his life, Elsie. Can you imagine the people who would give anything to wear those scars, those badges? He's the luckiest person in the world, we're lucky to be his parents. Our son was chosen, Elsie, by the universe, he is special, he hit the meteorological lottery! Can you understand a word I'm saying? One half of all farm fires—lightning! Our farm is one of them! Seventy-five thousand forest fires a year—lightning! Our woods and fields are smoking. Millions of tons of nitrogen released into the atmosphere, carried to earth on raindrops—every year, Elsie! On our property! Lightning is the source of life on our planet, our island home! Our farm, our son! They are the source of life!"

Leroy heard his mother's voice then. Something had changed, softened. She said, "Come to bed, Donald." Leroy came close and put his ear to the door. He heard a rustle of clothes. He recognized the sound as clearly as if he'd been in the same room with them. His mama was starting to undress. His daddy raved on and his mama was getting naked. "Think about Ishmael!" he heard his daddy shout. Elsie said, "Come to bed, Donald." Leroy imagined her outstretched arms. Swami Don's voice was almost a song, an incantation, now. He said, "'The palsied universe lies before us like a leper, a monumental white shroud, and of all these things the albino was the symbol. Wonder ye then at the fiery hunt?' Melville, remember that? Remember when we first saw the llamas and we were memorizing Melville?" She said, "We'll talk tomorrow, come to bed." He said, "Ishmael is saying Ahab has to chase the white whale, it might be crazy, but he has to do it, nobody can fault him. The whale is the strange beauty at the center of the universe, at the core of life, you chase it if you are a good person, it chases you if you are blessed. We're blessed, Elsie, honey, blessed, Leroy, all of us, no matter the pain, no matter the enormity of our mistakes, the blessing won't fade, it's ours forever, all the pain of love is worth it if you're blessed with what we have, through ourselves, our son, all our children. You decide for yourself what romance is, everybody does this—or innocence, whatever you long for—you pick out the best symbol you can find, whales, llamas, lightning, it doesn't matter, so long as it is magnificent. Llamas are magnificent, Mississippi is magnificent, the red clay hills, the hardwood forests and swamp elves and bear cats and possums and lightning, oh my God, lightning is the most magnificent of all, Elsie! You've got lightning in your own backyard, angels of fire in your living room, in your plumbing, in our son's head and out his heels! Lightning is the symbol at the core. Choose a symbol worthy of a good man's love! Choose lightning, choose llamas, choose me!" "Make love to me, Donald," Leroy heard his mama say. Swami Don was not finished. He said, "You know that story about Benjamin Franklin, the kite in the thunderstorm, remember that? Ben Franklin is a perfect example. He was one of the chosen ones, too, he was like us, when he started to fly that kite. Wasn't it raining? Did you ever think about that? How could he fly a kite in the rain? It can't be done. You can't get a kite to fly at the beach half the time, let alone in the rain. That's with a decent kite, too, modern materials, balsa wood, plastic, printed-out directions on the package. Imagine the piece-of-crap kite Benjamin Franklin was trying to fly. What did he use, bedsheets and a couple of his father's neckties knotted up for a tail? It's ridiculous. That kite wouldn't fly. Tubby and Little Lulu might be able to get that kind of kite airborne, but no real person ever did, not without being special. And yet the lightning found him. I'll tell you something else about Benjamin Franklin. What about his wife? Have you ever given a minute's thought to Mrs. Franklin. She was as wonderful as Benjamin. What if she thought flying a kite in a rainstorm was a stupid idea, which I grant you it is, is one way of looking at it. What if Mrs. Franklin had said, 'You are going to do *what*?' You are going to fly a kite in a rainstorm? Look at that ridiculous kite. You're not going to fly that piece-of-shit kite in a rainstorm. You're going to get your silly ass electrocuted, is all you're going to do. Forget the fucking kite. The kite is history.'" Leroy heard sounds after this that he understood very well. He covered his head with a pillow and blocked out the sounds of the bed and its inhabitants. He tried not to think of the ways a one-armed man makes love.

That night when Elsie came into his room, wearing her nightgown, to tuck Leroy in bed, Laurie was already in Leroy's room. She had heard the fight as well, and the aftermath, and she had been frightened. She had dragged a quilt and her pillow with her and made a pallet on Leroy's floor. She told him she had heard the shouting and was scared. They were lying in the darkness, looking out at the clear fall sky outside the window, where moonlight hung like orange crepe paper in the tree limbs. Elsie came in and found them there and sat at the edge of Leroy's bed. She said, "Come on, I think we can all three squeeze in here for good night." Leroy scooted over as close to the wall as he could and Laurie and Elsie managed to squeeze in beside him. They lay together in the silence. The new puppy was asleep at last. It had wet the floor a dozen times, it could never hit the paper, and nobody had the heart to make it sleep outdoors. Leroy began to feel sleepy.

Laurie said, "Tell the story."

Elsie lay still for a minute. She said, "Well, let's see, the story, how does that old story go—?" Leroy and Laurie knew she was just teasing, she remembered the story.

Laurie said, "Daddy was your boyfriend, and he had an old car—"

"Oh, yes, that's right, I remember now, he had an old car, and so one day, late in the afternoon, when our college literature class had let out, he said he wanted to take me for a drive in the country."

Laurie said, "You thought he wanted to kiss you."

"Well, I sure did, that's exactly what I thought—"

Leroy said, "He did kiss you."

"Later, he did, he most certainly did, but not right away,

that would be later, so okay, who's telling this story anyway?" The children snuggled down into the bed, they stayed quiet. Elsie said, "Daddy stopped the car beside a big field and turned off the engine."

"That's when you heard them," Laurie said.

"Right. We listened for a while, and then I heard them."

"You thought they were horses at first."

"You know this story better than I do."

Leroy said, "Their hooves were flying. They sounded like thunder in the hills."

"That's just the way it was. Thunder in the hills."

"Then you saw them," Laurie said. "They were magnificent. You had never seen anything so beautiful."

"Their slender bodies, their long necks, legs so thin you wondered how they held them up," Leroy said.

Elsie said, "I saw their pointed snouts and bulging eyes—"

"All colors—," somebody said. "Rust and pure white and pure black and mottled."

"—running for the fun of it," somebody else said.

"Yes, sweethearts," Elsie said. "Running and running, just for the fun of it."

They lay together for a while in Leroy's bed in the moonlight.

Laurie said, "And then you fell in love?"

"Yes, honey, that was what happened. I fell in love."

This was where the story always ended. Maybe sometimes

Elsie said, "And then my three little angels were born," but the story of the day she first saw the llamas ended here.

This night, though, Leroy said, "But what does it mean?"

Leroy felt Elsie turn in the darkness to try to look at him. She said, "Mean?"

He said, "What does the story mean?"

Laurie said, "Yeah."

Leroy felt his mama turn back and lean against the pillows again. He could hear her breathing. They were squeezed up in the little bed so closely he could feel her soft breath against his hair. She said, "Well, gosh, let's see. What does this story mean? Hm. Let me think— I never really considered it this way before. It means—I guess it means that true love lasts forever. That would be my guess. True love lasts forever, I believe that would be it. That's the meaning I suppose I'd have to give to the story about the day your daddy showed me the llamas, how beautiful they are when they run."

Lewis Nordan is the author of three collections of short stories and four novels, *Music of the Swamp, Wolf Whistle, The Sharpshooter Blues,* and *Lightning Song.* His prizes include the Southern Book Critics Circle Award for fiction and three American Library Association Notable Book citations. Born and raised in the Mississippi Delta, he lives now in Pittsburgh, Pennsylvania, where he serves as Professor of Creative Writing at the University of Pittsburgh.